Roses Bloom in June

By

Kathryn Larouche Imler

Kathryn Larouche Imler

ISBN: 978-1-962849-56-2

Dedication

I would like to thank my family who have been so encouraging with my writing; a new adventure in my senior years.

My husband Bart: thank you for everything you do to help me on my journey

My children and spouses:	*and my grandchildren*
Lenny and Jessica	*Mila*
Anthony and Corrie	*Jake and Michael*
Natalie and Shane	*Sam and Penelope*

A big thankyou to Jake my marketing manager whose enthusiasm and encouragement has been a delight.

Table of Contents

Chapter 1

Olivia and Millie

Olivia leaned over the bedside rail, trying to hear what her dying mother, Millie, was saying. "I forgive you, Livy," she says. "What are you talking about?" Olivia nearly yelled out loud. "Forgive me? What did I do?" "And don't call me Livy; my name is Olivia!" She hated that nickname forever. In her mind, Millie only called her Livy when she was giving a warning. "Now Livy blah blah blah," and Livy had better do as told or take a chance of Millie blowing her top.

Millie's dying was taking a long time, unlike her Dad, who graciously had a major stroke and died right with his boots on, well, his slippers, actually. Millie, who figured she was the centre of the universe all her life, a demanding presence, self-obsessed, and practically perfect in every way, was not leaving our world easily. Millie was 96 plus years old.

Millie had been living in an "Independent" living facility, where they tend to keep their private paying clients well past the independent stage. Millie, with her advancing dementia, decided to have a boyfriend. The problem was he wasn't just a gentleman caller, taking her out for dinner or the movies. Oh no, we found out the hard way they were sleeping together. Well, that was a shock as Millie always insisted on and maintained her independence after Dad died nine years ago. "I don't care who you are when you find your ninety-five-year-old Mom in bed with a stranger. Well, let's just say I didn't find it amusing," said Olivia.

The only problem was this gentleman who professed to love Millie must have had a lot of his own brain cells not functioning well either. He just couldn't understand how sick Millie was.

Despite growing weaker, Millie adamantly denied her inability to walk. Despite enduring four falls, one of which resulted in a broken hip, she insisted that she had been taking long walks around the Long-Term Care facility she was relocated to after numerous visits to the emergency room. Oh, plus dancing. Apparently, her facility had a dance the other night. Considering most residents could not walk, I found that to be an interesting statement. But as dementia care should be, there is no point in arguing when, according to the "patient's" brain, what they say is the truth, and arguing for the sake of arguing never helps the situation. So, Olivia agreed and went along with Millie's version of the truth. Except when Millie insisted, she could "darn well get up and walk to the bathroom" or out to the patio. So, Olivia learned to let her try, but as soon as she moved even a bit, Millie realized how weak she was. There was no getting back upright for this woman.

Dementia is a cruel way to finish a life. Millie's personality changed over and over throughout her years with dementia. It was exhausting.

Millie then told Olivia that she would be receiving letters and whatnot from her lawyer. Olivia just shook her head. "What's this about a lawyer and letters?" This is the first Olivia has heard about this.

"What are the letters about Mom?"

Millie didn't answer. She appeared to be asleep again.

"Oh well," Olivia thought, "I'm sure to find out soon enough," gauging Millie's diminishing presence. Millie was very pale and very small, almost camouflaged, shrouded under the white hospital sheet.

Olivia sat with Millie for another fifteen minutes, but she stayed asleep, so Olivia left, telling the nurse she would be back after dinner.

Olivia was tired of the facility's cafeteria food, so she set out for a good meal at one of the local restaurants along White Rock, British Columbia's beach area.

Olivia took a taxi from the long-term care hospital, not trusting herself to drive after several nights of lost sleep. Millie had a stroke three days before and was definitely on her last days or hours.

Olivia had been called to the facility twice since Millie's admission to the Palliative care floor. The staff had been sure Mom's time had come, but typically, Millie had rebounded twice, and Olivia was exhausted from the death watch or dying game she now figured it was. Olivia was the only family member left, and whether she loved her or not, she wouldn't abandon her.

After a delicious dinner and a couple of Cosmos at a restaurant overlooking the ocean, Olivia walked along the boardwalk and pier in White Rock, trying to sort out her complicated feelings for Millie. It was a warm evening, and the tide was coming back in. She could smell the brine from the water, but that didn't bother her. Olivia had always loved the nearby ocean, rivers, mountains, and forests, with the many trails for cycling or hiking that are found throughout the lower mainland and the rest of British Columbia.

Olivia and her brother Ben had been adopted as babies. Ben had been chosen by the adoption agency because his birth father was the same height and built as Larry. Olivia was chosen because her birth mother was short and petite, just like Millie. That's what happened in those days. Of course, the parents who would adopt went through several checks to determine they were "fit" to adopt. "Ha!" thought Olivia, "fit my ass."

Olivia had always been interested in what her "real" Mom was like and had put in requests at the adoption register in Manitoba, the province where she was born, years ago, but somehow, the file had gone missing, and she had to start again. Ben never wanted to discover his "real" Mom. He was very angry at being "abandoned" and furious at Millie since the day he was born. He drank himself to death by age fifty-seven, a slow suicide. Death may have put Ben out of his pain, but it caused a whole lot of emotional torture for everyone left behind after the unexpected death of a loved one who died from addiction.

Olivia remembers Ben at age sixteen, asking her to buy him some cheap wine and beer for a party. She always wondered if she had made a grave error in buying him that booze. An alcoholic friend said to her after he was dry. "I was an alcoholic right from the first drink I had in my teens."

Ben crashed his new, used Mustang car in a ditch by the highway. He escaped with bruises, and he never drove again. Millie and Larry probably grounded him. Olivia couldn't remember. What she did remember was Ben calling her from jail and having to go and bail him out. While driving back to her place, she saw the upside-down car in the ditch and wondered how much Ben had had to drink or how he managed to escape unscathed. At least he didn't take out another car and cause harm or death to another.

One night, before cell phones existed, Ben called Olivia from his house phone, which he had taken outside with him. He was determined to kill the huge tree that had been planted by his neighbor, who refused to trim it. The tree blocked Ben's view of the valley, and he was determined to kill the innocent tree. Ben managed to climb up on a ladder and hammer a nail into the tree trunk. Being so drunk, a nightly occurrence, he fell. How he didn't break his back was beyond Olivia. His wife was out, and his boys were too young to help, so he called Olivia. Not that Olivia could do much to help as she lived at least twenty minutes away, had young kids of her own, and was a single parent at the time.

Olivia seemed to be the only one Ben would talk to when he was stressed out and inebriated, upset about something Millie said to him that day or years before. Olivia hadn't realized how much he was drinking every day for years. He had a high-paying job, which he managed to do well for over thirty years. Alcoholism and depression often go hand in hand and can be very difficult to treat if the person refuses help.

All of them, well except Millie and Dad, tried to help Ben get help, but he always refused. At times, Olivia thought that Ben reveled in his hatred of Millie, blaming every negative thing in his life as her fault.

Olivia wanted to "find herself" by finding her "real" family. She didn't feel abandoned by her "real" mother. She knew there were reasons a woman had to give up their baby. It was heartbreaking, really.

Olivia never loved Millie either for as long as she could think back on her life. There was always so much drama and chaos when Millie didn't get her way or some minor issue that had pissed her off along the line of her day, and she would blow her top almost literally directed at Ben and Olivia.

Millie was a small woman, 5 '2" tall and 107 pounds exactly, with short, curly brown hair that she "frosted" but never colored her hair. She was as fierce as a pack of lions on a kill when she'd blow. Her eyes would shoot daggers, her body would go tense like a rattler ready to strike, and woe was the one who was near. It was ugly. Yet some of her last words were, "I forgive you."

This phrase rolled over in Olivia's head. She didn't understand what she was forgiven for or what exactly Millie was talking about. "Whatever, I really couldn't care less. I just wanted this whole process of mother's dying finished" declared Olivia

Millie had been a whirling dervish, a Tasmanian Devil, and an Energizer bunny rolled into one. About a year and a half previous, Millie had been on the go from early morning to late evening. She just never knew how to stop. Olivia wished she knew what Millie was running from.

After dinner and martinis, Olivia went back to the hospital and entered Millie's dark room, chewing on a piece of gum, hoping to cover up the booze on her breath, even if it was vodka. She knew you could still smell the alcohol smell, especially after a few.

Millie was awfully still and even paler. "Is she dead?" Olivia approached the bed slowly, not sure what to think. Millie, of course, wasn't quite finished with her drama, and her eyes popped open. "Thought I was gone, did you?" she said in her diminishing, raspy, hoarse voice. "No, Mom, I figured you'd draw out your dying for dramatic effect and to piss me off," said Olivia.

Olivia had to shake her head to realize, thankfully, that she hadn't said that out loud. "Gee, I was a horrible daughter," thought Olivia. But Olivia's mom's eyes closed again, and a long sigh left her body. Then, absolute stillness. "Oh, she's probably going to pop up one more time," Olivia thought. Remembering the children's story "Never Cry Wolf."

But everything stayed silent. Millie really had left the building this time. Olivia fell into the armchair beside the bed and felt a huge weight lifted off her shoulders. "She's really gone. Should I do a little dance or cry or what?" her emotions were definitely messed up.

After processing the situation for a while, Olivia pressed the call bell for the nurse. Then she walked out of that death room, moved quickly down the hall to the elevator, down three floors, and out the door, picking up her speed until she was running. Well, she was actually walking really fast, which was running at her age, down the street, which was on a steep decline, and if she didn't slow down, she would roll right into the ocean. Olivia was finally free of the woman. She could barely tolerate Millie after Ben died. But being the only family member left and either out of guilt or a sense of duty, Olivia made sure her Mom had a good end of life and was well looked after until she died. Millie's personality had profoundly changed in the past year. Instead of the high-strung, demanding woman, she almost had no affect or boiling anger inside anymore. She was a lot easier to be around, but the ugly memories still popped up for Olivia now and again. Olivia couldn't change history, but it was nice to see the person Millie could have been without her destructive anger toward herself, Ben, and Dad.

However, in the last six months before Millie died, her personality had several swings. She was stuck in a wheelchair after the second break of her hip. At times, she was delusional, seeing old friends, then crying and pleading with Olivia to "take her home," then yelling at Olivia to go away, or bored to tears remembering her former hyperactive self. Millie was locked in a nightmare. Her Energizer lifestyle never allowed for rest but had left her mind still wanting to get up and go.

Olivia often questioned herself as to why she was being so attentive and kind to Millie, visiting several times a week when she had been so hurtful to Ben and her even years after they grew up.

Millie had mastered the art of training Ben and Olivia to comply with her every request or instruction, making them aware that if they upset her, the tables could quickly turn against them. Was that the reason behind Olivia's feelings of guilt? It took her a while to unravel the confusion. Olivia had yearned for a nurturing mother-daughter bond with Millie, and when Millie's dementia temporarily softened her demeanor, Olivia dared to hope for a brighter future. However, it was short-lived. When Olivia asked her daughter why she was being kind to Millie, she simply responded, "Mom, you couldn't be any other way." This statement illuminated a part of her struggle—her persistent need to please everyone, often at her own expense.

Millie's parenting had a few positives as Ben and Olivia were growing up—she openly disclosed that they were adopted. This contrasted with the experience of a girl Olivia knew in high school who learned about her adoption in a heart-wrenching way. At the age of thirteen, she accidentally overheard a conversation among relatives, and understandably, she was devastated by the sudden revelation. Consequently, she encountered significant challenges in trusting others from that point onward.

Millie told Ben and Olivia about their adoption from a very early age. It was like a story she told every now and then.

Olivia resembled Millie, being 5' tall and anywhere from 100 to 115 pounds, which drove Millie nuts when Olivia got to the 115-pound mark. Millie would remind her all the time about gaining weight. Even when Olivia was on the skinny side, she always felt fat, hearing "Now, you don't want to gain weight, Livy" over and over throughout her life like it was the crime of the century.

Olivia had been happy to have lived all across Canada. It wasn't easy, though, growing up and moving every three years to another Air Force base where her Dad, Larry, served. The school systems were different in the way they taught, especially math, but Olivia would soon catch up. Moving to British Columbia and starting grade eight was an eye-opener in many ways.

Millie had always bought Ben and me the newest in fashion clothes. She saw us kids as a reflection of herself. So, when Olivia started grade eight in a small town outside of Vancouver, she was placed in the only class that had space, the one where kids who were constantly failing disappeared or where misfits were relegated in those days.

The kids in Olivia's class certainly didn't have leather dresses, hot pants, or go-go boots in their wardrobe. She couldn't help but feel like a "misfit" among the other girls, who seemed to have stepped out of a time capsule from the 1950s to the early 60s. Pointed bras, pencil skirts (which were definitely not in style in 1968, except perhaps for some older women), and beehive hairdos adorned their appearances. Olivia half expected to stumble upon the early Beatles hiding in their closets.

Olivia made it through grade eight with good grades. She was introduced to marijuana before she turned fourteen by the "misfit" kids. Olivia would try a few puffs in the woods with the other kids during break. It made her laugh and feel good, but it was no longer fun by grade ten. Olivia would pass out or go into a weird, phobic state, and that was the end of that. At the time, she preferred beer anyway. Olivia later was told by her RCMP spy Dad that the town they lived in near a river was a major drop for narcotics, and often the weed was laced with LSD or some other crap.

Ben and Olivia spent most of their time after school at home, avoiding Millie. Hiding out in their rooms or watching television in the wood-paneled "rec room" in the basement.

Olivia remembers Saturday mornings with fondness, sitting with her Dad, Larry, downstairs, laughing at Bugs Bunny and especially the Road Runner cartoons. Larry would laugh right out loud, not his usual demeanor, where he, as well as Ben and Olivia, would find quiet places to be anywhere but where Millie was.

But oh, did he love those cartoons. Larry also loved watching sports, so Olivia and Ben often joined him to watch football and hockey. That is where both Olivia and Ben picked up their love of sports. Millie was usually upstairs doing something, so it was fun, with just the three of them shouting at the TV for one team or another. Millie did bring them popcorn and Cokes, so she wasn't totally mean all of the time. Millie always joined them to watch the major events like the Stanley Cup, the Grey Cup, which is won by one of Canada's football teams, and, of course, the Super Bowl, the final contest between the American football teams.

Millie was usually quite the distraction, getting overly emotional and yelling for her favourite team. "Take a chill pill, Millie." But we would never say that or else…

Sunday morning was generally a good day for Millie. Olivia had wondered what her parents had done the night before; when she was older and thinking about such things, she figured it out. Eeeeeuw.

Millie loved music and couldn't live without some type of background noise. Or foreground noise as she always blasted the stereo playing records from all the musicals she had seen with Dad. Both Ben and Olivia grew up with a big appreciation for all types of music. Ben's taste in music was quite eclectic, as he had a friend in his early 20s who worked as a DJ and had hundreds of LPs that Ben somehow ended up with. He gave Olivia a stack, but unfortunately, she melted them in the back of her 1963 white Chevy Nova.

So, although Ben and Olivia couldn't connect emotionally with Millie, mostly because they couldn't trust her, there were some positive events. Millie was a very complex soul. She always seemed to be running to or from something. Olivia had only heard a few stories from Millie's youth. Millie had hinted at a couple of events from her past that sounded like they would have affected her personality or behavior, but she was never clear what had happened or when. She did grow up with four brothers, so Olivia could imagine the pranks they may have pulled on their only sister. However, those stories never seemed bad enough to make Millie the way she was, always having to be so perfect, always busy, busy, busy. Nobody could keep up with her.

Just as Olivia was reaching the age of independence, this small town on the outskirts of Vancouver, BC, became her final destination before setting out on her own journey toward a Nursing Degree.

<hr>

After speed-walking herself to exhaustion on the beach after Millie died, Olivia returned to the hotel where she had been staying the past several nights, close to the hospital. Her brain was turning in circles, so many thoughts in her mind. The funeral home would pick up Millie, and she would be cremated. Olivia was to pick up her ashes in a few days. "What the heck was I supposed to do with ashes?" It made her shudder thinking of handling her parents' ashes and finding a golf course to "dump" them, which she was sure was against the law. But that's what Millie wanted, and what Millie wants, Millie gets.

Olivia also wondered when she would receive the letters from the lawyer Millie had spoken about. Olivia didn't even have a name for this mystery person. "How would they know Millie had died?" Olivia's brain hurt. She was beyond exhausted. Too exhausted and in too much pain from running to even have a shower. Olivia felt like a ship-wrecked passenger pummelled through the churning sea and rudely tossed upon the beach.

The next morning, Olivia finally had a nice long shower, stretched her muscles, ate some breakfast at the café next door to the hotel, had a couple of cups of perfectly brewed coffee, and returned home to the countryside where she lived with her husband and two dogs. Olivia's own children and grandchildren from her first marriage lived not too far away, about an hour's drive into the city near Vancouver.

Thankfully, Millie hadn't wanted a funeral or memorial service; well, she did expect some kind of recognition of her death, but the problem was there was no family left except Olivia, her husband, and her children, who had already said their goodbyes. Most of Millie's friends had died before her.

Every day of Olivia's life, at least as far back as she could remember, Millie had been on her mind whether she wanted her there or not. Olivia was very tired of thoughts about Millie taking up so much space in her life, but that was Millie, a force that would not leave.

Eventually, there was a memorial, which for Olivia was horrible. She had spent two weeks preparing a slideshow of Millie's life, ordering memorial cards, etc. It kept Olivia's mind busy. People just "loved" Millie, so Olivia had the memorial for Millie's slew of friends and her kids. Memorials are always difficult, especially when Olivia is the one making the farewell speech. She had done the same at her brother's well-attended memorial. Giving his eulogy was the worst day of her life thus far. Olivia never thought she would have to do one more. Larry had died ten years earlier.

Everyone got over Millie's memorial service, but for the next several weeks, Olivia labeled herself with "AAHD," she was not at all poking fun at ADHD, which she definitely had as a kid, but her grieving self, Angry, Anxious, Hyperactive and Depressed. Olivia was up and down like a yo-yo. She was angry at Millie for living so long and for destroying Olivia and her brother. Such a whirlwind of feelings. The memorial felt like another abuse hurled at Olivia. Hearing over and over how much everybody loved Millie made her feel grateful that Millie had had so many loving friends but completely horrible at the same time. Not one of them really knew what Millie was capable of doing behind closed doors. Olivia shed a tear but for Ben and herself, not for Millie.

Finally, after several weeks and some counseling, Olivia was able to let go, well, mostly anyway. It still felt like pulling a squid off her face. Olivia found herself plunged into an existential crisis as if she had just started to truly live her own life now that Millie was no longer a part of it. However, Olivia was left grappling with the daunting questions of "who was she" and "whereabouts in the universe did she fit in." Plus, death. Olivia still had a bucket list of things she wanted to accomplish. Actors and musicians from her era were starting to die at a rapid pace in the past year or two, and she recognized life is short and goes by in a flash. Olivia wanted to experience so much more before she got too old to enjoy it.

Confusion reigned over Olivia's thoughts for a considerable time. She wanted to run away or climb a tree as she had done in her youth to get away from noise and people.

A little more than a month after Millie died, Olivia received the package from the lawyer Millie had talked about. "How mysterious and exciting." Olivia had already told her husband and kids that she had been impatiently waiting for whatever it was the lawyer would send her.

The package arrived in the morning. Olivia stared at the large box. So many thoughts had been rolling through her mind about what the package contained. "Why hadn't Millie been more explicit about what it was all about? Maybe she didn't know? Should I be worried? Was it good news or something else?" thought Olivia.

Olivia paced around the house, trying to get her nerve up to open the box.

"Take a few deep breaths and just do it." She always told herself when facing something stressful. Olivia opened the sealed box and pulled out the first set of letters and old, musty, smelling diaries.

She then poured herself another cup of green tea, cleaned her glasses, and sat down to read the first letter from the lawyer.

Chapter 2

The Delaney Family

Dear Ms. Harrison-McDonald

We at Longren-Kelly and Associates extend our condolences upon your mother's death, Amelia Barlow nee Delaney. We have enclosed the following letters in your name, which we have been entrusted with for the last fifty years. We have been instructed to deliver these letters to you after Amelia Barlow's death.

The sender is your great Aunt, your grandmother's elder sister Maybelle, or Aunt Belle, as you would have known her.

Also enclosed are several diaries written by your grandmother, Carys (nee) Delaney, and your great-uncle Percival Delaney. Your great Uncle's diaries are mostly from his time spent overseas in Europe during the First World War.

After your perusal of these letters and documents, kindly contact us, and we will send the next set.

Yours truly,

Martin Longren

"Aunt Belle, how strange." Olivia had known (great) Aunt Belle since the 1960s. She was the only sister of her grandmother's she had met. Aunt Belle was full of life, even in her eighties. If Ben or Olivia ever complained, "We've got nothing to do," Aunt Belle would tell them to "go play in the traffic." Olivia recalled seeing a photo of Aunt Belle at the beach wearing a bathing suit, and in 1920, she was one of the first women in the community to be so daring.

Olivia peeked into the box at the file folder containing letters written by Aunt Belle many years ago. "She was going to receive more letters after this? What about the diaries? Should I begin with them? Goodness, what was this all about?"

Olivia opened the first set of multi-paged letters and began to read.

Dear Olivia,

I wrote these letters for you to read after Millie's death. I also enclosed a few diaries I found in my mother's attic after she died. Some are from your grandmother, and the ones in ratty condition are from our brother, Percy.

When you receive these letters, I'll most likely be long gone, too. I'm sure it all seems bizarre and perhaps a little strange. Still, there are reasons I needed to keep this information from your mother as it concerns her. But the letter is mostly about your grandmother's (Carys) life. I hardly know where to start. As family stories go, it's no more or less sad and tragic as many others during WW1 and WW2. I began writing a diary when I was young, but they turned into letters about Cary's life, which truly was more exciting, or should I say, at times more tragic than mine. I loved her dearly. I never had children of my own. At first, I was going to give your mom these letters and diaries, but in later years, I decided not to. Instead, I saved them for you.

First, let me tell you about your mother's mother, your Grandma.

Carys Delaney was born in Chilliwack, BC, at the start of the brand new century in January 1900. She was a sweet little thing, born a few weeks early, but she was robust and gained weight rapidly to catch up. I was her older sister, and we had two older brothers and three younger siblings. Our mother and father came from Ireland via Montreal Harbour and Ontario, drawn to Western Canada with the promise of cheap, fertile land. "A paradise for farmers." the leaflets said. Carys was the middle child, more or less. I was the oldest girl.

When Mom and Pops arrived in Chilliwack from Ontario, they fell in love with the majestic landscape. The huge soaring mountains of the Canadian Cascades, the mighty (and muddy during the spring run-off) Fraser River. There were many lakes nearby, too, and when we were older, we loved spending lazy summer mornings fishing.

We raised sheep and cows. The shearing season was always a hoot. The local sheep farmers would hold contests to determine who was the fastest sheep shearer in the valley.

Percy and Joseph, our older brothers, always entered the contest held in one of the neighbors' barns. Joseph was a big, strapping fellow with muscles galore. Percy was smaller in stature but just as strong. The sheep were definitely not happy having their warm, woolly coats removed. They looked utterly naked. There was a lot of booing and laughter from the others watching the chaos. Joseph won again for the second year in a row. I don't remember how much he won, but it seemed like there was a lot of side-betting between the other farmers and sons.

Mom and Pops settled in Chilliwack in 1890 before they had any of us kids. Four of us were born in Chilliwack, and the other three were born in Alberta. They were newlyweds when they arrived from Ontario, looking to start a brand-new life in a beautiful province. There were lots of jobs to be had in forestry, fishing, and the railroads. Pops worked for a while logging and would be away for several weeks at a time, but they were saving their money to buy a farm. Mom, a small but mighty woman, stayed at the small home near downtown Chilliwack, looking after us children who seemed to pop out every year or two. I really don't know how she managed, but a few of the widows or single women would help out with the cooking or laundry. Mom was always so grateful for their help; after they moved to their farm, she brought them seasonal vegetables and fruits. Mom sure did have a big heart and was always trying to make others' lives a bit easier. Chilliwack became known for the sweet corn grown in the area, and soon, our fields were sky-high with cobs of corn. It would get so hot in the summertime we half expected the corn to pop right there in the fields.

After having lived in Chilliwack for only a year and a half, there was a huge flood in May 1894, covering all of Chilliwack. Thankfully, Pops was home when the flood waters began pouring in. They didn't have much time to get out of town to a higher location. There were plenty of hills to climb. After a few days of camping outdoors, they made their way back to their small apartment, which was on the third floor and had remained mostly dry. The market, the church, the school, and so many other buildings had been damaged beyond repair. Several men from New Westminster and surrounding communities made their way up the Fraser River to bring supplies and help rebuild. Hundreds of farm animals had been lost, and land wasn't plantable that spring.

The only good thing that came out of that for our family, and several more, was the silt deposit left behind on the land, which made farming even more fertile and abundant. There were farmers who simply gave up after the huge flood and sold their land at a bargain price. One never knew if there would be another severe flood in the future.

Pops and Mom eventually had enough money to buy their farm on a beautiful piece of land. They started from the ground up, building their home and barn. In the meantime, Mom now had four children. The clean air and proximity to a myriad of creeks, streams, and rivers made fishing easy, especially during the salmon runs. We also had plenty of water to care for our crops.

We had a nice, warm, and comfortable house with a huge stone fireplace with crackling wood, taking the chill off in the winter. We would put hot coals under the covers at the foot of our beds to keep us warm at night, but we'd wake up the next morning with frost on both sides of the window, and we could see our breath in the air when we spoke. Getting the kids up to go to school in the winter was a definite chore for Mom. We did not want to get out of our warm beds. But we did as there was work to do before and after school for all of us. Mom needed help with baking bread, doing dishes, sweeping the floors, and shaking out the blankets. The boys had their chores outdoors, feeding the animals, milking the cows, chopping wood, and saddling up horses for those of us who attended school.

Once a week, Mom made us, (well, that's the way the boys looked at it!) have a bath. She would heat up water on the wood stove, put it in a big tin tub, and from youngest to eldest, we would bathe. Two days for the girls and the next two for the boys.

Life was hard, but we didn't see it that way, as that's all we ever knew. We were always busy except in the evenings when we had time to study or read by oil lamp. We would listen to our Victrola, one of the early record players. Jacob had found one when he was in town buying supplies. The cabinet was damaged, and it was missing a few parts, but at $3, it was a steal. We had wanted one for years, but they were ridiculously expensive, too much for our family, so it was a blessing that Jacob, who could fix anything, was able to find or make the parts needed. He sanded down the cabinet, added a darker stain, and waxed it until it glistened.

Mom also liked to tell us some Irish folk tales before we went to bed. Some were too scary, but she would tell those to the older children on a rainy day when the youngsters were having their naps.

The following one was a favourite for all of us girls.

Once upon a time, there was a young girl in Ireland named Siobhan who lived near a fairy circle. She had grown up listening to stories of the fairies from her grandmother, who would tell her that they only appeared to the pure of heart. Siobhan had always dreamed of seeing the fairies, but she had never been lucky enough to catch a glimpse of them.

One day, as she was gathering flowers near the fairy circle, Siobhan saw a beautiful green light coming from the center of the circle. She cautiously approached, and as she got closer, she saw a group of fairies dancing and singing. They were so tiny and delicate, but they moved gracefully and sang so sweetly that Siobhan was entranced.

At first, the fairies didn't see her, but when they did, they were alarmed. They had not meant to let any human witness their celebration. However, Siobhan was different. Her pure heart and gentle nature made her a friend of the fairies, and they invited her to join their dance.

Siobhan twirled and spun with the fairies, and the more she danced, the more she felt like she belonged there. The fairies began to tire as the night wore on, but they did not want the celebration to end. So, they asked Siobhan if she would make a wish.

Siobhan thought for a Moment, and then she said, "I wish that I could visit the fairy kingdom whenever I wish, and I promise to always respect and protect it."

The fairies considered her wish, and then they agreed. They gave Siobhan a special coin made of moonlight and told her that with it, she could enter the fairy kingdom anytime she wanted. However, they also warned her that she must never lose the coin, or else she would be trapped in the fairy realm forever.

Siobhan thanked the fairies and made her way back home. She hid the moonlight coin in a secret place, only to be used when the time was right. From that day on, Siobhan often visited the fairy kingdom, always respecting and protecting it, and the fairies became her dearest friends. And if you ever visit Ireland, you might see her still dancing with the fairies in the moonlight.

Mom would also tell us tales of the Leprechauns, the mischievous little elves with their pots of gold. One St. Patrick's Day, he played a trick on his town and painted it green. It's been said that there's a pot of gold at the end of a rainbow, but we never could find it.

Some scary stories were about the Pookas or changelings. These tales were only for the older children, but even so, they would chill our bones, even knowing they were not true. The Irish had Halloween for centuries, although it was called the celebration of Samhain and was celebrated to mark the end of the harvest and the beginning of winter. People wore outfits to disguise themselves from the evil spirits and fairies.

Here's a good tale of the Pooka Dad would tell us on Halloween Eve.

Long ago in Ireland, there was a creature that lurked in the darkness, ready to strike at any Moment. It was called the Pooka, and it was known to be one of the most fearsome creatures in all of Ireland.

One night, a young man named Sean was walking home from the pub. It was a dark and stormy night, and the wind was howling. As he walked, he heard a faint rustling noise behind him. He quickly turned around and saw nothing. But he had an uneasy feeling that he was being watched.

He picked up his pace, hoping to get home quickly, but the noise persisted, growing louder and more insistent. Suddenly, he heard a growl so fierce that it made him shiver. Out of nowhere, the Pooka appeared in front of him.

The creature was a sight to behold — it was a black stallion with glowing red eyes and ragged breath. Sean tried to run, but the creature chased him down, huffing and growling behind him. He couldn't stop or slow down, or the Pooka would catch him.

Sean ran all the way to his village, gasping for air, and finally reached his front door. As he closed the door behind him, he heard the Pooka's growl and turned to see it standing outside, glaring at him with its fiery eyes.

The Pooka continued to torment Sean for many weeks, always appearing when he least expected it. The Pooka demanded Sean leave him three gold coins under the milk pail every morning. It wasn't long before Sean ran out of coins and pleaded with the Pooka to let him be.

It would chase him, growl at him, and leave him with nightmares that lasted for days.

The very next night, Sean saw the Pooka again. The Pooka was blowing fire and steam from his nostrils and furiously stomping the ground, flinging clumps of sod over Sean's front door. Sean pleaded with the Pooka to give him one more day.

Finally, Sean couldn't take it anymore and went to see the local priest.

The priest listened to Sean's story and decided to help him. Together, they prepared a special potion made with holy water, salt, and rowan berries. The priest blessed the potion and gave it to Sean, telling him to sprinkle it on the Pooka the next time he saw it.

The next day, he was ready. The Pooka arrived at the designated time and demanded the gold coins from Sean, or he, the Pooka, would tear Sean limb to limb and eat him for dinner.

Sean took out the potion the priest had made and threw it on the Pooka. Instantly, the creature disappeared, never to be seen again.

From that day on, Sean lived in peace and never forgot the terror he had experienced at the hands of the Pooka. It was a fearsome creature, but with the help of the priest and his potion, Sean had defeated it. And though he knew he would never forget the encounter, he was glad that the Pooka was gone, never to torment him or anyone else in his village again.

There was a teacher living on the farm close by, and we attended school in her enormous kitchen, sitting around the large wooden block table. There were ten of us. I remember Mrs. Gallantry as being very intelligent and humorous. She taught us in a manner quite different from most other teachers. Mrs. Gallantry seemed like a little sprite. She was always cheery, even when dealing with the Johanssen boys, who were a handful and a half.

Nothing was known about attention deficit disorder, autism, anxiety, depression, or post-traumatic stress syndrome at that time, and most people scoffed at anyone who had these problems. I heard Millie say more often than not that "so and so" needed to "pull up their bootstraps." If only it was that easy.

Pops knew his neighbors well. The Johanssen had been living on their land since before the flood. They were one of the few families who stubbornly defended their land as best as they could against the ever-increasing water level. They lost all their crops as well as many animals but were determined to let the past go and start again. After all, it wasn't the first time they had to start anew. Being Jewish, they had been forced out of two villages back home by the Russians.

The boys were now living with them. Their uncle left Russia ten years prior, bringing along his new bride, their Aunt. This couple was never able to have children, as Sonia was not able to have pregnancies last more than four months. After five miscarriages, her doctor advised her not to get pregnant again as the last event nearly killed her through blood loss.

Olivia put the letters down for a breather. She had always loved history, but by learning Jewish and Russian history as an adult, she was much more aware of the horrors done to others in the name of war.

Having lived past her sixties and been exposed to a wealth of experiences and knowledge, Olivia had witnessed the harrowing consequences of both warfare and the destructive forces of hatred and fear. The gripping fear of losing not only what rightfully belongs to individuals but also the insatiable greed that drives some to the madness of always wanting more. Regrettably, these circumstances often ended up in various forms of massacres, wars, and other atrocities.

The Russian Pogroms were one of those atrocities, a systemic assault on the Jewish population in Russia, Poland, Ukraine, and other locations. Over 100,000 Jews had died in the Pogroms even before the start of WW1. Not that that was startling news to Olivia. Olivia only remembered the Jewish history from the Holocaust of Hitler during WW2 taught in schools. However, having rewatched, probably for the hundredth time, Fiddler on the Roof, Olivia finally put more of Jewish history together.

Olivia had been born and raised in Canada, a Caucasian "Christian," and Jewish history way back then hadn't been thoroughly taught, or she just didn't remember. Olivia stopped and looked online at the history of the Odessa Massacre in 1905. "Why do so many people hate each other"? Olivia believed people fear what they don't understand, and they don't understand because they fear. This is what Olivia read from various online websites.

A carefully orchestrated plan was in place for a widespread massacre of Jews in Odessa, scheduled to occur on the day following Orthodox Easter. Shockingly, the mob was led by priests, and the chilling cry of "Kill the Jews" resonated throughout the entire city. Caught completely off guard, the Jewish community was mercilessly attacked and slaughtered. Several people were killed, and many more were injured. The scenes of horror that unfolded during this massacre defy adequate description. Infants were brutally torn apart by the frenzied and bloodthirsty mob. Despite the chaos and terror, the local police made no effort to intervene and curb the rampant violence. As night fell, the streets became strewn with lifeless bodies and wounded victims. Those who could manage to escape fled in sheer terror, leaving the city practically devoid of its Jewish population.

Olivia picked up the letters again.

The boy's parents had been shot down during the raid in Odessa. That fateful day on the busy streets, women started screaming and running past the boys, clinging to their children's hands. Men were shouting. There was a smell of smoke in the air. People were trampled by men and horses. The boys hid under a buggy, just having witnessed their parents and neighbours slaughtered. Some soldiers were even killing children and grabbing young women, dragging them screaming to a wall, raping then shooting them in the head. When the attackers finally fled, there was destruction everywhere. Dead bodies lay strewn up and down the street as far as the eye could see. Some were moaning and crying out for help, but what could two young boys do? They crawled out from under the wagon and began to run, never stopping until they reached their aunt's house several blocks away.

Thankfully, that section of town had not been raided, but by then they had all heard the screams and gunshots. Neighbors were cautiously stepping outside, waiting to hear if there would be more violent outcries or horses pounding down the road, indicating another attack.

Aunt Helga grabbed both boys in her arms and hugged them fiercely into her ample chest. Both boys dropped their heads and began sobbing when she asked them where their parents were. Eventually, the words came out that they had seen their parents shot down in the street.

After weeks of burying the dead and cleaning the streets, the boy's Aunt and uncle and eight children of their own managed to obtain passage on a ship taking them to Canada.

The boys ended up living with their other Aunt and uncle, who were childless and more than happy to raise the boys.

The boys never talked about that horrific day. It was like nothing that horrific could ever have happened. The boys were always the troublemakers in the town when they were teenagers. They were always drunk and often ended up in jail for a night to sober up, but the following weekend, they were determined to drink their memories away and provoke fights to release their anger on anyone in their way.

The really unfortunate thing is the boys were very intelligent and could have done well in school and life. I heard years later that both boys died in their early twenties, having been involved in a car crash or mishap. They were both drunk and ended up in the Vedder Canal in Chilliwack on their way home from a buddy's house.

Chapter 3
The Big Move

After living in Chilliwack for several years, all of us were tired of the almost constant rain from October to the end of June. We, the Delaney's, weren't used to the temperate climate of British Columbia, a rainforest. We wanted a proper winter.

Pops made the decision to sell our modest farm along with any other possessions he could part with. We packed the remaining belongings into a well-built wooden wagon, harnessed to four sturdy horses, accompanied by seven children, three adults (including great uncle John, who graciously joined to assist his brother), a dog, and a cat. It felt as though we were embarking on our own version of Noah's Ark.

The dog and cat were young and were purchased to try and keep the younger siblings occupied for the rest of the trip. They certainly did that. I don't think Pops thought about how active young children are, let alone kitties and puppies.

Mother insisted on bringing the beautiful hand-carved sideboard containing her Belleek China wrapped in sweaters and hay. It had travelled with them all the way from Ireland, and she was not going to leave them behind. Either it came, or she stayed. Mom had made that point very clear to Pops. Aside from linens, these were her only possessions brought from Ireland. If they had survived the flood, they would have survived a trip to the next province and their new home. It really was amazing that only one cup broke.

Deciding what to take and what to leave behind was heart-wrenching for Mom, having to give up piece after piece of her physical connections and memories, which connected all of us girls to her past.

The wagon proved spacious enough for the entire family's journey, and Pops, unsure of what awaited them in their new land, brought along an abundance of tools and saws. The majority of the boys opted to ride horses and sleep outdoors, while Mom and we girls found our rest inside the wagon, nestled on a bed of hay.

We joined several other families from Chilliwack, British Columbia, and towns further west and set out on the old gold rush trail, which was long and arduous. From Chilliwack to Hope, the Old Yale Road was fairly easy, at least compared to the Fraser Canyon, straight up from Hope, BC, following the mighty Fraser River.

I believe this stretch of the Cariboo Wagon Trail, the passage from Hope, BC, to the Fraser Canyon to Cache Creek, was the most harrowing part of the whole journey. As the road climbed steadily, it put considerable strain on the horses. We learned to avert our gaze from the edge, for if you glanced downward, a perilously deep drop awaited. Although there were wooden railings at the side of the trail in the mountains, they provided little reassurance in the event that the road should give way.

We certainly left at the right time; although there had been slides and floods in previous years, the past couple of years had been good. From Hope, we travelled north to Yale, which was known as the official start of the Gold Rush trail or the Cariboo wagon road. Yale was also the main train station for travelling further north and east. Not all the railways were convenient for getting the family and their possessions to east central Alberta. Plus, the cost would have been out of their reach.

The Gold Rush Trail had finished being built two or three decades ago. The land had been forcefully taken from the Aboriginals, who now mostly lived on reservations established by the Canadian and provincial governments. We would see few Indians, or First Nation People, as they were later known.

This was also the era of the beginning of residential schools, which turned out to be tragic for many who attended. The children were taken away from their families, usually at a young age. It is really hard to imagine the cruelty they endured. A generation of abuse, leaving marks on the body and soul only to be passed on to their children and grandchildren. A nation defeated, pushed down, and out of their own land. Breaking those chains of depression might take a century, but I sure hope they get there.

Olivia had been following the news lately about children being buried at the schools, often with strange death certificates that definitely sounded suspect, like a boy falling off his bed and dying but actually due to being beaten or sexually abused. Disease was rampant, and the children rarely had access to medical care. They would just waste away trying to stay upright in class lest they be beaten and starved. Often, their families were not told how they died. The children just disappeared. The death certificate often just lists their first name as given to the child by the school instead of their true name. Some children ran away only to be discovered frozen just a few miles from the school. Safety measures didn't exist, and a few fires swept through the schools, killing children in their beds.

150,000 First Nations, Inuit, and Métis children passed through the residential school system between the 1870s and 1997, according to the Truth and Reconciliation Commission of Canada. As far as Olivia was concerned, it was a cultural genocide.

Many crude burial sites have been recently discovered, and there are ongoing searches.

The odds of dying in Canadian residential schools over the years they operated were about the same as for those serving in Canada's armed forces during the Second World War.

Canada now has a National "Truth and Reconciliation Day, a day off work for many to listen and learn. Olivia was watching the special broadcast that day. It was sad, especially watching many of the attendants place tiny moccasins or running shoes on a platform to commemorate the loss of one of their children. Then, at one point during the ceremony, people carried a long red banner with the names of nearly five thousand children found so far in the "hidden" burial grounds of the residential schools. It was a stark reality too long ignored by too many people, not just in the government.

Back to Aunt Belle's letters.

The journey itself proved to be an almost overwhelming ordeal, surpassing any expectations we had. Every wagon was crammed with belongings, people of all ages, children, and animals of all sorts. The roads we travelled were nothing more than packed dirt, often resembling mere walking trails. However, the unpredictable downpours would occasionally transform these paths into raging rivers, forcing us to halt for a few hours or longer. Despite it being early summer, the threat of rain persisted for a few more weeks. We anxiously awaited the forecasted extended dry spell between British Columbia and south-eastern Alberta, hoping it would soon materialize to spare us from waterlogged trails.

Our family was just one among many brave souls embarking on this challenging journey eastward and then north through Alberta. It was fortunate that multiple families chose to travel together, as the combined strength of the boys and men was indispensable in getting our teams through the treacherous mud, relentless rain, and days of scorching sun. During the nights we huddled closely together, the men kept the fires stoked all night to ward off any unwelcome visitors from the animal kingdom. The echoing howls of the wolves provided a somewhat captivating evening soundtrack, adding a touch of both fear and fascination to our experiences.

Fishing opportunities were plentiful wherever a river or stream crossed our path near where we would settle for the night. To this day, I still love freshly caught fish steamed over a campfire.

The journey stretched on and on, a seemingly endless trail covered in dust, surrounding us in a brownish shroud. Originally travelled by hordes of gold prospectors seeking their fortune, the Cariboo trail had lost much of its appeal after the gold rush shifted to the Klondike in the late 1890s. We had heard tales of this dangerous and challenging trail, but it was believed that as long as we followed the horse-drawn carts and the lead stagecoach, we would reach our destination in one piece.

The most harrowing part of the trip was from Hope to Lytton, BC, along the mighty Fraser River. There were so many twists and turns it seemed as if we circled back on ourselves. As the canyon narrowed even more, we reached the small town of Yale, which was the furthest that steamships could reach from the coast.

The canyons were frighteningly deep. We passed by "Hell's Gate Canyon," and I was trembling. Mind you, the roaring waters through that canyon were quite a sight. The wagon trail was stunning, with steep rock faces of the Cascade Range on both sides of us, split with numerous waterfalls. Once we got to Clinton, the surrounding landscape changed to wider, dryer valleys, the southern edge of the Cariboo.

Before we set out, the stagecoach driver and their assistants cautioned each travelling family about the hazardous terrain, emphasizing the importance of maintaining order and unity, both figuratively and literally.

Sadly, not every wagon driver heeded the warnings with sufficient attentiveness. A devastating accident occurred just outside of Hope, revealing the consequences of one driver's excessive consumption of alcohol the night before. Despite the prohibition of alcohol on the wagon train, many men—and a few women, I noticed—could not resist its sedating and tranquilizing allure, although there were plenty of them who would become aggressive the more they drank.

The wagon cart driver likely dozed off and loosened the reins. The horses tried following the wagon ahead, but the wheels at the back of the wagon began teetering on the edge of the precipice. Gravity and momentum took over, tragically plunging the wagon, horses, driver, and wife into the depths of the ravine. The memory of that heart-wrenching incident haunted our thoughts for countless sleepless nights. It had a sobering effect on every member of the wagon train.

We carried on. There wasn't much of a choice. Turning back would leave anyone vulnerable to further catastrophes without the expertise of the stagecoach lead driver and the company of fellow travellers.

We often spoke of that trip in later years. It took us nearly two weeks to arrive at our destination in the Peace River, including stops along the way in the many small towns that had sprung up along the Cariboo trail. Sometimes, the stagecoach would lead us to the next stop, and that's it. Then, we'd have a new stagecoach and driver to lead the way. They were definitely used to this dirt trail and knew the pitfalls. We did feel safe in their hands.

At night, as you see in the movies these days, we would sit around a campfire after dinner, singing and socializing. It was on this trip that I met my best friend, Nellie Banks, whom I'll tell you about later.

The next and last incident occurred just outside of Quesnel, BC. The wagon train suddenly stopped. We were on a fairly wide trail, and thankfully, we didn't run into each other. We were about the fourth wagon in line behind the main wagon. We heard a bit of a scream from one of the women in the stagecoach. Our hearts lurched. Were we being robbed? Although stagecoach robberies were not that common anymore due to the patrolling of the Royal Canadian Mounted Police (RCMP), they still happened.

Joseph, our eldest brother, jumped off his horse to explore. He came back with a grin on his face. Apparently, there were four men at the side of the road who had flagged the wagon train down. Their cart, full of logs, had tipped over, and now the road was blocked. It didn't take long for the majority of the men belonging to our wagon train to pitch in and get the logs rolled to the side. We were near our next rest stop just outside of Quesnel. Actually, on one of the men's farms, our men had helped to clear the log spill on the road.

After we settled at our rest stop, the men whose cart had tipped over, their wives and children, friends, and neighbours started showing up, bringing meat and fish, stews, pies, and cakes. Of course, everyone was happy for a break and a party. A few guests had brought harmonicas and fiddles. You just couldn't stay still with that stomping rhythm, and soon, almost everyone was on their feet, having a great time. After the recent stressful events we had all been through, it allowed us to blow off steam.

We finally reached our most northerly destination in British Columbia of Prince George, then east to McBride. The wagon train continued eastward and headed to Jasper National Park. We were so close to our destination, and the worst was over. We only had one more creek to pass.

When we neared Jasper, it was as if we ascended to heaven. Jasper is surrounded by huge, towering mountains and glaciers. It was almost unbelievable that any land could be so beautiful.

We were told about natural hot springs nearby, so the ladies and children went first for a nice hot dip, then the men. We were so thankful for getting rid of all the dust caked in our clothes and on our bodies. We camped overnight and left early the next morning for the final leg of our unforgettable journey.

After crossing the British Columbia/Alberta border, the wagon train took another turn, this time leaving into the Peace River Valley area of Alberta.

This "Promised Land" was the latest incentive to populate mid-Alberta in Canada in the late 1800s and the early 1900s. Canada had been calling all pioneers to settle in the Prairies. The gold rush had almost petered out, so people were looking for other adventures, and the promise of cheap, fertile land was alluring. Of course, nothing was mentioned about the hardship of the weather in mid to northern Alberta, the long, harsh frozen winters, floods in the spring, clouds of mosquitoes, and black flies in the summer that bit chunks out of people and livestock.

Settling near a small town gave our family access to the Mercantile store, which sold everything one could think of or if not in stock, could be ordered. There was also a small one-room school and church.

Our land was beautiful. Pops and the boys quickly built a small house and barn to shelter us throughout the summer while a bigger, more permanent house and barn were built. Everyone worked hard, and over the years, along with the size of our house, the nearby community and our own family grew fairly quickly.

Eventually, we had a two-story white clapboard house with green shutters. In the late spring and summer, gorgeous deep red roses bloomed in the garden below, spreading their sweet scent through the gentle breeze into the open windows of the house. We were surrounded by green rolling hills that sprouted several varieties of wildflowers. It was a piece of heaven.

Mom, ever the poet, kept this poem of her beautiful fragrant roses.

(Enclosed was a short poem written by my great-grandmother on the back of an envelope.):

Fragrant dark red roses

In their beauty, they do delight

A symbol of love

And a joy to behold in sight

And read Mom's second, longer poem. She always loved to write. I guess that's where Carys got her love of literature.

Fragrant red roses, a vibrant delight,

Their scent in the air was a sweet respite.

Petals unfold, velvety and bold,

Aromatic whispers, stories untold.

Like flames of passion, their color aflame,

Eternal beauty, they proudly proclaim.

Each bloom is a poem, nature's exquisite art,

Captivating senses, touching every heart.

In their fragrance, love's essence unfurls,

A symphony of aromas, enchanting the world.

With every breath, a Moment held dear,

Fragrant red roses, an eternal cheer.

Olivia went back to the main letters.

It was a very busy summer. We all had to pitch in some way to get our land cleared and plowed. The boys soon turned dark brown, well, their faces at least. We all had to wear long sleeves and pants or skirts to keep the nasty black flies and mosquitoes from eating us alive.

We met life-long friends at the one-room school we started attending that fall. My best friend, Nellie, went with me to Edmonton to work after we graduated. We couldn't wait to turn loose in the city and get away from our parents and the hordes of flying insects.

I think back on those crazy years shortly before the First World War. Life in The Peace was hard. Hard work, hard land, and hard times, but the whole family did their part, and soon, the men and boys had fields cleared and planted with wheat and oats for our livestock. Mom and us girls, even the young ones, cleaned the house, shook out the quilts, and even in winter, washed clothes in a big old tin wash tub, of which we also took our weekly baths, cooked breakfast, lunch, and dinner for the hungry lot of us. In the meantime, from late September to mid-March, we, well, most of us, went to school. Joseph, our eldest brother, gave up school in grade eight. He wasn't much of a student but loved the farm and the animals.

We did have a horrific accident in spring a couple of years after settling in the Peace. Pops, some hired hands, and a few of our older brothers were felling trees perhaps a little too quickly. They wanted to get the land cleared to plant more crops by early spring. A couple of the younger boys were fooling around, something they had been told over and over not to do as they needed to be aware of their surroundings and the work at hand.

Carys, Mom, and I were making lunch when Carys suddenly groaned. She had been looking out the kitchen window, waiting for the men to arrive for lunch. She let out a weird sound, a frantic cry, and went dashing out the door.

Percy, our second to the eldest brother, was flying over the field on his horse like a bat out of hell, yelling something incomprehensible.

"Carys, Carys! Go fetch Dr. Kennedy. A tree fell on Daniel. Hurry." At that, he turned his horse around and practically flew back to the working area.

Carys ran to the barn to hitch up her horse, Daisy and galloped down the road to town, hoping the doctor would be at his clinic in his house. Thankfully, he was, which was a miracle as Mrs. Mitchell was due to have twins any day, but Dr Kennedy's wife was a trained midwife, so he was ok to leave, especially in such an emergency.

Dr. Kennedy grabbed his black medical bag and supplies while Mrs. Kennedy and Carys hitched the horses to the wagon full of hay to transport Daniel back to his surgery as quickly and comfortably as possible.

Daniel had been brought back home on a makeshift stretcher by the time they reached the farmhouse. Mom was crying and holding his hand while Carys and Dr. Kennedy held his other hand. Daniel was unconscious. There was some blood trickling from his nose, and the corner of his mouth was bubbling spots of blood-stained mucus. He looked ghastly. Everyone seemed in shock.

I guess Dr. Kennedy realized there was nothing he could do to help Daniel. The log had crushed his chest, and it was amazing and heartbreaking at the same time that Daniel was still alive. He was carried into the house and laid on sheets and comforters to wait for the inevitable.

Tears were running down all of our eyes. Sweet Daniel, sweet, sweet Daniel. The clown of the family, he always had us in stitches. He sure was one with the jokes. We missed him dearly.

I left the homestead in 1916. The war had been raging for two years already. Two of our brothers, Percy and Joseph, signed up as soon as they could and couldn't wait to go.

Nellie and I had finished school. We both wanted to get away from our parents and prying eyes. We rented a small apartment in Edmonton and were soon able to get jobs as most of the young men were overseas, already fighting the Huns.

I worked as a bookkeeper at an accounting firm, and Nellie was a secretary in a pool of secretaries. In her spare time, Nellie loved to write. She ended up writing a few fabulous books that were eventually published after the war.

Chapter 4
Carys and Henry

Carys loved learning. She turned seventeen in January and would finish school that spring. Carys wanted to be a teacher as she thought education was a never-ending journey of learning and discovery she wanted to pursue. Carys found reading took her to foreign lands, foreign people, and customs. What a great way to learn about the world and everything, really. She learned far more, especially about people, all through books. In her mind, she travelled to India, England, and South America. Although Glen, your great uncle, and I travelled to a great extent in later years, we didn't have children. Carys never did get to see other countries, the ones she had dreamed about through her books.

She was in love with Henry Bernard, a boy she had grown up with at the same small one-room school we all attended. She didn't know anyone who was "in love." Our parents and other relatives were much too old to be in love. No, her love of Henry was beyond the brightness of the stars. Carys never thought love could be anywhere this overwhelming. Her belly always had a warm tingling, an overpowering feeling of wanting to connect with Henry. To feel his strong arms around her. To love every inch of his body.

Carys felt she was an ordinary-looking child, medium height, with long golden-brown hair that shone beautifully in the summer sun. Carys was a tomboy and was constantly being told she couldn't do this or that because only boys did that. She loved being in britches or overalls and would groan on Sundays or holidays or even going to school when Mom insisted she must wear a dress and be presentable.

Carys always did her best to do her chores quickly so she could go read and write somewhere quiet. She also loved exploring the property with me when I still lived there, and on my many visits home, we would roam over the rolling grassy land that had been cleared of trees to build the house and barn. Their female dog had somehow gotten pregnant. Well, we knew the facts of life living on a farm; things were pretty obvious, but we hadn't seen another dog around. "Love will find a way," declared Clarys. The sweet little furry balls of fluff would run and trip over themselves, trying to catch up to her. We would wander down to the small creek where the puppies would splash about as Carys took off her stockings and joined them. We often had a feeling someone was watching us and hoped it wasn't a Momma bear. It was just a boy from school in love with Carys hiding behind a copse of trees, swooning over Carys with her stockings off.

Henry was the first child of four of the Bernard's, all boys. His mother, Corina, had died on the grueling journey from Ontario to Alberta. She had been pregnant for the fifth time. Corina hadn't even known she was pregnant that last fatal time. The journey turned out to be far too challenging. Although they travelled in groups, no one in attendance knew how to stop the bleeding after she miscarried. Both baby and mother died. It was a sad loss, leaving behind Henry, his brothers, and his Dad, Samuel, to fend for themselves. Considering Samuel was the only preacher within fifty miles at the time, the church ladies would take turns bringing food or helping out with "female" chores. It did add to the church women's already heavy daily chores on the homesteads, but they gladly took their turn looking after the handsome, still young, and now available preacher. Many were widows themselves, some still young. The war to end all wars had already taken a toll on many families.

Henry, the eldest son, would also go into the ministry after graduating from school. He was a good-looking boy and was definitely filling out his body working the fields. Henry was a tall boy with dark hair and "dreamy" eyes, according to Carys. He was smart in school and quite the athlete in school and community sports. He loved playing hockey, his favourite winter sport, and baseball in the summer. All the families in the surrounding area would flock to the outdoor games, especially during playoffs, to see Henry play. One winter, scouts from the Winnipeg Falcons professional team came to watch Henry and would have offered Henry a contract, but war was looming, and Henry wouldn't have wanted to leave his Dad with his three younger siblings, who were a handful. Maybe he would have another opportunity after he graduated high school, and the war would be over quickly, as the powers were predicting.

Carys wasn't always in love with Henry. Actually, she could hardly stand him when he was younger. He was such a teaser and prankster, pulling at her braids and throwing snowballs at her in the winter on their walk home from school or starting a race without warning so that he would always win and tease her relentlessly for being a girl. Like she could help that. Carys would rather have been a boy. They got to do so many more things without getting into trouble, like climbing trees and going off to war to fight Fritz, the Germans.

Henry wasn't so sure about the war. His Dad was a preacher and wanted his son to become a minister, as his grandfather had done. It was a family tradition for the eldest son to go into the ministry. Henry was not at all keen on killing a human being. He wasn't a coward at all. He just didn't understand how killing all of the Germans was going to solve anything. However, Fritz was killing Canadians, and that made him angry. Henry constantly told Carys he would go to France and stand with her brothers even if he wouldn't carry a rifle. Percy and Joseph were leaving in the next few days. Henry just needed to be one or two years older.

Carys remembers the day she progressed from "putting up" with Henry to falling in love with a big bang. It was a day like all the others in early winter. As usual, Henry walked home with Carys until the road forked one way to Carys's place and the other to Henry's. He grabbed her from behind and tossed her into the snowbank. Oh, she was mad. Henry lay in the snowbank beside her after a bit of a wrestling match.

"Carys, you are so beautiful," said Henry.

"You must be blind," replied Carys.

Henry moved over, facing her, and suddenly, they began kissing. And oh, did they kiss like they had been starved for contact. They were getting soaked from the snow by that time, but as they got up from the snowbank to go to their prospective houses, they realized a huge change had taken place. They were in love. Suddenly, the grey skies seemed to part just for them, and the sun shone on their faces, warming them all over. Their eyes lit up, and they hugged briefly. Without saying a word to each other, they separated, each running towards their own homes, feeling light and dreamy. Teenage hormones had been ignited.

Carys could barely wait for me to return home for the holidays. Thankfully, there was now a rail line that travelled from Edmonton to the Peace River area. Nellie and I were able to visit both of our families often now. We were both from large families and although we were together in Edmonton, we dearly missed our rambunctious siblings and parents.

Soon, it would be Christmas. As always, there was a heap of snow in December, and everything was frozen. It was -20 C, and the windchill made everything cold and miserable but, at the same time, beautiful and peaceful when the sun came out, making the landscape glitter like diamonds on the snow. Long icicles hung from the roofs of the house, barn, and windows. Carys and I would go for walks on snowshoes which Pops had made for us. It was a wonderland; all you could hear was the snow crunching under our feet, the breaking frozen branches of the trees cracking like a rifle shot, and our breath steaming like a kettle after we had walked some. We loved the crisp, clean air, and we were happy to be outdoors during the winter instead of combating freezing rain in our previous home in Chilliwack. In our homestead in the Peace, we would return from an outing in winter to a hot fire blazing in the floor-to-ceiling stone fireplace in the great room and have a cup of hot chocolate milk and biscuits. It was heavenly.

Your grandmother and I were always close, even though we were a couple of years apart in age. In some ways, we were totally opposite in character and, in other ways, pretty similar.

That Christmas, it was the Delaney family's turn to visit the Bernard's home for Christmas dinner and celebration. Nelly and I made it home from Edmonton just before the last big snowstorm.

Carys missed me a lot, and I missed her. Carys yearned for someone to confide in, to share her secrets and dreams as we always had done. Our younger sisters were still too inexperienced to understand, and she couldn't bring herself to discuss matters of the heart, matters of falling in love with her brothers, or even our mother. Heaven forbids what they might say.

Two of our brothers, Percy and Joseph, were leaving sometime after Christmas to join the Canadian 49th Battalion in Edmonton, which had already sent a group of soldiers to Halifax for training and sent overseas in 1915. To their great disappointment, the younger brothers weren't eligible to join the fight until both were eighteen in 1916. There was a lot of patriotism, and they would never think of not joining up. They just had to wait to be of age. Joseph had turned eighteen already but wanted to wait for Percy to come of age. Joseph never did anything without Percy.

Nobody spoke of it, but all realized it might be their last Christmas together for quite a while to come. There had been higher patriotism and hope for a quick end to the war when it began and through 1915. Too many men ended up as casualties, but through newspapers and town meetings, Canada still believed in the war, and there was a constant push for our men to remain faithful, strong, and proud to serve with Britain and the Allied forces.

Pops hitched the horses up to the large snow sled. The snow was falling lightly. It was already getting dark at 3:00 in the afternoon. Still, Pops had been out with the horses and sled every day for the past three, keeping a path cleared to town, the school/church, and their neighbors, the Bernards and the Wilsons.

Everyone dressed in several layers, including long johns for the ladies, too. Then we climbed into the wagon, piled a few blankets on top of us, and away we went, the horses prancing and jingling down the path as if they knew it was Christmas and a day to be merry.

The feast was wonderful. Samuel had cooked a turkey with help from his sons and our family, plus the Wilsons brought the extras, including Christmas pudding with rum sauce. The families ate until we were all more than satisfied. After dinner, we sang carols around the old piano that had somehow been transported from Edmonton. After dinner, we played games until the young ones started to nod off. So back on went our layers of inner and outerwear. Joseph got the horses from the barn, as Pops was a little loopy from the punch, hitched them to the sled, and Christmas was done for another year.

Carys and Henry tried not to be too obvious about their change of feelings for each other during their Christmastime together, but try as they might, their eyes found each other, and it was hard to look away. Carys had butterflies in her tummy every time Henry looked at her. She was on cloud nine. Mother certainly tried to keep her eye on Carys, realizing this was Carys's first experience of love.

It's a good thing Mom or Pops didn't see them hidden behind the staircase smooching away. I had to make sure that Cary knew about the "birds and the bees," although living on the farm was a lesson in itself. I had never been explained how pregnancy really worked until I met Glen, the man I would later marry. He was a pharmacist but well-schooled in medicine, too.

Chapter 5

Percy and Joseph

The following June, the older Delaney boys had been more than determined to sign up to join the military after reading a bulletin from Edmonton on June 10, 1915.

"A man enlisting for active service naturally prefers to go to the front with men he has known, and as part of a battalion whose fortunes may be watched by the relatives and friends, he leaves behind. One of the infantry battalions, the 101st, has been wiped out of existence, and its members are attached to battalions from nobody knows where. The process of attrition has begun upon another, the 51st, and the prospect that only the 49th may be allowed to get to the front as an Edmonton unit."

Percy and Joseph left for Edmonton to join the proud 49th. Finally, Percy turned eighteen.

Percy was the letter writer, and Joseph left him to it. He never could get his letters straight as in his ABCs. Things looked backward when he wrote, and his knuckles could still feel the ruler smacked across his fingers from their teacher. He dropped out of school. He didn't need it. He was the eldest and would take over the farm one day. He was good at math and could do figures in his head, which really was the most important thing to him. He had to make sure to keep the farms' accounts in order, and Papa sure didn't do a good job of that.

Percy and Joseph spent the first night in Edmonton and met up with me (Belle) and my girlfriend, Nellie. Boy, what a fun night we had. Prohibition hadn't started yet. That would happen in 1918.

Even when Prohibition was on from 1918 to 1920, alcohol wasn't too hard to find. All you had to do was go to the many bootleggers or ask your doctor for a prescription for a bottle of Gin or Whiskey, which they were happy to do. After all, they made a lot of money that way. Nobody seemed to care. There were some disgruntled people in our era who thought all of life's problems were caused by booze. After a few years, it was evident that prohibition didn't solve society's woes.

After a delicious dinner at the hotel, the girls took the boys to a bar hidden behind a fake front. Unless you knew it was there, you would walk right on by. Joseph and Percy had a bash of a time. Girls were dancing with girls, and some boys were dancing with boys, then there were boys dancing with girls. It was all so confusing, but there was definitely an excess of women, and that kept Percy hopping all night. Joseph was too tongue-tied to talk to the girls but chatted away with a bloke who would be on the same train as them, heading to Halifax the next day for training. They both disappeared for an hour or two, but Percy figured they went out for fresh air and smoke. In a couple of months, they would board a ship in Nova Scotia with others from the 49th Battalion and others across Canada.

The next morning, even though a bit hungover, Percy and Joseph were excited as youngsters at Christmas. They were at the Edmonton train station about to board the train to Halifax along with hundreds of other soldiers, or soldiers to be. All these young men and boys were really looking forward to the excitement of learning to be soldiers and travelling to England and France. Who would have ever thought they would get to travel to another country? They would fight off their enemies during the day, go drinking in the bars, and dance with the foreign girls at night. Oh, the beautiful foreign girls with French accents would love these boys from Canada. They were all feeling pretty cocky and full of themselves.

The following poem was printed in "The Forty Niner," and it was good the boys hadn't read it before taking off for war. It sounded very gloomy, but at the same time, they knew their duty to God and country. At least, that was the way of thinking back then.

Eager to go. Why! Why!

When going means forsaking

Home and friends and all that dearest seems,

Position, comfort, and farewelling

All fond ambition's dreams.

Eager to go. Why! Why!

Eager to go. Why! Why!

When eager means, perhaps,

Eager to die, eager for pain.

Eager, perhaps, to travel down the Western slope

Before the peak of life's full strength is gained.

Eager to go. Why! Why!

Eager to go. Why! Why!

Have all life's sweets proved bitter to the tongue?

Does hope lie slain?

Has evening's gloom attended morning hours,

And life held only shattered plans and longings in vain?

Eager to go. Why! Why!

Eager to go. Why Not?

Can we forget Belgium's brave vicarious grief?

Forget Louvain?

In a few short days, forget her ravished homes, her noble slain?

Eager to go. Why not?

Eager to go. Why not?

When mighty foes are drinking to

"The Day" of Britain's fall

Shall we not, for dear Empire's sake,

Hear and obey the call?

Eager to go. Why not?

Eager to go. Why Not?

When we believe the path of battle

Is today the path of God?

When we believe the Voice that calls us

Is the Voice of our Eternal Lord

Eager to go. Why not when God and duty call?

Yes, yes, thank God - eager to go. Unknown

Chapter 6

Off to Battle

Percy, the letter writer, sent his first of many letters from England and France to Mom and the family. Mom kept some of the letters and passed them down to me, although I gave them to Carys in later years. She was the writer and historian in the family.

Postcard: April 30th, 1916

Halifax, NS

Mrs. Delaney,

Dear Mother

Just a line to let you know we are alive and well, had a pretty good trip (on the train), and will arrive in Halifax in about an hour. I don't know whether we'll sail today or not, but others think we will. Have to close off now, with love to all.

Percy

The letters over the years of the war were sporadic, but Percy was dedicated to keeping the family informed. Postcards and pencils were given to the men from the Red Cross and the YMCA to write home, but some of the letters were often redacted. Paper was scarce at times, and letters were often written in small penmanship and on every available spot on the 3 x 4" paper or postcard. The men were encouraged to be positive in their letters and not to mention their exact location or what they were doing; it would be redacted, and they would waste their paper.

The boys didn't leave Halifax right away. They had to have training first. Being farm boys, they already knew how to shoot rifles, but they were pushed to their physical limits over and over again, running up and over wooden barriers, crawling on their bellies through mud while the drill sergeant yelled above them to "plant your face in the mud," "get down private, Fritz would have shot your skinny ass by now."

They were already exhausted and missed their warm beds in the Peace Country.

Finally, they boarded the ship headed for France.

Postcard June 1916

Dear Mother,

Just a line to say we are on our way to France. That is the same bunch except for Charlie. He had to stay behind, but it will be over pretty soon. Haven't got your letter yet.

Give my love to all.

Your loving son, Percy

Percy, Joseph, and the other men of the 49th soon found they weren't shooting rifles right away as they hoped. Rather, they walked for miles and miles through the elaborate trenches the soldiers had built well before their arrival. Their job entailed repairing and fortifying the tunnels with barbed wire and sandbags, digging latrines, and removing the dead and wounded. They built cubby holes fortified by wood like little cabins for the higher-ups and radio room but not for the lackeys like them.

Their duties bore no resemblance to the expectations and battle training they had been given. Their initial eagerness to fight had quickly dissipated, replaced by the grim task of cleaning up the aftermath. They found themselves as the "mop-up" crew, gathering the lifeless bodies of fallen soldiers scattered across the vacated battlefields, often dismembered and unrecognizable. The stench of charred flesh from incendiary devices and the acrid, metallic odor of blood overwhelmed them, triggering waves of nausea. These haunting odors invaded their dreams, leading many to shout out in their sleep, desperately seeking solace and comfort. Many turned to fervent prayers, yet their pleas seemed unheard, driving some to tears as they longed for the tender embrace and gentle kisses of their mothers.

No Man's Land

No Man's Land is an eerie sight

At early dawn, in the pale grey light.

Never a house and never a hedge

In No Man's Land, from edge to edge.

And never a living soul walked there to taste the freshness of
the morning air.

Only some lumps of rotting clay that were friends or foemen yesterday.

What are the hounds of No Man's Land?

You can see them clearly in either hand —

A mound of rag -bags grey in the sun.

Or a furrow of brown where the earthworks run from the eastern hills to the western sea

Through field or forest o'er river and Lea;

No man may pass them but aim you well, and death rides across

On the bullet or shell.

But No Man's Land is a goblin sight when patrols crawl over the dead at night; Boche or British, Belgium or French.

You dice with death when you cross the trench.

When the "rapid" like fireflies in the dark flit down the parapet spark by spark and you drop for cover

To keep your head with your face on the breast if the four months' dead.

The man who ranges in No Man's Land is dogged by the shadows on either hand.

When the star shell flares as it bursts o'er-head,

Scares the great grey rats that feed on the dead.

And the bursting bomb or the bayonet snatch may answer the click of your safety catch.

For the line patrol, with his life in his hand

Is hunting for blood in No Man's Land.

——-Captain J.K. Adkin, in the Spectator

The 49th Division, of which Percy, Joseph, and several men from the Peace River area belonged, saw their first real battle, "at last" they all declared.

Their time so far had been quiet in comparison to what would unfold at the Somme and later battles.

In September 1916, the 3rd Canadian Division, including the 49th battalion with Percy and Joseph, had been moved to the Flers-Courcelette sector in France and became part of the Battle of the Somme, a fierce battle intended to relieve pressure on the French defenders of Verdun.

"Well, dear brother, we're in for some excitement now. It will be a long walk through the trenches and on rural roads to get to the Somme, but we'll be heroes after we wipe out Fritz," said Percy.

"I'm tired of digging ditches and trenches. Every time it rains, not only are we sopping wet but full of mud too. Every time I hear that buzzing noise, I know there's going to be a shell exploding, and if it's close by, well, then we're eating mud." replied Joseph.

"We'll stick close by to each other and the other boys too. We'll be a force to reckon with."

The following morning, they set out one by one, following the leader on the long road to the Somme, onward to a long and bloody battle.

Soldiers on both sides of the battle fought along an 18-mile stretch around the Somme River in France. The grueling skirmish raged on from July to November 1916. It was a trial by fire for many as they mentally prepared themselves for what would become the deadliest and longest battle of World War I. The atmosphere was stifling, with an uneasiness that permeated the entire area.

Throughout the day, intense fighting continued, with neither side making significant advances, but both sides stubbornly pushed forward. As the sun began to set, the chaos and gunfire were intermixed with the sounds of birds chirping, creating a strange and surreal experience.

The British (and allied troops) began with an offensive, resulting in thousands of casualties, some 57,000 killed in the first day alone. The lack of preparation and inferior equipment, including faulty rifles, slowed down progress on both sides. However, a Canadian Brigadier General named Greisbach helped to provide better Enfield rifles, replacing the notoriously unreliable Ross Rifles. The Canadians were aided by the use of tanks in this battle as well. Aircraft became important for the first time in the Great War.

Hundreds of thousands of soldiers were injured or died, but not our brothers. Something happened to their brains, it seemed. It was the most horrific situation they had ever faced in their lives. When they were younger, the boys had seen and endured a lot, moving from one part of Canada to another, to an undeveloped area of Alberta. Sure, land was cheap, but it was a lifetime of hard work and tenacity. Both boys and most of their pals had butchered pigs or cows, so death was a part of life. For so many reasons, the death of another human was nowhere near the same. After a few days on the battlefield, knowing that it's "us or them," keeping yourself alive was the priority, and if killing or wounding another man prevented you from dying, well, it had to be done. The soldiers developed a sense of being in a nightmare that never ended. The shelling back and forth was relentless, and many men had been killed by "friendly fire" or explosives detonating at the wrong time. Nothing seemed to work the way it should. They were in a sort of trance. Ordered down at night, they crawled into any cubbyhole built into the walls of the trenches they could find or lay down as close to the sides of the trenches as they could. Bloated by food and garbage, huge rats ran over them at night, their tiny feet running from one soldier to another. Lice was an ongoing problem. Their bites spread disease, and many soldiers came down with trench fever, giving them high fevers and muscle pain. During the damp months, of which there were many, trench foot was common and had to be cared for immediately, or the foot may turn gangrenous and have to be amputated.

The weather was in itself another enemy for both the Allies and Germans. During the torrential downpours in spring and fall, their uniforms would get saturated with water, making them heavy and irritating on the necks and shoulders where they carried their heavy equipment.

Food was out of billy cans and never enough. Their ration of rum was a bit of a help at night when there were no nightly raids. At times, the rum didn't reach the men in the trenches, but they knew not to complain. Life was a challenge all around. The men lost weight from stress, lack of proper nutrition, and lack of deep sleep. However, at night, after the darkness arrived, after battling the enemy at dusk for a few hours, they were so exhausted it felt as if they were unconscious as soon as their heads hit the dirt floor or their coat if it was warm at night. After darkness arrived, there was a team of soldiers who crawled out onto the battlefield to retrieve the dead and wounded from No Man's Land. Nobody liked that task, but the brothers often volunteered. After all, they had started out in this war, retrieving the bodies of fellow soldiers.

They found they often faced the enemy in no-man's-land during the night, searching for fallen men. Instead of shooting each other, they realized the German body retrievers were hauling Canadian soldiers back over the line to the Canadians. The boys could hardly believe their eyes. That was actually more difficult for them to handle emotionally. This type of kindness was certainly not shown by all the Germans, but it gave the boys pause to realize that their enemy had hearts and had families just like theirs waiting at home, praying their boys would be delivered back to them alive and unharmed.

One private had his poem entered in an army magazine. It said all there is to say.

Aftermath

With Desolation and the Stars
I lonely vigil keep,
Over the garner'd fields of Mars,
Watching the dead men sleep —
Huddled together, so silent there.
With bloodless faces and clotted hair,
Wrapped in their long, long sleep!

By uptorn trees and crater rims
Along the Ridge, they lie,
Sprawled in the mud, without-spread limbs,

Wide staring at the sky.
Why to the sky do they always stare,
Questioning heaven in dumb despair?
Why don't they moan or sigh?

Why do I rave 'neath the callous stars,
At their upturned faces white?
I, surely I, with my crimson scars
Slumber with them this night!
Death, with shadowy finger bare,
Beckons me on to — I know not where;
But huddled together and freed from care.
We'll watch till the dawn of Light.

From the Somme,
1916

Pte. Frank Walker

When weather conditions allowed or under the cloak of moonless nights, night attacks became a constant reality. The soldiers would swiftly scramble over the trench edges and cautiously crawl forward, maneuvering on their bellies, slipping into holes or craters left behind by shell bombardments. Aside from the perils posed by the enemy, they had to be vigilant of additional hazards.

The craters, formed by the devastating bombs, often held stagnant water, rising to a soldier's waist or even higher. They knew there may be barbed wire unseen below the water. Although reconnaissance was done of the crater holes the night before, if a soldier leaped in the wrong crater, he could become entangled and injured by the unforgiving barbs. If the hole was full of water, it wasn't unusual for the men to drown. Most would not be rescued until after dark. Many had died by then.

Amidst the onslaught of Allied soldiers advancing against the Germans, as they rushed from their trenches to confront the enemy, the risks were always present. In an instant, you could be struck by a bullet, your leg severed by an explosion, or find yourself lying on the battlefield, clinging to life. The chaos of men running through explosions of body parts, mud, and blood or engaging in hand-to-hand combat with a German. If no comrade was near enough to offer aid or incapable of doing so, the trapped soldier would face a protracted, torturous demise, either bleeding out or succumbing to the chilling embrace of drowning within the rainwater-filled crater.

The night moves were tedious, the waiting and listening for the approach of the Germans. At times, the enemy seemed close enough to smell their fear. They spent long hours waiting in the cold and mud for their next orders to charge again. It left too much time for thinking, which was too much to bear for many. Some lads seemed to purposely pop their heads up from their holes and were promptly shot by one or more German soldiers, an easy suicide.

Only a month ago, a soldier was shot right behind our quarters by the military police. The dumb sod tried to flee one night. The lad looked only sixteen years old. Those fools, lying about their age to be heroes. And now they are dead. How horrifying if their family knew. Desertion is a deadly word.

Both sides fired shells and sniper bullets, often without a specific target, keeping the soldiers on edge and exhausted. Infantry and machine gunners bore the brunt of the fire, with hundreds suffering death or injury daily. The Front was a deathly place where souls wafted away like mist, hoping for a kind afterlife.

Flares would go off at night, lighting up the battlefield sepia. A bleak and hard land. Occasionally, a German soldier would sneak close to our trenches on his belly and open his blow torch, setting our men on fire. Those screams were the hardest to get out of your head. Same with the images. How do you not keep seeing and smelling the atrocities?

There was a rhythm to the war in many ways. Soldiers rotated duties and were usually at the front for a week or more, then rotated back to their resting and shower areas. The next rotation would put them at work fortifying and digging new trenches. Often, tunnels were dug directly under the German tunnels or beside them. If the Germans discovered the Allied tunnel, they would detonate their own tunnel after ensuring none of their men would be harmed but take out several of the British/Canadian soldiers.

At times, having pushed the Germans back, the Allied soldiers were astonished at the elaborate German trenches. Often brilliantly designed, with actual offices and rooms often fortified with cement. A startling discovery putting their own feeble trenches to shame.

There were some battles where a soldier could be kept at the front battling away for a month or more with no relief, often due to the huge numbers of soldiers dying or having been severely wounded. They constantly needed more soldiers; it was a revolving door between the living and the dead.

They battled on for months. Rotating from the front to the rear, round and round, they went, distressed each time they got to the rear of the YMCA socialization tent, which showed how many men of their division they had lost through their time at the front. Men they had practically grown up with. Men who helped each other with tasks on the farm that needed a lot of manpower, those they graduated with.

It was very wearing on the men of the 49th division, those that remained.

It was becoming a living hell. Percy and Joseph carried on as they knew they must.

Although there were lulls in the action, the trenches were never truly quiet. At times, each side had to either withdraw or make a limited advance. It was a relentless back-and-forth struggle, with neither side able to make significant gains. Battle strategies were constantly changing depending on reconnaissance and the state of the general's minds. The men often questioned among themselves the lack of mental stability among some of their leaders.

Many battles baffled the soldiers, for they seemed to have no strategic value or clear path to victory. Charging onto the battlefield meant climbing the ladders of the trenches, becoming a death trap for the first men over the top. It seemed impossible to emerge victorious under such conditions.

More than one new recruit was terrified and had to be yelled at by fellow soldiers or their captain to "get their asses over the top," only to be blown to pieces.

Those "lucky" enough to have lived through the terror had to repeat the same type of battle over and over, some for years. Percy and Joseph were only at the end of their first year. They had a long way to go.

Singing in the trenches during the lulls or at night was common with many a bawdy tune, but it helped lift their spirits, slamming the war, their enemies, or their superiors.

I Want To Go Home

I want to go home. I want to go home.

I want to go in the trenches no more,

Where whizzbangs and shrapnel they whistle and roar.

Take me over the sea, where the Alleyman can't get at me.

Oh my, I don't want to die. I want to go home.

I want to go home. I want to go home.

I don't want to visit la Belle France no more,

For oh, the Jack Johnsons, they make such a roar.

Take me over the sea, where the snipers they can't get at me.

Oh my, I don't want to die. I want to go home.

The Alleyman referred to the Germans at Allemagne, and the Jack Johnson were heavy shells.

Shelling and sniper fire were often random from each side. Sudden death was expected every day. This contributed to the high levels of stress that would eventually wear them down. Hundreds of soldiers were killed and wounded every day. The infantry and machine gunners took the majority of the fire. Death surrounded them on a daily basis, especially when fighting at the Front. If one believed in spirits or souls ascending, surely, they saw hundreds floating up as mists on the battlefield, hopefully onto a kinder, more beautiful, and more loving place.

At the rear of the fighting, there was time to relax in the YMCA tents, reading or writing and chatting with fellow soldiers waiting for new orders to move to the front or move the unit altogether to the next planned major attack.

They loved reading the Forty-Niner, their troops' own newspaper. A couple of limericks caught their eye and gave the boys a good chuckle.

We're dry as dirty bones

We speak in husky tones

Our tins and cups are here

We hate this smelly beer

But rum is what we pray and crave for now.

By and by, by and by,

In the sweet by and by,

We'll have some rum to drink

By and by, in the sweet by and by. Unknown

There were some fun times, though, with the boys of the 49th. A brief break from their duties of war. As reported in the Forty-Niner, we had another battle: Our "Football Match." The battle of all battles on which the fate of nations depends. A football match between the Pioneers, of which Percy and Joseph were part, and the Transport. What a glorious day, but not for the Pioneers, unfortunately.

An excerpt from the Forty-Niner spoke of the battle that day.

It had been a freezing night, and the round was in perfect condition for the game, which was to decide the destination of the rum issue. Many a quaking heartbeat under a service tunic, many a stalwart and thought of home and mother as he faced the opposing side, fearful of what would be his end once the battle was over. But each and every man was willing and ready to lay down his life for the issue of rum.

As the referee raised his whistle to his lips, a breathless silence pervaded the atmosphere. The battle has commenced on which the fates of nations depend.

In spite of wonderful tactical operations, the first death is to the Pioneers, who lost the first goal.

The Pioneers advance under cover of the dirt on their perspiring faces, determined to win or die.

Backward and forwards swayed the tide of the battle. Wounded men fought with too much at stake to quit.

At last, a rush that could not be stemmed by all the armies of the world, the Transports, with a mighty attack, bomb the goal of the enemy, reducing it to atoms, score that final goal, and with heads proudly poised march in column of route from off the blood-stained field amid the voluminous cheers of the admiring crowds.

Percy and Joseph hadn't played in that football game but cheered them on from the sidelines. It was times like these that gave men hope, even if it was just for an extra ration of rum. That small victory, or even the loss, drew the men together for a few laughs, a few hours to put the war in the back of their minds.

Percy wrote home as often as possible, kept a few diaries over the years of war, and sent them home whenever possible.

Although Joseph was never far from Percy, the loneliness and longing for home never truly left. The army tried to keep the soldiers busy with battle drills and everyday duties, but there were plenty of times for quiet reflection.

An excerpt from one of Percy's diaries talks of his depression and yearning for home.

"The war has crushed my spirit, and every moment of every day feels like torture. Since joining the Army, I have long longed for my peaceful life back home in the prairies. The mud, filth, and continuous gunfire had taken a toll on me - both physically and mentally. I miss my family so terribly. I feel the war has transformed me into a shell of my former self. Sometimes, when I have a few quiet moments alone, I cry, but most of the time, I need to keep my emotions buried deep. I'm so very exhausted, and I feel trapped in a thick fog with no clear way out. I can't even talk to Joseph about how I'm feeling. He's far braver than me. I want to go home.

I can't let ol' Sergeant McIntyre know how I really feel, or I might just be shot or, worse, sent to a mental hospital like that boy last week in the trenches. He plumb went off his rocker. Yelping and dancing around like some fool. He was babbling like a baby. Nobody could understand a word he was saying. I'm so tired, so so tired. I don't know how I can carry on with this fighting. Even when we get sent for rest, there's never much rest at all. We can still hear the shells and the gunfire from the front lines. You'd think I'd be used to hearing it by now, but the booms still make my heart jump. I haven't received a package or letter from home in many weeks. Have they forgotten about me? Joseph keeps telling me the war has to be over soon. I know he believes it, but I can't. There is no end."

Chapter 7

Percy Gets Injured

In November 1916, shortly before the end of the Battle of Somme, Percy got hit by shrapnel from a nearby exploded shell. He wasn't severely injured and was happy for the field hospital break.

According to what I could read from Percy's diary, it was the worst battle the two had seen to that point.

Percy had been transported to the mobile surgical hospital after being carried off the battlefield by Joseph, who really did have the strength of an ox. An ambulance arrived when they reached the muster point of safety. A woman was driving, which was not at all unusual as men were needed for fighting. They were brave women, certainly as brave as any man during war. Sure, they "just" drove the ambulance, but many times, they had to do so under cover of darkness with no headlights while possibly being targeted by the enemy. More than one ambulance had driven into an unseen ditch.

Percy hated to leave Joseph behind as they had been glued to each other for comradery and support all their lives. Percy kept his eye on the pretty female ambulance driver. He wasn't in that much pain, although his side hurt like heck. He figured a little bit of flirting wasn't too out of line. He had been injured, after all. Surely, he could only hope this angel would bring him out of his funk.

The mobile hospital was full. It was a horror. Percy realized how lucky he and his brother had been. It really was a miracle, a crap shoot, of who would be the next to be injured or killed.

In the hospital, which Percy wanted to get out of as soon as possible, there was a constant movement by the health care team and constant screaming from the operating room. Most soldiers' lungs were full of tar and nicotine, and the anesthetics used back then didn't always work completely on the blackened lungs. Percy found it hard to look at times. Men were missing half their faces, their limbs, everything you can imagine. Men of all ages would sob at night. Morphine and cocaine were the drugs of choice as long as the field hospital didn't run out, which happened often enough. At times, medical convoys bringing medicine didn't always make it from pick up to delivery.

Somehow, Percy saw how grateful he was not to have been as seriously injured as some of these poor blokes.

Important health measures were created during WW1. Triaging was introduced. Some men with more minor injuries were attended to on the battlefield or in the trenches. Other soldiers were classified into emergency or urgent care and attended to in order of priority. Some, like Percy, were taken to a relatively nearby mobile army surgical hospital via ambulance. Others were stabilized and sent on trains to established hospitals for added treatment.

Ether or nitrous oxide was used as anesthetics per face mask. However, new techniques, such as endotracheal intubation, were introduced, allowing for more complete sedation. Plastic surgery came into being as many men had severe facial wounds.

Other soldiers had been blinded or had their lungs injured by the horrible effects of the yellow-greenish gas that the Germans began to use. The Allied armies were horrified, but they ended up using it, too. All soldiers were supposed to have gas masks, but occasionally, they got lost or damaged, and a soldier had to wait for a replacement. All soldiers knew not to fall to the ground when a gas attack occurred because the gas was heavier and thicker near the ground.

The onset of the First World War introduced cocaine to the battlefields, where it gained popularity among Canadian infantrymen. This drug, originally developed in the 1860s, caused significant concern among the British population in 1915 due to its widespread use by Canadian soldiers stationed in the United Kingdom. In response, the British army distributed a medicine called "Tabloid" or "Forced March," which contained cocaine and an extract from cola nuts. It was believed to instill fearlessness and alleviate combat fatigue. Cocaine was also frequently consumed without medical supervision, as it proved to be an effective aid for boosting morale in the trenches. London pharmacists capitalized on the demand by selling medical kits containing cocaine and heroin. Women joyfully purchased these kits, advertised as "useful presents for friends at the front," and eagerly sent them to their loved ones serving on the front lines, including their sons, fiancés, and husbands. Becoming addicted to opioids was rampant, and there wasn't any rehabilitation help back home. You were a lousy down-and-out druggie, spurned by society, at least in North America and Britain.

Mental health problems went untreated. "Pull up your bootstraps and get to it" was the prevalent attitude for decades, even after the Vietnam War. Men became shell-shocked, a condition caused by the constant and catastrophic stress of warfare. PTSD, or post-traumatic stress disease, affected almost every man and woman who attended the war theatre.

Over the several weeks of healing at the mobile hospital, Percy was moved to a cottage used to rehabilitate soldiers. There, he got to see Angela, the ambulance driver. She really was a doll and would sit with him when she was not on a call, and they would chat for hours about his home in Canada and hers in England. Angela was like her namesake, an angel with soft honey-blonde hair that she would shake out of the bun she wore under her cap whenever she was with Percy. Angela wasn't that tall, but neither was Percy at 5'9. She fit perfectly into him, the top of her head reaching just under his chin. She was lean from the war but also very strong from lifting stretchers into the ambulance during her shifts.

Percy had never been in love, not like this. Maybe it was the urgency of the war that pushed men and women together. They realized at any moment, their lives could end. There was no time for long, drawn-out romance.

When Percy was doing his initial rehab, whenever Angela was available, they would walk around the cottage compound trying to find a few secret hideaways to be together. Just as many other couples did the same, they often had to walk away to get away from prying eyes, but they did it with a smile on their faces. Percy and Angela would kiss and cuddle; having sex was challenging, but they found their ways. On Angela's days off, she would show up with a picnic basket and blanket, and they found their favourite spot near a creek and spent hours talking and getting to know each other. There was an urgency between them when they found themselves alone. They wanted to engulf each other with their whole being. They never wanted to let go and eagerly awaited their next (not-so-secret) rendezvous. Several other soldiers had connected with nurses and other female support staff. Life seemed short.

While healing, Percy had been in constant worry for his brother, Joseph. He often asked the matron if she had a list of casualties, and she just laughed. Apparently, most mobile health clinics had a hard time keeping up with the wounded. Yes, somebody somewhere had a list, but she only knew the wounded in her clinic.

After a few weeks of therapy, Percy was well enough to join his brother and the division of 49ers again. His mood had lifted after meeting Angela; her joy of life had not been dampened, and her love for Percy shone through. They vowed to stay in contact as best as they could. Both hoped the war would be over by Christmas, although many thought the same thing the year before. Percy found a small piece of metal that he fashioned into a ring of sorts and, getting down on one knee, which still pulled the stitches at his side, he proposed to Angela, which she very happily accepted. They remained positive throughout, exchanging letters when they couldn't be together and making plans for their future after the war. They never ever mentioned the impossible to think; they may not live to be together as husband and wife.

Percy often sang this song, or part of it, to Angela. It kept their hopes alive.

I'll be seeing you in all the old familiar places

That this heart of mine

Embraces all day through

In that small cafe

The park across the way

In every lovely summer's day

In everything that's light and gay

I'll always think of you that way

I'll find you in the morning sun

And when the night is new

I'll be looking at the moon

But I'll be seeing you

Chapter 8

In Flanders Fields

Etaples France

Dec. 2nd, 1916

Dear Belle,

I just received your letter this morning, so I thought I'd better drop you a line. In fact, I got three or four letters from home and had about fifteen altogether. Thank goodness most of them were answered before I got them! I'm sorry you got scared about me being wounded. I don't know who sent the card if it was me, I don't know what I was thinking about.

It certainly is queer how such news gets about. It was the 10th of November when I got hit. It has healed up, and I'll be going back to the trenches in a few days.

Mother said Mildred told her that Eddy said I was very thin, well I was pretty rough looking when I saw Eddy last, it was after we got out of the hell-hole that there was so much news about in the papers, it was rather trying on a fellow's health, but I'm feeling fine now and looking good too. Of course, I didn't come out here to get fat.

I haven't heard from Jim or Ed for a long time or Charlie either. Maryl said she heard he was wounded. I wish I knew where he was.

I'm sorry to say that the bunch of men (from the 49th) is getting small.

We may have more of the boys with us one of these times. Tell Hanson I got his letter but didn't answer; I'm not sure where he'll be.

Harold wants to know how many Huns I've killed. It was some question, but I told him I had one to ask. Ask him if he wants me to bring one home.

Well, sister, I'm very sorry I can't get some little things sent home for Christmas, but I can't get any money over here. However, I will send along some little souvenirs from the front as soon as I can.

I got the book this morning, but none of the other parcels.

Our company has a rule that if a man is not here (if a man has died), his parcels are divided amongst us boys.

Thinking of you in advance

Your loving bro.'

Percy

P.s. I met the fine doctor who wrote that beautiful poem about Flanders Field, John McCrae. I'll send it to Mom as I know it would mean so much to her to learn I met him. I didn't realize he was an older gentleman. He told me what inspired him to write this and other poems. A mate of his had been killed. Dr McCrae was serving as a gunner and a surgeon, so he saw and did it all.

He personally buried his friend. He said he was so overwhelmed watching p oppies blossom around the graves of fallen soldiers and felt compelled to write. I've enclosed his poem.

In Flanders Fields

In Flanders Fields, the poppies blow

Between the crosses, row on row,

That marks our place and in the sky

The larks, still bravely singing, fly

Scarce heard amid the guns below.

We are the dead. Short days ago

We lived, felt dawn, saw sunset glow,

Loved and were loved, and now we lie,

In Flanders fields.

Take up our quarrel with the foe:

To you, from failing hands, we throw

The torch be yours to hold it high.

If ye break faith with us who die

We shall not sleep, though poppies grow

In Flanders fields.

"For seventeen days and seventeen nights, none of us have had our clothes off, nor our boots even, except occasionally. In all that time while I was awake, gunfire and rifle fire never ceased for sixty seconds... And behind it all was the constant background of the sights of the dead, the wounded, the maimed, and a terrible anxiety lest the line should give way."

—McCrae

Back to the horror of trench life and rotations went the boys, those who were left from the 49th and other divisions that formed the company. It really was a war of attrition.

Resuming duties in the trenches was no better than braving direct assaults from the enemy. Even in the periods of lull between active combat, the relentless tasks persisted. The soldiers lived in a constant state of danger while stationed just 300 meters away from the German troops, who were occupied with similar activities. The smallest lapse in concentration, inadvertent exposure of even a fraction of one's head over the parapet, could result in a fatal gunshot. The trenches demanded hard physical labour from every man, even those who had once been hard-working farmers. Digging into the dense clay or mud and hauling it over the 8-foot barriers was an incredibly draining task.

The constant presence of rats, lice infestations, the constant mire of mud, and the unrelenting onslaught of sleet and rain seeping through their scratchy wool uniforms were elements the soldiers could never grow accustomed to. Every man scratched almost incessantly. When they were sent to the rear, they gladly shook off their uniforms to be deloused by chemicals, had showers, and put their uniforms back on, only to become infested the minute they returned to the trenches.

OUR LITTLE WET HOME IN THE TRENCH (Tune:

In my little grey home in the west)

In our little wet home in the trench

That the rain storms continually drench

There's a dead cow nearby with its hooves in the sky

And it gives off a terrible stench.

Beneath us instead of a floor

Is a layer of cold mud and some straw.

The Jack Johnsons we dread

As they speed overhead

In our little wet home in the trench.

Tom Skeyhill

Battles were often carried out by the Allied and Germans at dawn or dusk. The call to engage would send out men in the first line to attempt to blow through the heavily fortified German lines through reams of barbed wire. Often, most of these frontmen were shot and killed or wounded. Then the next line would charge, and so on. This type of trench warfare was a major part of the First World War.

The soldiers on both sides endured their time at the front sweating or freezing, depending on the time of year. They endured the stench of men and fear.

During the rainy seasons, they soon realized their heavy gear and overcoats were an impediment. They would become caked with heavy mud and had to be left behind or on the battlefield. They barely noticed the cold and wet until the fighting had stopped, and they returned to their trenches without their overcoats for warmth when they needed it. They would spend the night shivering from the cold and fear.

The seasons did go round and round, and there seemed no end to the environmental onslaught each season could bring.

Day after day, month after month, the boys carried on as ordered. The boys from the 49th fought in all of the major battles, including Ypres, Passchendaele, Vimy Ridge, and the Somme.

Anticipating the arrival of parcels from loved ones back home was always a source of excitement for soldiers stationed in various locations across Europe. However, due to the unpredictable circumstances, such as damaged roads and crossings, along with the soldiers being in different places at different times, it often took weeks, or even longer, for the packages to reach them. Whenever the men found themselves in the grim trenches, the arrival of a package would evoke intense emotions, bringing tears to their eyes. It represented a tangible connection to their homes, simultaneously evoking both aching longing and heartwarming comfort. Amidst the harrowing experiences of bloodshed, pain, and death, receiving a letter or package felt like receiving a heartfelt embrace and a tender kiss from the familiar surroundings of home.

Finally, Joseph, Percy, and the few boys from the 49th division were sent on Furlough in

Bramshott, England, where cities were also being bombed. But at least they got away from the front lines for a week or two.

Chapter 9

England

October 17, 1917

Dear Belle,

Received your welcome letter on August 25th, last night, and was very glad to hear you are getting along fine.

Yours is the first letter I've had in some time, and Joseph has had none for three weeks. I'm darned if I know what is wrong with the mail service, but it is quite worrying now, and I almost quit writing, too.

Well, we are having some real English fall weather these days; it's cold, windy, and rainy. Gee, I would like to get into a decent climate again. This blooming weather doesn't agree with me.

I had a letter from Eddy a few days ago, and one from Paulie, they were well. Paulie had been on working parties. Eddy said they had a very hard trip. I guess Fritz is shelling pretty heavy these days. I hope they don't, for I'm _________if I want to go out there at this time of year.

Well, Belle, I can see by the papers that crops are good in Alberta.

Gee, this is an awful day, rainy and pitch dark and cold as H_______. Rain is running down both sides of me now. I sure hope Fritz gets licked pretty soon and let us get home and out of this mess. Joseph is not feeling very well these days. I hope he gets better again.

Well, Belle, I think I'll ring off at this time. I have many letters to write. So, thanks again for your letter.

Your loving Bro.'

Percy

October 22, 1917 Bramshott, England.

Dear Mother,

I just received two most welcome letters from you, also from Belle, and am mighty glad to hear from you as this is the first correspondence for quite a while now.

I'm glad you are all well and getting along fine with the harvest. You sure have been lucky to get along so late without a frost and to have a good crop.

Yes, Mother, it was certainly too bad about Harold. I heard he was killed but was not sure of it. It would certainly be hard on his people, but I hope they are over it again. Yes, it is pretty bad out here, but I think the people at home have the worst of it; at least we have the excitement of the thing. Things don't look very good the way those blasted Russians are going, but let's hope it will be over soon.

I was put on draft again last week but was taken off again, but I guess I can't always be so lucky.

Jim left here three days ago on his way to Canada. Had a few lines from him today saying he expected to sail soon, so I hope he makes it alright, as he was in very bad shape for a week or more. They should have sent him home long ago.

Haven't heard from any of the boys in France lately. I hope they are alright.

Eddie A. is having a long stay out there. I guess he and Mr. K are the only ones out there now.

Belle tells me a lot of the Dunvegan and Camrose boys were wounded, as well as a bunch of Lamont. Boys.

Oh, it is sure some war alright and getting no better fast.

Mrs. Andrews sure must like the farm. It will be quiet, a change for her. I hope she won't work too hard.

We have a very good theatre in camp now. I was up there to see Severn Days the other night. It was pretty good, and it sure helps to pass the time away. And this is a very quiet spot; nothing here but soldiers.

I have met a fine lady named Angela. I can't wait until you meet her. We plan to marry back at home.

Well, Mother dear, I think I will ring off and go to bed. So, give my love to all and wish you all good health and good luck.

Your loving son,

Percy

p.s. write to the address on the headline. YMCA and Canadian War Contingent Association with the Canadian Forces.

Percy and Angela were able to spend two weeks together in Bramshott England as she had taken leave at the same time Percy and Joseph had been granted their leave. Percy was absolutely delighted as he could now show off his sweetheart to his brother, Joseph, and his pals.

Entertainment in England was full on. There were many dance halls, movie theatres, and musical stage shows.

Percy and Angela stayed at her sister's home, while Joseph and Arny stayed in a billet close by.

During WWI, entertainment in England was largely focused on boosting morale and patriotism. Popular forms of entertainment included music hall shows, where comedians and singers provided comic relief and escapism from the war. Theatres staged patriotic plays and variety shows, while cinemas became increasingly popular. Sports events, particularly football matches, were also seen as an important diversion from the realities of the war.

It was a fun time, but so many in Canada had no idea of the true picture of war. It was easy to be patriotic when not surrounded by death and suffering. Nevertheless, the boys, Angela, and her widowed sister, made every minute of their leave count. They slept in and had a lazy brunch at the nearby cafe. In the afternoon, they would go for long walks along the river, enjoying the clean air, the breeze, and the warm sun on their faces. They saw many bombed-out buildings, but there hadn't been air raids for several weeks.

In the evening, they would go to a comedy show or one of the musicals in town. The shows were mostly patriotic, keeping the soldiers positive, upbeat, and proud of their part in the "war to end all wars." The whole audience would sing the words to each song as seen on the wall from the projector. Songs like "It's a Long Way to Tipperary", "Pack up Your Troubles in Your Old Kit Bag", "Keep the Home Fires Burning" and many more.

It was so much fun they were in stitches, especially when they went to see Harry Lauder with his hilarious skits and Scottish accent. Percy and Joseph had seen Harry perform before while at the front. Harry Lauder was well known for entertaining the troops. He'd hitch his piano to a truck and make his way from one zone to another, entertaining troops. His own son had been killed in December 1916, halfway through the war.

Angela's sister, Annie, put her and Percy in separate rooms upstairs of her house, fully knowing there was a connecting door between the two. Annie was happy and supportive of their union. Angela had not yet told Percy that a year and a half previous, during the London raids, her sweetheart was killed by German bombers in 1915. Her heart had been broken. That's when she joined the ambulance crew. Angela felt she needed to contribute to the war effort in some way.

Although she loved Danny, her high school sweetheart, she definitely didn't love him the way she loved Percy. Angela and Percy were drawn to each other like bears to honey or hummingbirds to flowers. It was a deep internal need. Angela wanted to care for Percy. He was the most generous man she had known. Not with money and gifts, although there were some of those too, but his generous spirit towards her and others. Percy had a way of making everyone feel comfortable with his polite but humorous ways. She knew Percy to be a very brave man. Joseph had told her a few stories about rescuing men from no-man's land amongst German gunfire. Although Joseph was usually right with him, there were times Percy was sent out on reconnaissance at night due to his keen sight and slim build. He managed to go to many dark areas on the battlefield unseen. It was like he wore an invisible cloak. So, his commander kept sending Percy out when risks were high.

Angela and Percy made love every chance they got. They used fancy French "letters" or condoms handed out to the soldiers. They didn't want to bring a baby into the world until they were married and living in Canada. Angela had no other family but her sister, who declined to move to another country. Annie had lost her husband; well, he was "lost," was how the army put it. He was missing in action (MIA). He could be in some hospital without his ID or dog tags. He could have been taken prisoner but hadn't been reported as captured. Who knew how long this war would take to be over? It had already been two years by this point.

Chapter 10

Getting Lonely

Another year goes by with letters exchanged back and forth, although months could go by without receiving any letters or packages depending on the manpower overseas and the ability to get them to the soldiers.

All of the men from every allied nation were sick and tired of the war. I'm sure the Germans were also tired of following their crazed master. The Canadian men had been so enthusiastic when the soldiers first arrived. But after years of not knowing if you would live or die when out on the field, battling not just the Germans but the constant loss of men, extreme weather, rodents, fleas, scabies, and the lack of decent meals when in the trenches wore a person down. It was always a guessing game when you rotated to the safety of the rear. Who would be left? Who lived, who died, and who were the lucky bastards who got to go home even if wounded?

THE NEXT MAN WHO DIES

We meet 'neath the sounding rafters

And the walls around are bare

As they echo our laughter

T'would seem that the dead were there.

So, stand to your glasses steady

'Tis all we have left to prize

Quaff a cup to the dead already

And one to the next man who dies.

Time was when we frowned on others

We thought we were wiser then

But now, let us all be brothers

For we never may meet again

Cut off from the land that bore us.

Betrayed by the land, we find

The good men have gone before us

And only the dull left behind.

So, stand to your glasses steady

This world is a web of lies

Then here's to the dead already

And hurrah for the next man who dies.

Here's an end to this mournful story

For death is a distant friend

So, here's to a life of glory

And a laurel to crown each end

Unknown

April 13th, 1918

My Dear Mother

I received your welcome letter written on the 8th of March, a few days ago, and also one on February 18th. I'm very glad to hear you are getting along well and are all in good health.

I have been under the weather the last few days but am alright and will be back to health tomorrow.

I have been very busy lately, so I haven't kept up my correspondence very well, but there's nothing much to write home about anyhow.

Things seem to be changing a lot in the Peace, and I guess we won't know the country when we get back home again.

I'm glad to hear that you made out so well with the crops last year, and I hope you do as well this year.

Had a letter from Belle, and also some photos. She looks very thin- she must be working too hard. Haven't heard from Pete for quite a while. I hope he is getting on well.

Well, Mother, I guess I'll sign off now. Hoping to hear from you again soon.

Love to all.

Your loving son,

Percy

France

July 27th 1918

My Dear Mother,

Just a few lines in answer to your letter of the 5th.

I am so very glad to hear from you and to know you are all as well as me, haha.

Also had a letter from Agatha.

I'm glad they are going to be staying with you for a while; you will be able to have a rest.

So, Bill has gone to camp. I'm glad he is getting on alright. It will be hard on account of his hearing, but he may get a job of some kind. Has Bobby had to go yet?

Had a parcel from Mildred a few days ago and a letter not long ago from Tom. They seem to be getting along pretty well on the homestead. How is Freddy making a go?

Haven't heard from Pete for quite a little while now. I hope he is alright.

How are the crops doing around Lamont? I see by the papers that it has been too dry down south and in parts of Saskatchewan.

We are getting plenty of rain around here these days, but it's rather late in the season to do much good. Some of the farmers are —— now. We still have it quite yet, but we hear rumors. Things are going pretty well for us these times, so this war may finish sometime after all.

Well, Mother, the news is as per usual, so I guess I may as well bring this to a close. My mail is coming along at a pretty good time now.

Now, Mother, don't work too hard, and don't worry, everything is looking as good as old Pendleton said.

Love to all from your loving son,

Percy

France

August 1, 1918

Mrs. J. Delaney

My Dearest Mother

Just a few lines as I haven't heard from you since I wrote last, and the news is the same as usual. Haven't had any mail lately, and haven't even heard from Pete. How is Button getting along in camp?

Tell him to write to me and send his address. He will be able to see Pete if he gets to England.

Well, Mother, we are still lucky, but things look like they are changing now. Let it come. Things are going very well for us out here these times, so there may be a chance of this job coming to a close this winter.

How are the crops doing around our country? The papers say it has been a very dry summer down south.

I'm glad Belle is going to stay with you for a while; it will give you a well-earned rest. I understand Henry will be signing up soon as a minister. I can't wait to see him if it's possible.

We are having very hot weather these days, and we have lost plenty of our sweat, but it's much better than rain for this job.

How is Amy getting on? I hope she is over her troubles by this time.

I can't wait until this blasted war is over and we return to you. I'll be bringing home a surprise, and there very well be wedding bells in the future for your second son. That's all I will say for now. Don't want to jinx it.

Well, Mother, I guess I will close. I am hoping to hear from you again soon. Love to all.

Your loving son,

Percy

August 17th 1918

My Dear Mother,

Well, Mother, I guess it's about time I dropped you a few lines as I haven't written for a couple of weeks.

Mother, as you will see from the papers, we have been rather lively the last week or so, and I'm glad to be able to write home about it.

We certainly slipped one by the old Fritz this time, and our casualties are very light, so everybody is well pleased with himself, for it was a good move.

Had a letter from Pete this morning. His category has been marked as B11, so I guess there's not much chance of him coming to France. He is one lucky bloke. Haven't had any mail from Canada for two weeks, but hope to hear from you soon. How are things going anyhow? Guess they will be busy harvesting by this time. I hope the crops are turning out well.

Is Belle staying with you now? You will be alright with both girls at home, so you want to have a good rest. Say, Mother, could you send me a parcel once in a while? Mail seems to be coming through fairly well these days. Send some cocoa, milk, cigarettes, and stuff like that out here now, as all our canteens get their supplies from Canada and run out of stock fairly quickly as there is such a demand. I see by the paper that they are mobilizing all the soldiers in Canada and are going to send a bunch to Russia, so Bill may be sent over there. That would be a pretty good place to be. I wouldn't mind going over there, but I guess there's not much chance.

Well, Mother, there's not much more I can say, and I have a lot of letters to write, so I may as well ring off, so if you see anyone who wants to send a parcel to a soldier, tell them I am very lonely. I am quite well after the —- and hope this finds you all the same. Write soon too.

Your loving son,

Percy

September 10th 1918, somewhere in France

Mrs. J. Delaney

My dear Mother,

Just a few lines while I'm in a place where a fellow can write. We sure get into some funny places these times, and we don't get much of a chance to do something like this. I'm writing this on a piece of paper that Winnie sent with her last letter. Paper is very scarce, and she can wait until I get more paper. Well, Mother, how are things going at home? We hear some very bad reports about the crops being frozen. I hope it is not true and they are good as usual. You will be pretty well on in the harvest by this time. We are getting some rain and wind at these times. I suppose we must expect some bad weather after such a fine summer.

I'm afraid it will spoil the big offensive quite a bit; it will make everything much harder for the men.

Well, Mother, I guess we will be spending another winter here so I hope you will send me a really good pair of leather gloves, something that will stand plenty of rain! Write to everyone and ask them to send a parcel once in a while as they have cut our pay down again and things are hard to get. You have to line up at the canteen and wait an hour and then maybe not get anything if they run out. Well, Mother, this is all the paper I have, so I will have to ring off. Hope you are all well.

Love to all

Percy

Embroidered Postcard

Carys,

Dear Sister,

Just a little bit of France. Expect to be in England soon. Have been under the weather for some time, but I am feeling really good now. Will write to you..........

(Remembrance card - Embroidered pansy on the front)

To Mother

Compliments of the Season

From: Percy

Fond Wishes

Just a card in glad remembrance

Sped today with wishes kind.

That the sunshine bright

Before you

And the shadows fall behind

September 14, 1918

Dear Belle,

Received your most welcome letter of Aug 18th yesterday, so will take a few minutes and drop you a few lines to let you know I am quite well and hope this finds you in the best of health. You didn't take a very long rest as I thought you were going to, but I guess everybody works these hard times.

I was very sorry to hear that everything around our part of the country was frozen. Let's hope it turned out better than was expected.

Well, Belle, everything is going pretty well out here these times, and we are kept fairly busy, and Gee, but I'm lousy. I am trying to write and watch The Brutes at the same time.

Haven't heard from Pete for quite a while now, and guess he must be on leave.

Winnie tells me Bill had sailed for overseas; he will be in Blighty for quite a while now. I'm sorry to hear Ted was forced to sell out. It will be a hard blow on him, alright.

We are having rather miserable weather these times, cold and wet. I suppose we have to look for bad weather this time of year.

Well, Belle, there's nothing new to write about here, so I guess I may as well ring off for this time.

By the way, all the young married couples at home seem to be doing well. Wish I'd thought of that sooner.

Write soon to your loving Bro' Percy.

Chapter 11

"Time to Get out of My Head"

Olivia put the letters down for a while. With her great uncle Percy's letters, she could vividly picture what real life must have been like for the men and women during WWI. There have been many movies about the "Great War to End All Wars," and Olivia had seen many, but actually reading the letters with her great uncle's words was so personal. She felt his pain deep inside of her.

The world is just coming out of several deadly waves of the COVID-19 pandemic. Olivia wondered if Percy and Joseph were sick in 1918 because of the Spanish flu, the pandemic that started near the war's end. Olivia took a break and went to her tablet to check on the history of the Spanish flu.

"Wow," she declared out loud. The dogs jumped up, all excited, thinking something good was about to happen, like walkies or a treat. "Sorry guys, you have to wait a few minutes."

Olivia wondered if she had ever been taught about the deadly Spanish flu in school. She had heard of it, of course, but until we went through our current/recent pandemic, it hadn't stayed in her mind.

Apparently, the deadly influenza of 1918-1920 killed almost as many people, mostly those between the ages of twenty and forty, as those killed during WW1.

The experts in 1918 knew nothing about handling a pandemic. They flew by the seat of their pants. It couldn't have happened at a worse time. By the end of the war, soldiers and support staff were packed together in camps awaiting transport by convoy, train, and then ships back home. The overcrowding led to rapid-fire transmission back to Canada and to every country involved in the war.

By the time the Canadian soldiers returned home, the medical experts in most provinces had closed down public spaces, schools, and churches. People were encouraged to wear masks and wash their hands often. Canada put a Health Department in place to oversee the chaos the (misnamed because it didn't start in Spain) Spanish flu caused worldwide. It was bad enough that so many men and some women of child-bearing age had died overseas. Now, young men and women were being wiped out by a deadly virus. To many, the past four years had been like living in hell, if that could be said back then.

Just like the Covid 19 pandemic of 2020 onward, people didn't like being told what to do back then, and there were many protests. Does anything change? People will be people.

The dogs were getting restless. Olivia had been reading about events and the history of the Peace River before and after the First World War for over an hour. Time for a break.

She hitched up the dogs; one was as big as a horse, well, a small bear, and the little white fluffy one at ten pounds, and took a drive and a walk in one of the nearby parks they loved. There's a waterfall, and occasionally, Olivia could make it to the top. Otherwise, the dogs would run around the fields, one trying to burrow and catch mice, the other one chasing sticks, then jumping into the creek to lie down in the water to cool down. Olivia always ended up wet, but it was just water and sometimes a bit of mud. That's what you'll get with dogs. It's almost impossible to stay clean. "You certainly couldn't eat off our floors like I probably could have in Millie's house" thought Olivia

Olivia and the dogs were back home after an hour or so, and she picked up the letters once again. It was like reading a history book but about her mother's family. She loved it.

France

Sept. 26th 1918

My Dear Mother,

I just want a few lines as I do not have much time this morning to write. Haven't heard from you since I wrote last.

Had a letter from Carys, also one from Belle, and one from Pete. He says there are a lot of the Peace boys over here now, but he hasn't seen Bill.

Well, Mother, I have been presented with an M.M. (Military Medal for Bravery in battle on land) since I last wrote. You were lucky when they dished out the rations.

Things are going well these times for the Allies, but let's hope it continues.

The weather has been very wet and cold but has cleared up in the last couple of days. It may be a while before you hear from me again as it looks like busy times soon but don't worry, as everything is lovely. I suppose you are all through the harvest by this time. I hope it turns out better than you expected.

Tell John I will write to him one of these times.

Well, Mother, drop us a line whenever you can and give my love to all. Well, I must close. I hope you are all well, as this leaves me.

Your loving son,

Percy

He truly was a humble man, thought Olivia

Chapter 12

Carys and Henry

Back home in the Peace Country, Carys and Henry finished school in the spring of 1917. Henry would be at a college in Edmonton studying to become a minister like his Dad. Carys, wanting to be a teacher, went to the Camrose Normal school for a few months to learn how to teach elementary children the three "R's," reading, writing, and arithmetic.

They found it very hard to be apart, but Carys was hoping to get a job teaching at one of Edmonton's elementary schools after her teaching course. There definitely was a greater chance of procuring a teaching job in the big city compared to the small towns where they grew up. Mom and Dad let Carys go because I lived in Edmonton with my girlfriend, Nelly, and we made room for Carys to join us. It was a small space, but we managed.

You may be, or not surprised by, my telling you I'm a lesbian. Don't faint!

Olivia, I hope by the time you read these letters, times will have changed, and we queer folks won't be whipped, thrown in jail or killed. It was a very difficult time for any homosexual. Literally, for me, it has been all of my life.

I got engaged to a homosexual man. We never consummated our marriage, but nobody knew that. In later years, when we did live together, we just declared I couldn't get pregnant and decided not to adopt. Glen was a pharmacist. We had a good life, and I did love the man; he loved me, just not in a conventional way. Glen passed away in 1972.

Carys seemed quite happy in Edmonton. She and Henry were able to see each other every weekend. They were so much in love it was like watching the sunrise. Their eyes lit up every time they were together, and it was incredible to see such honest and pure love.

Henry was determined to enlist to join the very depleted 49th division to which Joseph and Percy belonged. Carys, of course, was terrified of losing him to battle.

"Carys, I love you with all of my heart, but I cannot look myself in the mirror knowing that I'm old enough and proud enough of our country to join my "brothers-in-arms," and I must go. As your brothers have said, the war should be over by Christmas, and I'll be back to marry you, now don't you worry."

But worry she did, as the months went slowly by. Carys had been receiving letters from her brothers, well Percy mostly, as Joseph didn't like writing but would send a postcard every few months. The letters never said anything about being killed, killing, or wounding other men, but she read the papers every day, and they were gruesome at times, trying to imagine life in the trenches they spoke about. She was still a bit of a tomboy and liked to go fishing, hunting, and working in the barn with her Dad, but going to war didn't sit right with her, and she was surprised at Henry as he had been mostly against going a couple of years ago, but he'd be a chaplain in the army so maybe that wasn't as bad.

They went to another bash before he set off for England, where he was first posted. They both got a bit drunk, unusual for Carys as she really didn't like drinking all that much, but the champagne was so delicious and light on her tongue that it just slipped down her throat.

They left the party early as Henry was to embark on the train at 06:00 hours. Nellie and I stayed at the party with the other blokes and blokettes leaving on the same train, but they would be up all-night partying. With the number of wounded and killed in combat being reported, they knew the odds were against them returning home safely, but that was not ever talked about. Most of the men of fighting age had been conscripted in the past year, so some had no choice in the matter if they passed the physical. Often, a blind eye was turned when, at times, it was obvious that the men enlisting were actually still underaged boys, all pumped up and determined it would be them who won the war for the allies.

Carys and Henry returned to my apartment. Carys fell crying into Henry's arms, inconsolable. Henry held her tightly until the tears subsided.

"Oh, Carys, it's going to be fine. You just have to believe I'll be home all in one piece. I need you to be strong for me."

Carys stopped crying, and they lay on her bed in each other's arms. They realized making love and completing the act hadn't been done yet, but they couldn't hold themselves back this last time. Henry had always been so tender and loving towards Carys, and he never pressured her to go farther in their love-making than she was comfortable with. Plus, they had no forms of birth control. French letters/condoms were not easy to find these days, at least according to a few of his pals more experienced in the art of love-making than he was. Carys was to be his first and only love. He could never imagine being with another. Carys was his beacon in life.

They lay awake talking or making love the rest of the night. Carys was sore, not being used to this full love-making, but Henry was so loving and tender. He took his time and made sure Carys was as comfortable as possible. They absorbed every minute of each other. Trying to capture and hold on to each tiny piece of themselves that held so much love. But in the end, they had to part with a few tears from both.

Letters from Henry Bernard to Miss Carys Delaney

C.A.M.C. Camp

Western Hangar, Kent,

England

June 4th 1917

Dear Miss Delaney

Carys! How I love thee! I will bring you a beautiful, great big ring, and Carys, I'll make you my wife. I miss you more than your Mom's pancake breakfasts, and you know how much I love them.

I was more than pleased to receive your newsy and interesting letter a few days ago. I am surprised to know that you were surprised, haha, to receive my letter.

Indeed, this is a time for surprises, and one never knows just what to expect.

A little while ago, I heard that the S.S. Canada had been sunk on her return trip from India, but there was no report of it in the papers. I am inclined to think that it was a mistake, for the S.S. Canadian was sunk about this time last year, too. It keeps coming back to life, only to be sunk all over again.

Summer has arrived, and "Dear old England" looks at her best just now. The summer weather and refreshing rains have acted like a spell in woodlands and thickets by river banks in pastures and meadows. Everything is in bloom. The fruit trees are lovely, all messy pink and white. The blossoms shed their fragrance, refreshing the senses. All the migrant warblers are back again. The cuckoo is heard every evening, and the nightingale charms me with his deep passionate song. This place is indeed a "flowery, leafy Paradise". But oh, you Canada for me.

It was another surprise for me to hear that you, or the folks, have moved to Lamont. This, I hope, will be so much better for you all. I wonder who has taken the farm that you have left. They will miss you at P.

No doubt you will have read of the "Raid on Folkestone". On Friday evening, I was on my way to Folkstone. At about 6 pm, I heard a strange humming of planes. Suddenly, I heard a terrific explosion. The ground shook beneath me. The animals were frantic and ran in all directions for protection. Bang! Bang!! Bang!!!. Bomb after bomb, coming nearer. Upon looking up, I saw and counted sixteen German planes; they were just visible, and the sun was shining upon them, making them look like beautiful white gulls. Believe me, I held my breath as they passed over my head. I saw a bomb explode in the air, then one dropped in the churchyard at Hythe. When I got to Hythe, I went to the churchyard and saw the damage to the gravestones. The caretaker, coming out of the church, was hit with a piece of shell, and his leg was almost severed from his body. A woman was killed a short distance from the church. The church, which is a fine historic building, was not damaged at all. At Folkstone, the scene was too horrible to describe. Bombs and high explosives were dropped in the center of the town. The property was destroyed. Women and children were lying dead on the streets, about 46 in all. Two hundred soldiers lost their lives. It was simply fierce. I shall never forget it. I do not wish to be any nearer a raid than I was to this. I had got so used to our own planes flying over our heads that I was quite calm. I am amazed at myself, for I did not think of running for protection; I was in the middle of the road on a country lane. It took days to quit shaking. I wake up in my sleep shouting and thrashing around the narrow bed I was allowed in the church rectory.

Yes, I heard that Percy was wounded, and I often wondered how he was getting along. I suppose that he will be back with his own unit now. The Lamont and Peace Valley boys have certainly been getting it. I thank you for such interesting news. Kindly remind me of Mr. Hansen when you write to him. I hope that he will remain one of the favoured few and come through O.K.

I received six days' leave and had the privilege of visiting my cousins in Manchester. I dropped in on them unawares, for I had not written a line. Haha. I sure had a swell time. It passed too soon. I spent a day in London visiting the various places of interest. Both houses (not public houses) ha. St. Paul's, Buckingham Palace, the King's Mews, Westminster Abbey etc.

Did you hear the story of the woman who took a course in First Aid, and after long and anxious waiting, the street accident she had longed for and waited for took place? It was a bicycle accident; the man had broken his leg. She confiscated a walking stick of a passer-by and broke it in three pieces for splints. She blushingly took off her undershirt for bandages and was enthusiastically cheered by the crowd. When all was completed, she hailed a cab and took her patient to the hospital.

"Who bandaged this limb so creditably?" inquired the surgeon with a glance of admiration. "I did," she blushingly replied, her bosom swelling with pride. "Well, it is most beautifully done," said the surgeon, but there's just one little thing wrong, one little mistake—nothing in itself. She felt terribly self-conscious. But you've bandaged the wrong leg!" Haha.

We have an Irishman in our hut. He is the limit. We had meatballs for supper the other day, which did not look very appetizing. Paddy sat opposite to me and looked down at them—bowing his head. He said solemnly, "For what we are about to deceive ourselves with, may we be truly thankful, for it is all that we can get!" Haha.

I miss you so very much, but I'm sure I'll be home soon. There are rumors of plans to get this war over by Christmas. I can hardly wait to be in your arms once more.

Sincerely yours,

Cpl. Henry Bernard

Carys and Henry continued exchanging letters over the next year. Carys kept teaching in Edmonton and kept herself busy, but the time seemed to go slowly.

I don't know what happened to the rest of the letters. I only found a couple at Mother's house.

Olivia, a very sad thing happened to your grandmother, Carys, three or four months after Henry left to fight. It turned out she got pregnant that last night she and Henry were together. I don't know if what happened next was the stress of the war, the constant worry about all the boys of the 49th, her brothers, and most certainly, Henry, but tragedy struck.

Carys woke up one night and called out for me. She had been having cramps but thought she was getting her periods, which were never regular anyway, and when they happened, they were often heavy with lots of cramps. But there she was, her tiny little baby on the bed.

Carys, of course, was devastated. I never thought she would recover from the grief. She decided not to tell Henry. Life was hard enough overseas. She didn't want to add to his worry. Carys would tell him when he returned, whenever that may be. Henry was sure he would be home that Christmas, but it looked unlikely. This war was dragging on and on, and we were losing our boys by the dozens from our Peace River area.

Some of Henry's letters spoke of meeting up with the brothers now and then when they were on furlough in England. It seems that Percy had been wounded a couple of times but not seriously. To Percy's horror and embarrassment, Joseph has had to haul him off the battlefield more than once. Apparently, Percy had found himself a sweetheart. Her name is Angela, and she is an angel to him, working as an ambulance driver going onto or near the battlefields over and over to collect the wounded. A very brave woman indeed.

C.A.M.C. Depot

Risborough barracks

Shorncliffe, England

July 20, 1918

Dear Miss Carys Delaney,

I am sorry to be so late in answering your sweet letter, which reached me a few weeks ago. Your letter was delayed somewhat owing to it being sent to France - and I wasn't there. This reminds me of an Irishman who sent a letter to his sweetheart something like this:

Dear Maggie

I met you at the stile last night as arranged, but you were not there. I will meet you at the same place tomorrow whether you are there or not. If you are there first, put a stone on the stile, and if I am there first, I will knock it off.

I arrived in England on March 12th, and was sent to the East Sussex Hospital, Hastings, after being a bed patient in this hospital for a month after an explosion sent shrapnel into my leg. I was transferred to the Buchanan Hospital at St. Leonard on Sea, where I spent another month. I was then able to walk and was sent to the Princess Patricia Canadian Red Cross Hospital and convalescent camp, where I stayed for ten weeks. Since then, I have had ten days of sick furlough and visited my cousins in Manchester and friends in Huddersfield.

You will be pleased to know that my health recovery has been completed. I'm settling down once more to administer care and prayers for our soldiers who have been wounded or are close to death and expect to be at the depot for at least three months in training. Needless to say, I had a pleasant time whilst in the hospital. I was fortunate to be kept away from the military hospital.

I enjoyed your parcel's contents, especially the cake De Luxe. It was just it.

I smiled to read your remarks about the returned soldier. Ha, Ha!

Canada is playing her part well. England is proud of Canada's share in the war, of her achievements and her splendid record.

Personally, I do not regret it. I have never regretted the step I took in January of 1917 when I enlisted for service overseas. I believe that every minister who is eligible for active service (unless hindered, unless he has a good reason for not doing so) should enlist and go to the battlefield. I do not believe the Kingdom of Christ could be brought in by bayonet and shell, but it is out there that the world's pain is being borne, and it is where Ministers of Christ should be.

Indeed, the soldiers are a cheerful crowd. A smile is often the surest weapon of victory. Fun is the sunshine of life. It makes just the same difference to a grey life as sunshine does to a grey street. I wish the old gentleman (whom I strongly suspect to have been a soap manufacturer!) had written, "Cheerfulness is next to godliness." Ha, ha!

I am pleased to learn the children are doing their share of sending "sunshine" to the boys out there. It helps considerably and teaches the children to sacrifice.

Three thousand or more miles away, the Canadian boy, plucky and merry but often homesick, gets a parcel from the Canadian Red Cross in France or in England, which breaths of home and its anxious, loving people.

"Some parcel," he remarks appreciatively as he opens it and finds a comfort bag. It may be cigarettes of his pet brand, stationary, a razor and other toilet articles, a pencil, and similar small gifts.

Anything in the reason for which a Canadian soldier asks is supplied by the Canadian Red Cross. Great-hearted Canada helped thousands of French hospitals, and many thousands of pounds of supplies went to the French wounded as well as to the British. She maintains motor ambulance convoys in France, she organizes and equips hospitals in England, and yearly, she makes her offering to the British Red Cross to be used as the parent society sees fit. We are proud of the Maple Leafs Red Cross.

I cannot speak too highly of the Y.M.C.A. They are right up the line with the boys. Their Captains and workers often occupy a small lean-to, a pill box. They often work under shell fire and always under difficulties, but they are at the service of the boys. They are doing a splendid job. I do not know how we could have carried on at Passchendaele but for the assistance of the Y. I shall never forget Passchendaele!

I have nothing but admiration for the brave girl motor ambulance drivers in France. In the great yard of the motor convoy, where the big Buick ambulances are parked in dark looming rows, the girl drivers are busy. Only a dim light must show for the German planes are often busy here, of a moony night, but the girls know every inch of their cars, of the long road to the station, and of the complicated maze of the hospitals, a whole township in themselves.

One after another, the cars swing out into the road, going at a good pace, and the dark station is soon reached, where they all draw up in order to await the coming of the hospital train.

It steams slowly in at last; through its windows, you catch glimpses of its white-painted interior, fitted with shelves, on which the straightly laid forms of men are seen as things dark and muffled. The Red Cross orderlies lift them out swiftly on the stretchers and slide them into the ambulances, four in each, as one might slide precious and fragile parcels.

There is something very shocking as seeing a man lying flat and helpless, shoved here and there, in spite of the care and kindness with which it is done. It is a thing shocking in essence; somehow, it seems all wrong, an outrage of nature, and you get an odd feeling that the very posture of lying down has something unnatural about it you did not realize before......

The girl at the wheel pushes back the little window in front of the car and looks into its dimly lit interior. She sees the tops of four heads and the jut of the brows beyond them, heads wearily still or moving from side to side, moaning in pain; she sees the peaks of the upturned feet under the grey blankets; she sees the pale hands that lie helplessly or are swathed in bandages, and whatever else she sees, she knows she is looking on pain, pain, pain.

She closes the shutter when everything else is disposed of safely in that grim interior, gets her orders as to which hospital she is to go to, and again she is off through the night, this time so slowly, so gently, for she carries a burden that must not be jolted more than can possibly be avoided. She finds the hospital unerringly in all that web of new roads and then, relieved of her load, speeds up and back again to the station.

So, she goes back and forth all night long. At a time like this, and all day long too, for in many parts of France, there is no man running an ambulance. Still, every wounded soldier carried from the train to the hospital is carried by a girl. Tired as she may be at one convoy during a time of heavy fighting, the girls did not take off their clothes for two weeks, merely sneaking a couple of hours of sleep when they could. All she says is what every girl I met in France says- "It's the least we can do. Think of what the men are doing for us."

I am interested in learning about your pupils at school. Oh well, you are doing a good work. Your work is so important, and you are achieving so much. So many human lives are an unsolvable mystery in their apparent uselessness. To live long and achieve so little, therein lies the pitifulness of life. Even failure to achieve success is a step upward and onward. The only real failure is never to try to achieve anything at all.

I have never heard from or of Mr. Hampton. I met John Draper whilst in France. Our ambulance was in charge of the Corps Rest Station, and he came to the Dressing Station to have his hand bandaged. He was quite well and cheerful. He gave me much information concerning the boys from the 49th.

Write to me soon. I love reading your letters. They warm my heart. I can hardly wait to be in your loving arms again.

Sincerely yours,

Cpl. Henry Bernard

It was clear that Henry was a prolific writer, and it pleased Carys. She was proud of the fact that they both loved literature and the arts, as well as fishing and mucking about repairing farm equipment. They really were made for each other. Not that they didn't have arguments. Carys was stubborn, as was Henry. They would get locked into some battle or another, and things would get heated. But they loved to make up. I think they sometimes argued just to rile each other up, as Henry had teased her when she was younger.

Chapter 13

Percy and Joseph

In mid-September of 1918, Joseph was injured and sent home. He and Percy had been at the front line in Cambrai, northern France, as it was their turn in the rotation. The Germans had been bombarding their company with exploding shells and horrific mustard gas. Joseph, being the kind of guy he was, and being Percy's older brother, insisted Percy wore the mask when they ran out of supplies of all sorts, including the badly needed life-saving gas masks, which was not at all uncommon. How can anyone win a war with such little regard for the soldiers? It makes me mad every time I think of my brothers.

However, this time, the mustard gas exploded beside them in the trench. Percy kept trying to give his brother the mask, but Joseph kept it pressed on Percy's face. Joseph was sent to one of the military hospitals after that attack, then home, which sounds good, but he would never speak again. His hearing mostly came back, but it took a long, long time. Joseph remained unmarried and ashamed of his injuries. He not only lost his hearing; he lost an eye. He stuttered when he tried to talk and kept his answers short. He stayed with Mom and Pops until he died.

With Joseph sent home, Percy did not envy him, although he would have sold his kidneys to get home. Being injured, perhaps forever, was not on Percy's list of things to do while at war. Sure, he had been hit by shrapnel, but he was ready to go again after a few stitches. This war was dragging on too long. The boys from the Peace seemed to be all over the place. The division in "C" company had been depleted of men over and over. Some were in military hospitals in France or England. Some were in make-shift field hospitals. Percy was lonely and depressed. He hadn't been able to see Angela for several weeks, and the mail from home was so slow. He missed Joseph. He hadn't realized how much they had depended on each other to stay safe, the comfort of their conversations about home, and all they wanted to achieve when back home. Joseph wanted to keep working on the family farm. That was his joy. Percy wanted to become a doctor. He was so impressed by the medics and surgeons. He found it fascinating: the human body. He knew lives could be saved and wounds healed even in the middle of the war. Think of what he could do back home. He and Angela will get married, have ten kids, kidding, and she could work beside him as a nurse. Angela was fully capable of dealing with injuries and tragedies.

All the boys were homesick and beyond shattered. Of course, they were still patriotic. After all, it had been drilled into them well before they left for the war. But at night, one could hear men shut out from their nightmares and crying for their mothers in their sleep, especially the younger boys who hadn't been here long. The boys who had been there from the start of the combat or soon after knew their odds of living were decreasing each day. They had just been lucky so far. Or their fervent prayer to God had protected them.

In the last days of the First World War, a series of relentless attacks took place, forever known in history as the "Hundred Days" Offensive. This brilliant offensive by the Allied forces set the stage for the German forces' retreat and ultimately led to the signing of the armistice on November 11.

A resounding blow echoed through the war-torn landscape on August 8, 1918, at Amiens, France. Side by side with their equally battle-hardened comrades from the Australian Corps, the Canadian forces unleashed a devastating assault, tearing open a twelve-kilometre hole in the German line. This monumental breakthrough forever altered the rest of the war.

The renowned German General Erich Ludendorff would later dub this day "the black day of the German Army." The reason was clear - a considerable number of German soldiers, facing overwhelming odds, chose surrender over a futile fight to the death. The Battle of Amiens inflicted a crushing blow, one that left the German Army reeling, unable to regain its former strength.

For the first time since the war's inception, the glimmer of its end appeared on the horizon, casting a ray of hope upon the weary hearts of the Allied forces.

Percy and Joseph and the dwindling 49th Division were determined to push through. The end of this damn war was nearly over. Every man, woman, and child had been affected, especially in Europe. So many sacrifices had been made to beat the Germans.

As the final months of World War I drew near, Percy found himself surprisingly still alive. All the ranks of the Canadian and British forces were battle-weary. The war had taken its toll on the body and spirit, but a glimmer of hope burned within them, fuelling their dwindling spirits with determination to see this war through to the end and return home to their loved ones.

The 49th division from Edmonton had weathered countless battles, each leaving its indelible mark on their souls. The camaraderie forged amongst the chaos had become the strength of the resilience of the Canadian men, overcoming the horrors of the frontlines. They were a band of brothers, bound together by shared experiences and a common purpose.

It was during those final months that the 49th received orders to push forward in northern France, to deliver the decisive blows that would shatter the enemy's resolve. The weight of the mission settled on their shoulders, for the men knew that every step they took, every bullet fired, would inch them closer to the peace we all longed for.

The landscape the men traversed was scarred by the ravages of war, a desolate testament to the unyielding brutality they had become all too familiar with. Shell craters pocked the earth, serving as stark reminders of the violence that had consumed this land. The air was heavy with the acrid scent of smoke and the haunting echoes of gunfire.

Their battle experience and courage propelled them forward in the face of adversity. They pressed on through the mud and quagmire, through the incessant autumn rain that never seemed to end. There were new challenges each day as bullets whizzed past, exploding in bursts of earth and mud, the final assault to win the war. The deafening cacophony of artillery fire reverberated through their very being. Together, they fought, shoulder to shoulder, a united force against the storm of the last battles.

As the days turned into weeks, the landscape shifted. News of victories reached their ears, whispers of hope in the darkness. The realization that the war was nearing its end infused their spirits with a bittersweet mix of relief and sorrow. These men had endured so much and sacrificed so greatly, and now the end was within sight.

With unwavering determination, the Canadian and Allied troops shifted their focus to the Arras region in their relentless pursuit of the retreating German forces. Their target was the formidable Drocourt-Quéant Line, an impregnable fortress of German defenses along the front. Undeterred by the formidable obstacles, the 1st and 4th Canadian divisions pushed forward, braving heavy casualties, until they emerged victorious, capturing the entire German position.

Emboldened by their triumph, the Canadians pressed on, surging ahead to the Battle of Canal du Nord. On September 27th, a daring strike once again shattered the German resolve, forcing them into a hasty retreat. Each inch of ground gained exacted a heavy toll on the Canadian forces, with thousands of brave soldiers sacrificing their lives. However, their unwavering spirit and resolute victories dealt a severe blow to the morale of the Germans, who now faced the harsh reality that the war was irretrievably lost.

The indomitable Canadian forces had proved their mettle on countless battlefields, paying a steep price in bloodshed and sacrifice. Their triumphs, though costly, served as a testament to their unwavering dedication and resilience. As the echoes of battle subsided, a sense of inevitability settled upon the war-ravaged land. The end was drawing near, and the Canadian contributions had played a pivotal role in hastening the arrival of a long-awaited peace.

The focal point of these final battles was the heavily fortified city of Cambrai, where Percy was posted with the remaining soldiers of the 49th Division of Edmonton and fortified by British divisions.

Cambrai stood as a formidable stronghold, guarded not only by determined German troops but also by an intricate network of man-made canals that posed a daunting obstacle to both infantry soldiers and the emerging weapon of war—tanks. These canals, surrounded by enemy machine-gun posts, barbed wire, and various defenses, formed an impenetrable barrier.

To breach the defenses of Cambrai, the Allied forces faced the daunting task of crossing the Canal du Nord, situated to the west of the city, as well as seizing control of the heights of Bourlon Wood—a forested hill overlooking the canal banks. The responsibility of capturing these formidable obstacles fell upon the brave soldiers of the Canadian Corps under the skilled leadership of Lieutenant General Arthur Currie. Complicating matters further, the Germans had deliberately flooded much of the surrounding land, making the mission even more treacherous.

In the latter part of September, Currie devoted his efforts to meticulous planning. Canadian and British engineers received increased resources and manpower to work on the crucial task of constructing bridges to facilitate canal crossings and tramway lines to transport essential supplies and artillery to the battlefield. On the fateful morning of September 27, the Canadian Corps, supported by British forces on their flanks, launched their assault on a dry stretch of the partially excavated canal. They followed the wake of a relentless, moving artillery barrage, which kept the German defenders in their dugouts and their concrete machine-gun posts. As the day wore on and fierce fighting continued, the Allied forces succeeded in crossing and securing the canal while also capturing the small town of Bourlon Wood, a significant triumph.

In the following days, the Canadian soldiers heroically defended their hard-won positions against relentless German counterattacks. Engineers played a vital role in supporting the troops, tirelessly repairing roads and hastily assembling bridges to aid the movement of infantry and artillery across the challenging, often-flooded terrain. With the outer defenses of Cambrai overrun, the Allies made their final push, ending in the liberation and capture of the city on October 11.

The fall of Cambrai marked a turning point in the war, symbolizing the crumbling strength of the German forces and the imminent Allied victory. The heroic efforts of the Canadian Corps, supported by their British comrades and the resilience of the engineering teams, played a crucial role in the success of the "Hundred Days" campaign. As the guns fell silent and the echoes of battle faded away, the world witnessed the beginning of the end, paving the way for a new era of peace.

Then, the worst news came.

Postmark Oct. 8, 1918

4 General Hospital B.E.F. France

Oct. 1st, 1918

Dear Sir,

Your son, Cpl. P.J. Delaney, No ***** 49th Canadian, has been admitted to this hospital, suffering from a gunshot wound to his head.

I'm very sorry to tell you your son is dangerously ill. We are doing everything we possibly can for him here. I will let you know again shortly how he is going on.

Yours sincerely,

M. Law for

The Matron

4 General Hospital B.E.F. France

Oct 2nd, 1918

Dear Sir,

The condition of your son remains about the same. I am sorry to tell you that he is dangerously ill. Everything possible is being done for him. I will let you know shortly how he is going on.

Yours sincerely,

M. Law for

The Matron

4 General Hospital B.E.F. France

Oct 3rd, 1918

Dear Sir,

The condition of your son, Cpl. P.J. Hull, is just about the same as when I wrote yesterday. He still remains dangerously ill. Everything possible is being done for him, and I will let you know again shortly how he goes on.

Yours sincerely,

M. Law for

The Matron

4 General Hospital

B.E.F. France

Oct 5th, 1918

Dear Sir,

I am sorry to tell you that there is no improvement in the condition of your son, Cpl. P.J. Hull. He's still dangerously ill.

Yours sincerely,

M. Law for

The Matron

4 General Hospital

B.E.F. France

Oct 7th, 1918

Dear Sir,

Your son, Cpl. P.J. Hull is not as well as when I last wrote, I am sorry to say.

He's dangerously ill.

Everything possible is being done for him. Here.

Yours sincerely,

M. Law for The Matron

Minister's Office

Ottawa

Dept of Militia and Defense

Canada

December 10, 1918

Dear Mr. Delaney

I desire to express to you my sincere sympathy in the recent decease of No. ***** Corporal Percy James Delaney C.E.F., who sacrificed his life at the front in action with the enemy, has rendered the highest services of a worthy citizen.

The heavy loss that you and the nation have sustained would indeed be depressing were it not redeemed by the knowledge that the brave comrade for whom we mourn performed his duties fearlessly and well, became a good soldier, and gave his life for the great cause of Human Liberty and the Defense of the Empire.

Again, I extend to you my condolences and heartfelt sympathy for your bereavement.

I am,

Yours faithfully,

____

Minister of Militia and Defense

For Canada

Note:

The Honourable, the Minister of Militia and Defense, directs me to present you herewith the enclosed engraved Death Certificate with the sympathy of the Militia Council in your sorrow.

Major General

Circumstances of Death or Missing Report

Reg't No. ***** Rank: Corporal

Name: Delaney, P.J. Unit: 49th Can: Btn

Casualty: Died of wounds: 9.10.1918

Circumstances:

Private Delaney was wounded by an enemy Machine Gun Bullet during an attack on Tilley on September 29th, 1918; he was immediately attended to and evacuated but succumbed to his wounds ten days later at No. 4. General Hospital, Camiers

Major Lieut.——

I had tears streaming down my eyes. I had known great uncle Percy had died in the war, but reading the letters Percy sent home broke my heart. He sounded so alone and sad near the end. He was so very close to making it to Armistice Day, a little over a month. I again picked up the papers to continue reading.

Percy's death broke Mom's heart. It broke all of our hearts. Percy had been fighting that God-awful war overseas for nearly three years and was so close to the end. Three weeks until Armistice Day.

Then the next tragic "I'm sorry to inform you" letter came to Henry's Dad. Carys died that day. Or felt like it.

Carys sunk into a depression. She didn't want to do anything outside of her teaching job. Didn't care about anything. She lost weight and barely slept. The school gave Carys leave to return home until she healed. While Cary was healing, she wrote this poem. I'm so glad I kept it for you.

1918: A Woman's Grief

In a world torn apart by war,

A woman mourns, alone and raw.

Her boyfriend was gone, a casualty of a fight,

Her heart shattered in the midst of night.

She weeps for the love that will never return,

For the kisses and whispers that now only burn.

Her hopes and dreams crushed by war's cold hand,

Leaving nothing but ashes in its command.

But that was not all that she had lost,

For a baby she carried was also the cost.

A miscarriage that no one could understand,

A pain that only she could withstand.

She feels a void, a hollowness inside,

A deepening chasm that cannot be denied.

But she soldiers on with strength and grace,

Trying to find meaning in this heartless place.

Her grief, a thing of beauty and pain,

A testament to a love that will forever remain.

In a world that has lost all sense of care,

She wonders if love could still be found somewhere.

Joseph was at home now, not talking; his vocal cords had been too damaged, and he seemed most depressed too. However, being the era it was, nobody spoke about mood disorders, and if you got too depressed, then you got sent to an asylum. Nobody ever wanted to end up in that torture chamber.

So, Carys, Joseph, and the other younger children in the Delaney family surrounded each other with love. They were definitely not the only grieving family. 60,000 Canadian men died, and another 150,000 were wounded in the War to end all Wars.

Slowly, the ragged few from the 49th Division returned home.

So much happened towards the end of 1918. Everyone was reeling from the sudden change of the men returning and wanting their jobs back that had been taken over by women during the War.

In the spring of 1918, the Spanish flu pandemic hit the world. With the sudden movement of soldiers from many countries during the war and the long wait for ships to take them home at the end of the war, it was no wonder there was a pandemic.

Olivia put the letters down after realizing it really had been one in a hundred-year pandemic. The world had seen a lot of changes when our most recent pandemic, COVID-19, whipped around the world, catching most unaware that such a thing could occur in the 21st century. It had been a life-changing couple of years, especially where Olivia and Tim lived in the valley. At one point, due to an "atmospheric river," which caused days of heavy, unrelenting rain, roads, including major highways, had been washed out, leaving them in an area where they could not drive out of. A river breached its dyke and wiped-out hundreds of crops but, worse, killed thousands of farm animals. The flood happened fast. The past summer had gone on well into the fall months, with temperatures at least ten degrees Celsius above normal. Their small farming community had dense smoke covering everything with ash and making it very difficult to breathe. It was like an apocalypse was occurring and not about to stop. "Next thing, we'll be getting so much rain it will put out the fires but probably cause a lot of floods and landslides from the parched ground and weakened firma," said Olivia to Tim.

Back to Aunt Belle's letters again with her third cup of tea. Olivia feared she might float away.

After the war and murder at a nearby farm, Mom and Pop bought another farm near Camrose, Alberta. They were compelled to leave for a few reasons, one being the multiple homicides nearby that shook them all. Plus, they wanted to start with a new home and a smaller farm. Too many sad memories at their former farm.

The story we read about in the newspaper gave us shivers, knowing that our family had been so close to where six men were murdered on the next farm. It was almost unheard of to have multiple homicides in Canada.

The Grand Prairie Herald: summary

In June 1918, a series of gruesome murders occurred just northwest of Grande Prairie, Alberta. Six men of Eastern European descent were killed in two separate locations, making it the largest unsolved mass murder case in Alberta's history. The murders remain a mystery to this day.

The first indication of the multiple murders came when a settler named Dan Lough rode to the Alberta Provincial Police office in Grande Prairie in the early morning hours of June 20, 1918. He reported hearing a loud argument, cries for help, and a commotion at a neighboring farm owned by Joseph Snyder and his nephew Stanley. Lough mentioned that he saw a fire at the Snyder farmhouse, prompting him to notify the police.

When the police arrived at the Snyder farm, they found the building burned to the ground. Examination of the scene revealed traces of blood near the door, and it appeared that a heavy object, possibly a body, had been dragged from a nearby log to the shack. The bodies of Joseph and Stanley were discovered—one charred inside the dwelling and the other shot in the head.

The police believed it was a case of murder-suicide initially, as a.38 caliber revolver was found near Stanley Snyder's body. However, this theory was later ruled out, as it was improbable for a suicide victim to throw a gun onto the roof after the act. The revolver belonged to Ignace Patan, one of the victims discovered at the second site.

Three days later, another farmer, Alex Peebles, raised concerns about his neighbor Ignace Patan's farm, approximately four miles northwest of Snyder Place. When Peebles went to the Patan house, he found it deserted, with the door locked and a vicious dog present. The police were dispatched to investigate Patan's property, and they discovered multiple decomposing bodies, including Patan, James Wudwand, Charles Zimmer, and Frank Parzychowsky. All the victims appeared to have been murdered, with gunshot wounds in some cases and a slashed throat in Patan's case.

The investigations yielded little concrete evidence, leading to frustration among the community and speculation about the identity of the murderer(s). Various theories were proposed, including the possibility that returning war veterans or individuals with strong anti-German sentiments were responsible. However, no one was charged with the murders.

Over the years, the case remained open, with periodic interviews and investigations conducted by the Alberta Provincial Police, but the mystery of the unsolved mass murder in Grande Prairie, Alberta, persisted. Numerous suspects were considered, but none could be definitively linked to the crimes. The case remains one of Alberta's most enduring unsolved mysteries, with no resolution to date.

Pops was getting older, but Joseph wanted and needed to keep his hands busy, to forget, to repair, to plant and sow, and to find life in the soil. He had to push the blackness, the smell, and the sight of dead soldiers out of his every thought, both day and night. He worked hard, punishing himself for not protecting Percy as he should have. He had already been sent home severely wounded and wasn't there to take the bullet Percy got.

Angela was devastated. Although Joseph wasn't much of a writer, the two kept in contact until they died or were too feeble to write any longer. Angela never married. She had seen too much needless death and suffering and never wanted to get married and have children without Percy beside her. He was her shining star. She always looked to the heavens on a clear night and invoked the gods of love to let Percy shine brightly to fill her heart once more. Angela always remembered Percy singing their song from the war in his off-key voice.

And when the night is new

I'll be looking at the moon

But I'll be seeing you

Life on a farm had to carry on. There was always so much to do every day. In many ways, it was good for Joseph and Carys to be home to keep busy. Slowly, the good cooking and baking and just being with family helped to heal them all. It was a slow process.

The community held picnics and baseball tournaments to lift people's spirits.

Here is a write-up from the newspaper.

One beautiful summer day in 1919, our small community called Camrose in the Peace River Valley was buzzing with excitement for the annual baseball game. The town had been preparing for weeks for the event, with banners and decorations flying proudly from every storefront and lamppost.

The game was set to take place in the town's park, which had been transformed into a makeshift baseball field with wooden bleachers and a freshly painted diamond. Everyone in town was looking forward to the game, and it was said that even some folks from neighboring towns had come to watch.

As the sun began to set, the players took their positions on the field. The Camrose team was made up of some of the town's best athletes, including the star pitcher, Billy Johnson. They were set to face off against the team from nearby Ponoka and Wetaskiwin, who were known for their strong lineup of hitters.

They held a "round robin" style of tournament, and they were down to the final two teams. One was a team from Camrose, making the game all the more exciting for the townspeople.

The crowd cheered as the first pitch was thrown, and the game was off to a thrilling start. It was a close match, with both teams putting up a good fight. Billy Johnson was on fire, striking out batter after batter with his lightning-fast pitches. The Ponoka team, however, was relentless, and their batters were hitting the ball with incredible force.

In the end, it was a nail-biting finish, with both teams tied in the ninth inning. The tension was palpable as the Camrose team hit the field for one last chance to win the game. With two outs and a runner on third, the pressure was on Billy Johnson to deliver.

Everyone held their breath as Billy wound up for the pitch. He threw the ball with all his might, and it sailed towards the batter with a loud crack. The ball sailed high into the air, arcing toward the crowd. For a moment, it seemed like the game was over.

But then, to everyone's amazement, the Ponoka outfielder fumbled the catch. The ball bounced off his glove and flew over the fence, allowing Billy to score the winning run. The crowd erupted in cheers as the Camrose team and many spectators rushed the field, hoisting Billy Johnson up on their shoulders in victory.

It was a day the town would never forget, and for years to come, the annual baseball game would always bring the community together to celebrate their love of the game and their pride in their town.

Carys was well enough physically and emotionally to return to Edmonton to her teaching job that, thankfully, hadn't been taken over by a man. She really loved challenging young minds. Schools were popping up everywhere. After initial labour unrest, the 1920s brought rapid change to every sector of Canada. Automobile factories opened up, the first radio broadcasts happened, and Canadians moved away from rural areas into cities. The Roaring Twenties had begun.

Chapter 14

Belle, Nelly, Glen, Carys, and Tom

Glen, my "fiancé," Nellie, and I were a bad influence on Carys. We would take her out partying to the hidden gay clubs or even the regular clubs. Just as nowadays, with the hippies and free love, it really wasn't a lot different, just a lot more discrete.

The notorious "flappers" gave women the freedom of expression, especially sexually. You wouldn't have thought there were ever any "naughty" girls back then, and we really weren't. We wanted to spread our wings and get far away from the dowdy Victorian-styled women of the last century.

I should be embarrassed to discuss the crazy things we did in our youth, but I'm sure by the time you read these letters, your Grandma and I will be long gone. When I take a look around me and the recent past, I see the great tragedy of the Vietnam War, and I thank God every day that Canada had the sense to stay out of that one. The needless death of so many young men who never wanted to be there and then to be practically abandoned after their return, well, it was tragic. In my lifetime, I have seen too many wars. The first war to end all wars was never the last, nor the Second World War, nor Korea or Vietnam.

Also, I saw that movie Woodstock, and let me tell you, at least we kept our loving out of sight of others, well, except for the Petting Parties popular in the Flapper era. Those were something else, alright.

"Petting parties, what the heck are those?" Olivia briefly put Aunt Belle's letters down, shaking her head. "I wonder if petting parties were what I was thinking. Couldn't be." According to Millie, nothing like that ever happened during her lifetime as everyone just held hands, and no hanky panky was had, well, except for the naughty girls who got "in trouble". "Geez, I must have been so naive to have believed her when I was young." By the time Olivia was a teenager, most of her friends and she went to parties, drank booze, or smoked weed. Some got pregnant. Millie had Olivia convinced she was a skank of some sort, not having had a regular boyfriend in high school, well, at least until grade twelve. Olivia's whole sex education when she was a teenager was Millie telling her not to let boys touch her "down there." Down there, it wasn't exactly explained to Olivia. It took until she was in nursing school to really understand sex, the female body, and pregnancy. Once, Millie found some birth control pills in her room.

Yes, she had been snooping as the pills were well hidden. She threw them out, as well as Olivia, after slamming her around. Dad and Ben pulled Millie off of her. She really was insane. If Olivia hadn't disliked Millie before, well, she hated her now.

Back to the letters.

Thankfully, the fashions also changed. We were delighted to remove the old heavy clothes worn to our ankles and wrists, far too hot and cumbersome. Of course, when visiting home, we were sure to put on "proper attire" so as not to upset Mom.

We continued going to the clubs. We probably hit everyone in the next few years. It really was a bash and a half. We faced our futures with glee and hope. Times were changing fast.

Out in Camrose, there was a friendly but competitive baseball tournament down to the last two teams from the surrounding towns.

The Petting Parties we attended were exactly what you might have envisioned. Men, women, and everyone in between went to these fairly fancy private clubs where almost anything could happen, especially after a few glasses of champagne. We did everything but full-on sex. We were free of our parents, the war was over, and we had money in our pockets and a ton of energy for partying. We were free, and we needed to forget the past, all the pain and sadness.

Girls who had boyfriends or who decided to take their loving further would find ways. I don't quite know how because I was always with Nellie, Carys, and Glen, even though Glen would find himself somewhere entangled with some guy. Such a flirt he was.

One late evening, Glen came home very upset. He didn't want to talk about what had happened, but by then, the women were awake, too. They pleaded with him to say what happened, so after a slug of whiskey. Glen calmed down enough to explain what had happened that evening.

Thursday evenings were when he and his pals went to their "underground" gay bar. They had been meeting there for over a year. It was a fabulous place, great music and if you didn't know how to find it, well too bad as you had to have a special invite to show at the door which was behind another door which was down an alley. From the outside, it looked like just an old wooden door to an old building.

Glen always took a taxi to the closest hotel to the bar. He would walk through the lobby and exit the back door, walk to the end of the alley, walk another block, turn one more corner to the entrance of another alley, and if you knew which door to knock on, you would be admitted if you had the special invite card. It had worked smoothly until that night. Glen turned the last corner near the final alley, and he saw a scene of police brutality. Their clubs were out, and men were being bashed on the head, their arms, and their backs anywhere as they tried to escape the onslaught of violence. Blood was coursing down into their eyes from the wounds on their heads. Some were lying inert on the ground. Glen ran towards one guy he recognized sitting down by a wall. That's how he got the blood on his shirt and jacket. He wasn't injured but helped his friend home.

Apparently, the police had discovered the hide-away bar due to the attitudes and the law regarding gay people, especially men, in the 1920s. Somebody had snitched, and the police planned their strike well on a Thursday night, the busiest of the week. However, they hadn't taken into account that the bar didn't open until ten and really didn't get a full house until midnight, so the club, thankfully, was not full, maybe half. But a lot of them were taken to the police station, fingerprinted and photographed like criminals, then surprisingly let go.

The men were left terrified of ever being outed by the information the police had, and they knew if they were caught again in a gay bar, well, they would lose their families if married, their jobs, and their reputations.

Glen was still shaking, even more so when he realized how very lucky he was to have arrived when he did, near the bar but after the police attack. The adrenaline was just setting in.

Being gay and minding one's own business, hiding one's true self was difficult enough, but living in fear, a pervasive fear like a shroud following you everywhere.

Carys, Nellie, Glen, and I often went to the other bars with the petting parties, which were never raided by the police because half of the force attended.

Carys spent most of the evening dancing. It wasn't a habit of hers to engage in the dark corners of the Petting Parties, but after Henry's death, dancing her heart out seemed to make her a lot happier. It seemed everyone we knew lost someone during the war.

Now, you may wonder how all of the "straight" women didn't get pregnant. The birth control method at that time was advertised in women's magazines. It was a mixture of Lysol and water. Yes, you heard me! Can you imagine that? It's amazing anyone could get pregnant after doing that!

So, I made sure to instruct Carys what to do, not just before partying. Douching with Lysol was also advertised as a method for women to "be fresh for their man." Unbelievable in this day and age.

It must have been three years when we were all happy. The war was over, and the Spanish flu, too. The world was our oyster, as they say. But as life goes, nothing ever stays great all of the time. Carys got pregnant again.

She met a man, William, at a nightclub one night, and according to her, he was Henry's doppelganger. She immediately fell for the guy. William was a travelling salesman or something, as he had to go out of town for four or five days at a time. Nobody really ever thought about it. He seemed like a really nice bloke, and Carys was head over heels in love again.

There were differences, of course, between Henry and William, but Carys seemed to overlook these issues that others could see. We tried to talk to her and tell her to go slow. There was something not quite right about William, but we couldn't put our finger on exactly what it was. Maybe we were being overprotective, knowing how long it took Carys to get over Henry and their lost baby.

And then she got pregnant. Carys hadn't been sure until three months had gone by as her periods were still not at all regular. Carys told William one evening after dinner. She was nervous but felt William was just as in love with her as she was with him. That was the very last time she ever saw him.

One of Glen's friends was a detective with the Edmonton police force. He tried to track down William, but he was like a ghost who never existed. He probably hadn't even used his real name and most likely had a family elsewhere.

By this time, it was after Thanksgiving weekend. Carys, Glen, Nellie, and I always went home to the Peace country for the major holidays to be with family. It was always such a warm celebration being home with the ones we love. Carys, of course, was a little peaked but told Mom she had been working long hours, not that she was pregnant. That particular detail was never going to be told to Mom. Mom had had enough heartache for a lifetime.

After we got back to Edmonton, Carys and I discussed her limited options about having this baby. Going to a back street abortionist was out of the question, being four to five months pregnant already. Carys would just have to hide out at our place, and Nelly, Glen, and I would look after her. She could take another leave of absence from her job, make up some excuse, stay away from our family, and hope Carys never runs into anyone from home who might spill the beans.

Glen was making good money, and we rented a bigger house in another neighborhood. Carys was my "married" sister who lost her husband in a logging accident. Nelly was a "renter" of one of our rooms. Nobody seemed to care anyway.

We had to come up with an excuse for Carys not being with us at Christmas when we made our trek north to the town where the family now lived. It was still a long journey by train. Fortunately, there was a big snowstorm a few days before Christmas, and the train didn't get through. Glen and I visited Mom and Pop on New Year's, and we said Carys was preparing for the restart of school.

We found a lovely white cottage where Carys could spend her last month of pregnancy, which had been uneventful and healthy so far. The cottage was run by a few midwives for women without husbands. The only questions the midwives asked had to do with the health of Mom and baby. Nobody ever asked where the father was, which was a huge relief for Carys as she was still mortified at being pregnant and being dumped by a jerk. How could she have been so gullible to think William was anything like her beloved Henry? Her heart ached so badly for Henry still after all this time, and now she was having Henry's doppelganger's baby. What a mess she was in. She thanked me, Nellie, and Glen, for looking out for and after her so well.

Carys's room reminded her of home. Pretty flowered wallpaper on the walls, a porcelain commode, and a sink. There were plenty of books to read and other women in the same or similar situations to talk to. The deep red roses, just like at home, pleased Carys's senses. Their intense aroma filled her with joy and made her a bit homesick at the same time.

Finally, the day arrived when Carys went into labour. I was there to be with Carys, and it sure was a long day, but sweet Rose was born in late June, a couple of weeks late but such a healthy girl, a head full of dark curly hair, just like her Henry.

Carys knew she wouldn't be able to keep the baby, she wasn't married and couldn't afford to raise her on her own. Glen, Nelly, and I tried to tell her we would help, but the midwives at the home where Carys delivered her baby often found private couples wanting to adopt. Carys had met one such couple more than once while recuperating after her delivery. They were both close to thirty and had been married for five or six years and couldn't get pregnant. They were soon moving to Winnipeg, Manitoba, or to a smaller town closer to the woman's sisters. Glen knew the man somewhat; they had gone to college together, and he gave Carys's confidence that her baby would be well looked after with lots of love and care.

Carys reluctantly let go of Rose when she was just one month old. The couple who were adopting Rose needed time to pack up and sell their belongings in Edmonton, travel to Manitoba to buy a house and property, and return to Edmonton to get Rose. Carys had agreed to continue breastfeeding Rose until the couple's return, but that just made the separation much more difficult.

That loss of Rose nearly destroyed Carys again, and she quickly spiraled down. She lost her pregnancy weight too quickly, didn't sleep well, and was crying a lot. We tried giving her some herbal teas to brighten her mood, but they only worked a bit. Carys began wearing overalls with shirts and cut off all of her beautiful golden locks. She had such beautiful, thick hair and had never wanted to cut it because Henry had always loved her hair. But I guess she didn't care at that point. Carys wanted to go home to be with Mom. Whether she ever told Mom or anyone else about the baby, I wouldn't know, and I never asked.

Carys recuperated at home with Mom and Pops and one or two siblings, and within a few months, she got hired as a teacher in a nearby small town. Her mom tried to be a matchmaker with any of the single men in town, but Carys wasn't interested until she met a boy or man who was a couple of years older than herself. He and his family had recently arrived from Michigan to begin a new life in Canada. His Dad opened a garage for the many cars now on the road. Tom, as his name was, had spent some time overseas near the end of WWI but as a mechanic. He was almost the opposite of Henry, although he was still a decent-looking fellow, a bit short, maybe 5'7, but funny as heck. He liked to joke about, and that reminded Carys of the good times she had when she and Henry were young.

Glen, Nellie, and I made sure to visit the whole family often. That summer following Rose's birth, Glen and I were married at the small chapel in Mom and Pop's hometown. I know Mom had missed the countryside when they moved from their first farm shortly after the murders. The town just seemed too crowded and noisy these days. They felt they could manage a small farm along with Joseph and any other siblings that may remain at home. They were still traumatized by the recent murder of six men at a nearby farm.

Some reports suggested the murders were a racially motivated crime. After all, the men were German, Polish, and Russian. However, a lot of money was taken out of the bank earlier by one or more of the men. A large amount in those days, about $2500, but only $150 or so was found. Bills with splashes of blood were found in circulation later.

After two trials, the loss of police officers and investigators from the Spanish flu, and a lot of talk about incompetence regarding securing the crime scene, the perpetrator/s were never found, although there were suspicions.

After the move to the farm closer to town, Carys seemed so much better in every way. She had gained weight from Mom's phenomenal cooking and looked nice and brown from the summer sun. Carys had met a new guy named Tom, and they just clicked together. I thought it was a good thing that he didn't resemble either Henry or the nasty bloke she got pregnant with. He's best forgotten.

Tom gladly took Cary's fishing and hunting and let her help him work on his new invention, a snowmobile of sorts. It was a small truck mounted on gliders and definitely went faster than the old horse and buggy. He delivered the mail to all the homesteads in the winter months. He loved working in the garage with his father.

It wasn't long before Carys and Tom were an item and became engaged. Carys was happy, maybe not quite in love in the same way as Henry, but Tom was a steady, solid guy who let her be a tomboy when she wanted. He liked it when she dressed up in overalls and helped work on the cars in his Dad's garage.

They had a small wedding in September at the local church where Glen and I had married. Carys got pregnant within a couple of months, and she was very happy and looking forward to starting anew.

Life was looking good again until Carys had her first child, Amelia or Millie, with Tom. It was a girl that came out red and screaming, which didn't seem to stop forever. Poor Carys couldn't connect with this child. She felt dead inside and couldn't stand the constant helplessness of this demanding child. But she did her best. She couldn't keep breastfeeding for more than a few weeks as this baby wanted to devour her. Carys's nipples were raw and bleeding, and Carys was in so much pain everywhere. So, she turned to the modern method of feeding Millie with bottles.

Life carried on. There were hard times during the depression for everyone, but especially to the south of the Peace River area. There were severe droughts, more than one, and infestations of grasshoppers that occurred in the Peace area, too. Life was a challenge again. Life never seemed to stay the same. Just when things got comfortable, we were hit with major event after event. It was exhausting, but unless you wanted to end up in the "loonie bin," as we called it back, then you just kept going and hid your feelings. Sad.

Hundreds more families gave up on their farms in the southern areas, and the Peace in the north saw another surge of people hoping for better conditions to farm or the other developing jobs in forestry and the discovery of oil in Alberta. It would eventually make Alberta roll in the dough and oil.

In the late 1920s, the prices of grain and cattle dropped significantly. Many women lost their teaching positions in elementary schools due to the men returning home after the war, but mostly because the women did not work after marriage. It wasn't the norm. Women had been paid just half of what the men had done the same job, whether in teaching or labour. It was definitely a man's world back then.

Chapter 15

Young Millie

Every year or two, Carys had another child and ended up having four boys after Millie. The boys were always a handful, and Tom quickly used the strap. Carys didn't like to see physical punishment, but she was running on empty trying to keep up, so she let Tom handle the boys' behavior. Except for Millie, nothing seemed to work with Millie. Everything asked of her was met with a resounding NO. Carys didn't know what to do with her. Millie should have started school already, but she was so disruptive in kindergarten that she always ended up sitting in the corner. When Carys went to pick Millie up at noon, towing the boys along with her, she always got an earful about how naughty Millie was, and Carys just simply needed to get that child in order.

Carys would go home and cry. She had no answers. She and Tom had discussed Millie's behavior over and over. Carys finally turned to her mother, who always seemed so calm, and asked her for help.

Mom knew of a "spinster" who lived in another town closer to Edmonton. She had never married and was a retired school teacher. Miss Hogge would know what to do.

Unfortunately, this spinster's methods were cruel and demeaning. Miss Hogge had two other "naughty" girls staying with her. All three girls were terrified of Old Hogge. She surely suited her name. None of us knew until years later, and after a second stay when Millie was a young teenager, exactly how horrifying her "teaching" methods were. The girls were beaten often. They were taught over and over to be perfect in every way. They were taught etiquette and strict obedience to every situation they were in. Oh, such a heavy load for a six-year-old.

After a year, Millie was sent home. She entered kindergarten again, two years older than the other students, but she obeyed.

Until Millie turned thirteen, she started thinking she knew better than everyone, including her teachers. As always, Millie's brothers were enough of a handful, so Carys, not understanding because she had not been told about Miss Hogge's abusive ways, sent Millie back to be "taught" some manners again.

When Millie returned the second time after another year or more, she actually did seem calmer. Maybe because she was now fifteen and well settled into adolescence. It was hard to know.

Millie entered high school when she turned 17, always two years older than her classmates. She became the leader of the pack, so to speak. Millie could be very manipulating and always seemed to get what she wanted, and all of her friends idolized her. When Millie didn't get her way, she would have a tantrum behind closed doors. It seemed Millie knew how to behave in public, but behind closed doors, oh boy, she was a handful. Carys is usually so exhausted that she lets Millie get her way. It was so much easier than getting into an argument with her. Millie would yell and scream, kick at the doors. She actually broke her foot once, and nobody dared go near her during her outbursts. I, unfortunately, witnessed her behavior more than once when I stayed with Carys and Tom. Millie was like Dr Jekyll and Mr. Hyde, but her meltdowns were unpredictable and woah to anyone in her way.

I don't know if Millie ever got help from a psychologist or even her own doctor, but probably not. She was supposed to be perfect, and admitting she wasn't was beyond her grasp of reality. It was like she was in a fugue state during her outbursts. Millie never apologized to Carys and never ever talked about her devastating behavior, and I'm sorry, dear, but you and Ben probably have suffered at her hand. I could see it in your eyes when I visited your mom, brother, and dad.

Olivia put the papers down. She was relieved in one way that at least one other person in the world knew that something wasn't right with Millie. No one had ever said anything, well, except one of her Aunts when she was visiting alone. "You don't get along well with your mother, do you?" Olivia certainly agreed, and the Aunt went on to say that she felt Millie was a spoiled princess. So, there was that. "But why didn't Dad ever stop Millie from hurting Ben and me? Didn't he hear our screams"? I thought all families were the same. It never occurred to Olivia until years later that being terrified of living with a person was NOT OK. But Ben and Olivia grew up in that chaos. It was unlikely anyone would have called the cops even when Millie and their Dad were fighting like cats and dogs and sounding like they were killing each other. What went on behind closed doors was private. Ben and Olivia rarely had bruises because Millie was an expert at shaking us to death. She would grab them by the neck or shoulders and shake until they felt their brains wobble.

Olivia needed a break from all of this unexpected information from Great Aunt Belle. She had always thought Aunt Belle was a hoot and a half. She was brave and spoke her mind. Apparently, she was one of the first women to wear a bathing suit, at least at Edmonton's surrounding lakes. Olivia could picture Belle and Nellie in their old-fashioned skirt-type bathing suits running in and out of the water, having a ton of fun, and Great Uncle Glen with his bathing trunks on chasing the women into the water, or maybe he was the kind of guy who preferred to sit on a beach chair suntanning while smoking a cigarette in a long holder watching the beach "traffic" especially some of the men strolling by.

Olivia had a smile on her face when she read about Belle's girlfriend and the lengths they had to go to hide the fact they were gay. Those must have been crazy times. Olivia remembered meeting another great Aunt, Mildred or Matilda or something, when our family lived in Ontario. The great Aunt was living with another woman, "not so strange," Olivia thought, but there was an awkwardness when Ben and Olivia met the other woman for the first time. Something felt weird. It turned out that this great-aunt's daughter was gay, so maybe her Mom was as well. Olivia remembered this great Aunt's daughter staying with them when the family lived in Ottawa. At age 13, Olivia already knew this woman was gay. She dressed like a man and had a man's haircut. Olivia thought it was absolutely ridiculous that Millie was flirting with this woman, didn't she know? Well, Millie did flirt with every man she came in contact with, so maybe it made sense in a weird way.

Olivia had always loved Grandma Carys and felt such empathy with her having lost her soul mate and their baby. Olivia suffers from chronic depression, so she had tremendous empathy for her Grandma, but at least she had significant help from her doctors and specialists, plus medication. During Olivia's Grandma's era, people, especially women, were sent to the horrible conditions of a psychiatric unit or hospital. Olivia remembered as a young nursing student going on a "field trip" to the notorious Riverview Psychiatric Hospital in British Columbia. Just entering the very old building was very depressing in itself. Olivia and her fellow nursing students were told that the ward doors were never locked. Still, when the nurses removed an unruly female patient from the common room who was screaming at us to go away, she was dragged out of a door and locked behind her. Olivia was shaking in her boots, and although they had just been told the inside doors were never locked, the nurse definitely locked the door after the patient was herded out of the room where they were meeting. Restraints were often used. A few years later, watching the movie "One Flew Over the Cuckoo's Nest," it was like taking a peek back to Riverview.

Carys had lost herself in the horrible depression she endured after each loss and pregnancy. Olivia was beginning to understand her mother a bit more. It sounded like Millie was a firecracker right from the start. Then to have lived with that old hag Miss Hogge. Why didn't Millie ever tell Grandma about the abuse? It would have made such a difference in their relationship. Again, Olivia felt it was due to the era that Millie grew up in. Plus, the fact it went against Millie's belief that she was perfect. She would never admit she needed help after Ben and Olivia were adopted.

Olivia suffered from chronic depression for years. It began after the birth of her second son. It was a complicated time. Olivia wasn't getting along with her first husband, and it brought her so much stress that she sunk into a depression that lasted years. Medication helped her, and Olivia had done a lot of research on the subject and learned that most chronic depression is caused by an imbalance or the lack of certain chemicals in the brain. Olivia couldn't imagine the deep, soul-robbing pain her Grandma must have gone through without medication and counseling. It's a darkness deep inside. At times, it feels terrifying, suffocating, and pervasive. Breaking out into tears at the drop of a hat. It is not a good way to live. Olivia could think of times when suicide seemed preferable to enduring the pain. But Olivia was still here, still moving forward, and maybe for Carys, it seemed she found her way too.

When Olivia thought back on her life, she figured she had had depression since she was in high school. Olivia had gotten really sick in grade eleven, and her exhaustion dragged on forever, and it seemed to take months before she was back to her normal self. In grade twelve, Olivia was very exhausted in the mornings and never seemed to sleep all night. However, she loved to party on the weekends and worked part-time, which was a big load together, but Olivia liked earning her own money. Millie was non-stop action, so Olivia fell into the same kind of pattern.

Olivia also thought about her great Aunt and all the other gay people throughout the times. Olivia was sure, now that she was older, that she was probably bi-sexual. But the years when Olivia may have explored my sexuality with women came and went. Olivia had been attracted to a few women over the years, but they were strangers, and there was no way she was going to approach anyone she didn't know. Olivia felt she had missed the boat and realized how unfortunate that part of her life had been. Homosexuality was completely frowned upon and joked about when she was younger. Also, Olivia really did like men, so for years, she never thought about it. Such is life; people don't change, but fortunately, attitudes do, even if it takes decades. We no longer burn "witches" either.

The other thing Olivia pondered over was Millie. Her Mom sounded like a little hellion and most likely had ADHD, but again, during her school years, children with learning disabilities were thought of as either lazy or just plain stupid. Olivia, having two sons, one with ADHD and the other with ADD, knew the struggles of trying to find help for her boys in the 80's and 90's

Olivia had even gone to the school board begging for help for her boys, but unless she could afford mentors, which she couldn't at the time, there was no help. Every child was taught in the same way, and expectations were the same for every child. Now, how much sense does that make? But education is a business, an industry, and although teachers deserve a medal and a higher salary, it would be so helpful to have individual learning plans and goals. Well, that's what Olivia thought anyway. Olivia had been a nurse and an educator, but she had thought about teaching instead. But Olivia needed to get out of the house and away from Millie as soon as possible, and the nursing program was shorter than teaching. So, her need to get away from Millie trumped everything else.

Olivia heard the front door open and the dogs going crazy. Apparently, her husband, Tim, was home.

"Hey honey, how's it going?" Olivia inquired, above the racket of the dogs.

"Hi sweets, I'm doing A-ok. How did your day go? I see you have received the letters from Millie's lawyer. Wow, that's a lot of letters to read. What are they all about?"

"Shit, I didn't realize the time, how can it already be 4:30? I've been reading and thinking about these letters most of the day. I'm kind of overwhelmed?"

"Good time for a glass of wine. I'll pick out a bottle after I wash up."

"We're going to have to order pizza or Chinese food. I didn't take anything out for dinner. I'm telling you all this information has turned my brain to mush. Go get cleaned up and I'll fill you in with what I know so far. I want to read more after dinner."

Olivia and Tim ended up cooking up some pasta and had some raw veggies, and that was good enough for supper.

Olivia spent the next hour or two talking about her grandmother, her great Aunt, her great-uncles, and the one who died so close to Armistice Day. Olivia's great Aunt was gay, and her Mom's behavior now made a little more sense. That certainly didn't mean that Olivia had forgotten all the emotional and physical pain Millie inflicted on Olivia and Ben. For years, she thought she'd never be able to forgive Millie, but after reading these letters, Olivia hoped she would.

"I wonder if Millie ever knew about her mother's lost babies, one stillborn and the other adopted out? Did Millie understand her own mother's depression?" I asked Tim.

"I doubt it, Liv." Tim was allowed to call me Liv but not Livy. He often called me Oly, which was OK as long as it was never Livy.

"I doubt Mom had ever spent time thinking of anyone else but herself. She never shut up long enough or stayed still long enough to reflect on her actions. She had no insight into herself except to think she was so much better than everyone else." I said. "Everyone she ever met was judged by her very high, unrealistic ideals. Millie could never understand why more people weren't perfect like her. Even in her later years while living at an Assisted Living residence, she would shake her head at anyone who didn't want to participate in all the activities from morning to evening. She believed anyone with a walker shouldn't be allowed to live there. Lord save us all from Millie's critiques."

"I agree, but she's gone now. You don't have to listen to her any longer," said Tim.

"Ah, but that's where you are wrong, my dear. Reading these letters has brought back a lot of memories for me, and not a lot of them are happy. Ben and I were always miserable around her. On the other hand, reading about how she was and what she went through as a child helps me understand her a bit better. I don't know if I will be able to ever really forgive her or ever really forget the terror Ben and I had growing up. How can anyone not know that hurting children the way she did was not acceptable? I could never hurt my kids like that. I remember when Dion, my youngest, was young. I only knew how to discipline kids by learning from my mother. No, I didn't shake their brains about it, but I used a wooden spoon to spank him. He was a handful, and after his Dad and I divorced, his behavior got worse. The spanking never worked, so I stopped. It only hurt him physically, well maybe mentally too, that I could hurt him like that. But I was desperate and couldn't control him. You know I never got over those spankings. Maybe he did, but I did not."

"Oh, hun, don't be so hard on yourself. You know my Dad used a belt on us boys. He was tough and often cruel with us." said Tim.

"Nope, I really should have known better, but I did learn better methods of discipline for the next two kids. But their personalities were different, not quite as hyperactive." I replied. On the other hand, they became awesome adults and parents.

"I'm going to walk the dog once more before the sun goes down. Do you want to come? We'll just go down the creek." asked Tim

"Absolutely, I'll go with you. My brain needs to take some deep breaths in the green forest and listen to the creek. Plus, it's absolutely beautiful outside. The sun was out all day, and I missed most of it."

Tim and Olivia got the dogs ready and set out for the creek. It must have been just the right time of day for other wildlife to venture for an evening rink of fresh water. Three deer, two smaller than the really big one, ran up the creek beside us. It sure scared them although their big dog, Oscar, thought it was great fun chasing the poor things up the creek. He's fast, but they were much faster. That was what Tim and Olivia loved about living in the country. Not scaring the deer part, but the wildlife they constantly saw in the trees or fields. When Olivia was driving home last summer, she turned the corner to their street and saw a bear sauntering down the road. She followed it in the car, wondering where it might go. It went into a few open garages and snooped around but didn't find any food. The young bear continued up the street toward the woods again, so Olivia turned her car around. Near Olivia's house were young children getting off the school bus. Thankfully, the bear must have been able to tell the time, to have missed scaring the kids half to death. That bear had surely given me a start.

Olivia and Tim returned home, and she felt much better getting the cobwebs out of her head.

"Tomorrow, I'll start reading again." Olivia figured she should set the alarm when reading tomorrow, every hour, to take a break from reading and stretch her muscles. It was a history lesson plus.

Chapter 16

Millie

A new morning arrived after a good sleep. Olivia got up, fed the dogs, then herself, put on some coffee, gathered her thoughts, and picked up the letters where she had left off the day before.

During WW2, Carys took Millie and the boys to her Mom and Dad's farm to stay until Tom returned home. He was working as a mechanic in the army, but he never had to leave Canada to fight overseas. He was close to forty years old or so. I'm not sure where he was based with the army. I've long forgotten.

Millie had often talked about her stay on her Grandparent's farm. She loved it there. There is so much room to run, fresh baking every day, from the bread to the pies. Millie would brag that in the summer, she would eat a dozen cobs of corn in one sitting. She would help churn the fresh milk and cream into butter. She was in heaven. There was always so much to do and explore. It kept Millie occupied from morning to night.

In the winter, Pops would tow her with his car and a long rope while Millie showcased behind on skis. Millie and her brothers would play hockey on the frozen pond. Her brothers did tease her a lot, and in the summer, they locked her into the outhouse, where she stayed until one of the adults heard her scream. Boys!

Olivia remembered her older son hanging her younger son upside down in a tree. Luckily, it was in front of their townhouse, and she could hear a quiet "Help me, Mom." Olivia was a single parent and had been since her daughter, Olivia's youngest, was two years old. Life was hectic.

After Millie finally graduated, she went to Edmonton to take an accounting course. She was good with numbers. Millie lived with three of her friends who graduated at the same time but was two years younger, so Millie was still the leader of the pack. Millie and her friends were just like any other generation of young women. Working full-time and going out most evenings. They really loved going to the service clubs to dance and meet guys in the armed forces. The second world war was over, and the same was true during the Depression years.

As Millie became a young adult, others her age became known as "the silent generation." Generally, hard workers were very careful with their money and possessions and had been instructed by their elders to be frugal and thrifty. Couples married younger than the last generation and bought homes in the post-war and post-depression boom. Outlying neighborhoods were built to accommodate all the newlyweds and "baby boomers," as your generation is known. People moved away from the cities to buy land in growing areas called suburbs, which are more family-like and away from the cities.

A few years went by, and I don't know much about Millie's lifetime during those years. She worked with her friends in Edmonton and, according to Carys, was happy in the big city.

Millie did meet your Dad at one of the servicemen's dinner-dancing clubs in the city. He was four years older. At the time, Millie was twenty-three, and Larry was twenty-seven. He was in the Air Force, and all the women loved a man in a uniform back then. Larry had been dating off and on and had just broken up with a long-time sweetheart. He was enthralled with your mother. He would do anything for her. He treated

Millie like a princess, and he sure took a lot of shit over the years from her. He was blindly in love with her.

In many ways, they were a perfect match. If Millie said jump, well, your Dad said, "How high." Your Dad was an intelligent guy (except with Millie) and worked in communications in the Air Force. One of his early jobs was a post in the Northwest Territories spying on the Russians after the Second World War. The "Cold War" had descended upon us.

Your Mom and Dad married in the early 1950s. You would know the date as I've long forgotten these things.

As you well know, your Mom and Dad were transferred all throughout Canada. Starting a new school every two to three years must have been challenging.

Chapter 17
Ben Olivia, Larry, and Millie

Again, Olivia put down the letters, tears coming to her eyes as she remembered life on the Air Force Bases. It definitely wasn't easy.

The first base they lived in was Whitehorse Yukon. Olivia didn't remember too much from that time, just from photos and Millie's stories.

Millie used to pull her on a toboggan, both of them bundled up in the freezing cold, to trek to town to collect the mail and buy a few groceries. Millie said it was a scary walk in the dark. They lived in the land of the midnight sun except during winter when the day seemed like night. The wolves in the nearby forest would howl as they walked by. No wonder Millie was nervous.

Olivia's parents adopted Ben that year. Shortly afterward, they moved to Southern Ontario, which Olivia didn't remember a lot about those years. But she remembered many significant events during those "Cold War" years.

When Olivia's family first arrived in Nova Scotia, they lived in a motel room for a couple of months. That's when Olivia's nightmares and lack of sleep began.

Years later, when Olivia was in her early thirties, she was learning how to meditate. Ugly images kept intruding into her brain. Olivia could never understand why she hated closets, and they had to be kept shut if she was in a room, or she would get very anxious. During the move from Southern Ontario to Nova Scotia, a moving van worker had done nasty things to her in the bedroom closet. Olivia remembered but didn't understand what happened. She was terrified and confused. Olivia couldn't tell Millie because, as usual, Millie was flirting with the moving guy. Olivia went outside and faced the brick wall of the house. She stood there for a very long time in the sun until her friend, a little boy with dark hair, came and stood with her, not uttering a word, as if he knew something significant had happened. After a bit of time, they left to play. The incident was totally forgotten, or so Olivia had thought.

She remembered being terrified about going to a new school every time the family moved to another location. Math was so confusing, and Olivia thought she'd never understand the strange method taught in Nova Scotia. Plus, there was a hurricane. When you are a family of four and staying in a one-floor small motel room and hear that storm rush in, it feels like you could get blown away or blown up any second. Millie didn't help with her screaming at Larry to do something. The only thing he could do was what he was told to do: park his car at an angle. Seemed a little strange to Olivia, but that's what everyone in the motel did. What else could he do? There was a lot of destruction. Tree branches and whole downed trees covered the road, and the power was out for hours. It sure got cold in that motel room. It was a memorable event.

After living in the one-room motel, the family rented a draughty apartment in Kingston near the Air Force base. It was a very old house with rickety stairs to the upstairs two-bedroom apartment with a tiny kitchen and living room. Olivia didn't remember if there was a bathroom or maybe a shared one with the two "working gals" who lived in the bottom apartment. Their house on the base wouldn't be ready for a couple of months.

About a month after the hurricane, Olivia was picked up at school by her Dad in the middle of the day. It was Larry, her Dad, who told her President Kennedy had been shot. Shot? That terrified Olivia. How? Why? Where? Their questions were soon answered over the next few hours. The TV was on all day broadcasting the news, and they watched the president flop down in the backseat of the convertible, bleeding over his wife, the incredibly brave Jaqueline Kennedy (Onassis). Olivia could not understand why anyone would shoot a president. It was beyond her comprehension. She grieved right along with the adults. Three more prominent men were assassinated in the next five years.

Olivia's early years were marked by a series of assassinations of prominent men, as was the case for many of her fellow baby boomers. However, in Canada, occurrences of this nature were less frequent. Nevertheless, as our neighboring sister country, the United States' struggles were felt by all. We Canadians avidly consumed American news and were significantly influenced by the authorities in Washington and California, including the media industry in Hollywood. Millie held a deep admiration for President Kennedy and, in particular, his wife, Jacqueline.

Millie thought Jacqueline was the cat's meow and dressed like her and probably wanted to be her. Olivia hoped Millie realized how emotionally abused that poor woman was. Jacqueline had tolerated her husband's philandering with the "females" of the day, including Marilyn Monroe. It seems that individuals in positions of power are never content and seem to require a constant influx of adrenaline to maintain their grip on the power they hold. This is a generalization, of course, as some in power have not behaved in the same manner. However, it is a fact that many powerful men have been driven by their desire for dominance and control, often at the expense of others.

Christmas was spoiled for Olivia that year. She was six and a half years old, and at Christmas time, Millie and Larry had an epic fight and woke her up. Olivia went running into the small living room and saw the unwrapped presents that Santa was to bring. No Santa. Ben, who was just three at the time, was crying his little heart out. Olivia went back to her room, terrified her Mom was about to kill her Dad. Every time they fought over the years, Olivia had the same terrified feeling that Millie would harm or kill her Dad, never the other way around. Or worse, she would turn her anger on Ben or Olivia, which their Dad never tried to stop. Why? Was he that afraid of her destructiveness, too? Or a coward not to protect his children.

Strangely, Christmas Day turned out to be better. Millie would never say no to an invitation for coffee or a drink at a neighbor's; she loved to show off how well-dressed she and her perfect kids were. Their house was very small and stinky. Olivia was glad to get out of the place when the boy who lived there asked if she wanted to see the horses. Off they went into the muck to feed the horses some carrots. Later that evening, Millie told Olivia that the young boy, maybe ten or eleven years old, was a pyromaniac and was their nephew living with them at that point. Thankfully, he didn't set any fires when Olivia was with him.

There were several events that shook their lives, especially as children who cannot process tragedies as well as adults. Olivia and Ben didn't know what questions to ask to clarify the event.

Olivia got married in grade one. It always makes her smile thinking about it. During recess or lunchtime, some of the kids in her class would climb onto the bleachers outside, hold hands with the opposite sex, and jump into the snowbank. Then you were married. Easy peasy.

In the summertime, Olivia and a couple of girls from school would go for long bike rides through the countryside. They would pack a lunch and either find a field near a stream or sit on the low eave of a building near our school. They could reach it from the top of some rickety stairs. Sitting up there gave them a different point of view, something everyone should do once in a while.

Nova Scotia was a beautiful place to live, and Olivia remembered a lot about it. In the summertime, they would go on vacation throughout Nova Scotia, Prince Edward Island (PEI), Cape Breton, and New

Brunswick. Almost everywhere was the Scottish influence. Tartans and bagpipes. Olivia loved it. On Fridays, they had fish delivered door to door. The poor fisherman was pretty shy as he would jump down the front stairs and practically run away when anyone answered the door. But the fish was fresh and always delicious. Lobster and crab, too. Once, they stayed at a cottage on the ocean that Millie and Larry's friends owned. They ate so much fresh-caught lobster they could have burst.

Olivia and her family lived in Nova Scotia for three years. They travelled to PEI to visit the Heritage Home of Anne of Green Gables, and Olivia was in heaven. She had been an avid reader since grade one and had read Montgomery's famous books over and over. Olivia had lived there in her mind for many years. The rolling green hills, the white house with green shutters, large deep red roses that bloomed against the house on trellises, and in the summer, they spread their sweet scent through the gentle breeze. It was heaven. It reminded her of her Grandma's first house that Olivia saw in the Okanagan. She hadn't realized how much Grandma loved her red roses until she read about her in Aunt Belle's letters.

Olivia's Dad had to go on work courses every once in a while, and she hated it when he was gone. Millie was always okay, with no outbursts, but she would make Olivia sleep with her. She hadn't liked Millie for quite a while at that point and could hardly stand to be around her, so sleeping with her was torture. It took years and years of therapy to try and understand why Olivia hated Millie so much. Ben hated her, too. They couldn't trust Millie. When would she blow up next, and how badly would we be hurt the next time? Olivia really was terrified by Millie and her mixed messages. She would tell them they were the best kids and how proud she was when Olivia got on the honor roll but then turned around and hurt them.

One education course took Olivia's Dad to Bermuda. That afternoon, Millie was on the phone for quite a while. Then she turned on the news. An Air Force plane that had taken off about the time Olivia's Dad's plane took off had gone down in the Atlantic Ocean. Millie couldn't get any information for several hours. Of course, she kept the news on and close by. There were no survivors, and the newscasters spoke about sharks. Olivia was frantic, imagining what might have happened to her Dad. Larry and the rest of the crew had landed safely, and they hadn't known about the crash for several hours. Nobody wants to imagine their Dad, or anyone for that matter, getting eaten by sharks. Olivia never knew what plane had gone down with no survivors.

The last stop before moving west to British Columbia was Ottawa, Ontario. Another fun location for Ben and Olivia. Millie and Larry bought their first house, a true 60s house. It was a split level, a few stairs up to the bedrooms and a step or two down to the living room, which had the ubiquitous shag rug. There was a ton of snow in the winter to go tobogganing down the hills, build forts, and skate outdoors. Olivia remembered the smell of the warming hut at the outdoor skating rink, the pot-bellied stove where the kids would inadvertently singe their mittens. They often got a little roasted if a person wasn't paying attention. The odor of wet burning wool. Olivia can still smell it. She and her friends could purchase a watery cup of cocoa, too, for a nickel.

Olivia would help Danny, her best friend, alongside her best girlfriend, deliver his newspapers to the nearby farms, and they would spend time with the horses or see the newborn kittens in the barns. Olivia and Danny lived in a city but far enough from downtown to be surrounded by farms. There was a copse of trees behind Olivia's house, where she and her friends often built forts, climbed trees and played hide-and-seek.

Olivia had my first crush at age twelve for Danny. The very last night they were to be in Ottawa before moving to British Columbia, a few of them were playing hide and seek in her girlfriend's basement. Olivia was lying on a padded bench, and Danny came to lay beside her. She knew he was ready to kiss her, but she had just eaten garlic bread for supper and was too embarrassed to kiss him as it might gross him out. Big mistake. Olivia always regretted not sharing that sweet first kiss with him.

It was in Ottawa that Olivia began to think more independently and be more objective about Millie, who she was, what she didn't like about her, and why she didn't love her or even like her. Quite a drastic view for an eleven-year-old.

Olivia also began to learn what she liked to do and what her interests were. Olivia loved reading and had been taking out a maximum of six books from the library every two weeks. She loved Nancy Drew and the Hardy Boys books, Anne of Green Gables and other books in the series, and almost anything. By the time Olivia finished high school, she'd run out of fiction books to read at times, so she read all the classics, then maritime history. Weird, she knew for a teenager.

Olivia had been in Brownies in Nova Scotia and graduated from Girl Guides in Ottawa. One of the most excellent days she remembered was going on a hike with the Girl Guides in the fall. Millie and Larry golfed and curled, but a walk in the woods wasn't posh enough, she guessed. But Olivia loved the outdoors. That hike on a trail opened her senses to the autumn aromas, the smell of trees and moss. The deep brown earth, the colorful leaves that fell softly to the ground. Olivia was in love with the outdoors.

One other memorable experience while living in Ottawa was on a field trip with the school to a maple tree farm, where they watched the syrup drip from the maple trees into buckets. The students could smell the syrup gently boiling in the large vats in the hut.

Millie returned to part-time work in the accounting department at a bakery in Ottawa. Olivia was only ten at the time and had to look after Ben during the summer. Larry did work shifts, but Olivia and Ben were left to their own devices at least three days a week. Olivia did love Ottawa, though. It was fun to go downtown with her Mom now and then for an appointment of some sort. It was right in the mid-1960s. Flower power ruled. Olivia loved the fashion of that time. Mini skirts, as well as granny dresses, are such extremes. Bright, beautiful, flowery dresses or "bell bottoms" are everywhere.

Tim and Olivia had gone to Ottawa a few years ago for a medical conference. They had a couple of days to explore Ottawa and hopped on a bus to find Olivia's old house. She loved living there, but when a family is with the Armed Forces, you are constantly moved from province to province and base to base. Larry had nearly been posted to Germany, which Olivia and Ben would have loved so much, but Larry wanted out of the Air Force and took a job with the RCMP doing spy stuff. So, the family headed west and bought another new house near Vancouver. There really isn't anything to describe moving into a brand-new house. Everything is so brand new, you can even smell the new paint, especially in the kitchen and bathroom, where semi-gloss was always used back then. The brand-new wall-to-wall rugs also had a distinct new smell of chemicals.

On their move from Ottawa to Vancouver, they drove the whole way and overnighted in many small hotels along the way. Ben and Olivia always made sure that their Dad rented a motel room with a pool. Olivia ate pancakes with real maple syrup every morning. She never forgot the trip across Canada. They lived in a very large country, and it was a treat to see it all. Olivia and her family had been from one side of the country to the other and north and south. In the late sixties, travelling through Northern Ontario via Highway #1 was long and boring. One never wanted to get out of the car due to the horse flies that would take a chunk of your skin away.

When they were driving through Saskatchewan, Larry decided he wanted a beer. Their car definitely didn't have an air conditioner, and it was very hot and dry. Larry stopped on the main street with a bar across the street. Millie went with him. She had to enter the women's door as they were not allowed to go in the same doorway back then. How ridiculous it was because once inside, they sat at the same table. Ben and Olivia were left in the car. The hot car. No fluids allowed. No food either, for that matter. Millie wouldn't allow it. So, Ben and Olivia sweated and got stuck in that car for a couple of hours. They were allowed to have the windows down part-way. Olivia was getting worried when their parents finally came back. That was a rotten thing to do.

Larry, their Dad, loved driving, which was a good thing as it took at least five days to get to Penticton, where Millie's parents, Carys and Tom, lived then. Years ago, their Grandma and Grandpa decided to get out of the Peace River valley with the freezing temperatures in the winter. They bought an orchard in the Okanagan Valley. They grew cherries and peaches.

It took some time for Ben and Olivia to fit in when they moved to their new home outside of Vancouver. Ben was still in elementary school, which was fairly close by, but Olivia had to walk down a long hill to the middle school. She had stopped taking ballet after the move from Ottawa, and she had gained weight during her early teenage years. It was no big deal, really; she only gained around ten to fifteen pounds, and it wasn't like she was morbidly obese. However, Millie never seemed satisfied with Olivia's weight, constantly criticizing her for being either too skinny or fat. Despite this, Olivia didn't let it affect her too much; She simply walked to school every day, even though it was a bit of a hassle to climb back up the hill afterward.

The Barlows had moved into their new house outside of Vancouver in November after Ben and Olivia stayed with Millie's parents in the Okanagan, BC for a few months, while Millie and Larry bought a house. The school Olivia attended in Penticton had over 1,500 kids. She had never attended such a large school. Olivia felt constantly lost trying to find her next class in such a large school. Another situation that has given her nightmares of roaming down halls and never knowing what classroom was next.

After they moved to BC, Millie returned to work full-time. Olivia was thirteen then, and Ben was ten, but Olivia still thinks that she was too young to be left alone. However, they got used to it. They even got used to the weather, which was a huge change coming from provinces where it often snowed up to the roof. The fog was always an issue in the town they lived in, especially in the fall and spring. Olivia never forgot poor Ben wandering around and around one day after school during their first week after moving there. The fog was so thick Olivia could barely make her way home, but she was walking with other kids from the school who lived in the same area. Olivia had been home a while, but Ben still hadn't arrived. Finally, Millie donned her coat and set out to find Ben. The poor kid. She did find him, thankfully.

The Barlows settled in their new house and community. Larry never talked to us much about his job except occasionally to tell Ben and Olivia not to go here or there. "But why not, Dad?" Working with the RCMP in communications was about the same as being a spy in the Air Force during the Cold War. He wouldn't explain. Olivia would take the family dog for a walk, and if she was walking on the wooded path near their house, she constantly looked over her shoulder, certain she was being followed by some unknown criminal ready to stab her. Olivia always had a very active imagination. The "Colony Farm," the prison for the criminally insane, was literally just five miles away from where they lived, and at times, there were escapees.

It was many years later that Olivia found out what her Dad really did during the war years. Larry was in his late eighties when he finally began to tell us of his part in the war and onward as a spy in the Canadian Air Force.

After he entered the Air Force when he was eighteen or nineteen, he was trained as a radio operator but mostly how to "spy." Larry was sent to Camp X, a covert military training base, to learn about sabotage, hand-to-hand combat, intercepting enemy communication, and killing "silently".

Winston Churchill, realizing the importance of espionage in this war, was keen on training others across the Allied Nation. One of Churchill's friends, William Stephenson from Winnipeg, Manitoba, also known as Intrepid (fearless), was station chief for Britain's Secret Intelligence Service (SIS) in the United States. Stephenson was in charge of training men and sometimes women in North America.

They were a fearless bunch, and all were skilled in all espionage tricks of the trade, including how to disguise themselves with larger noses, wigs and adding a layer of newspaper to their shoes or padding for coats to appear different.

Larry, having great skills in radio technology at that time, left Camp X's training but ended up working on the secretive Hydra project, the state-of-the-art telecommunication system.

Olivia could never understand her Dad's fear of the house catching fire. He would completely turn off the heat in the house at night. It never mattered if it was -10, plus our bedroom windows had to be open an inch.

Larry had a fear of fire; he seemed a strange man at times, very quiet, but he would always laugh out loud at funny jokes. Ben ever, the comedian, would keep us in stitches. His fear of fire, though, was hard to understand, and for years, he never explained, and Millie would just shake her head and say, "Do what your Dad says," which meant keep the furnace completely off at night.

We would all wake up with clouds of breath coming out of our mouths, especially during the cold winters in Nova Scotia and Ottawa, until the furnace heated the house.

Then Larry told Olivia the story of his time working on Hydra. The buildings were mostly wooden, and one night, the mess hall caught on fire and spread to their sleeping quarters. Now she understood. Why hadn't he just said so before? But he was sworn to secrecy until late in his life.

After Hydra shut down, Larry was sent to Manitoba to the far north, called the Dew Line or Distant Early Warning Line, at the northern border of Canada, following the Arctic Circle to carry out spying on the Russians. They built a series of outposts with radar stations, and Larry was sent to one or another. The Cold War began soon after the end of WW2.

Larry once told Olivia "There was always an armed guard on patrol, not just watching for enemy submarines or aircraft sneaking towards

Canada, or even more worrisome were the Polar Bears who loved to wander in and get into any garbage. They soon learned to keep the garbage inside. The adult bears had huge paws; one swipe from them, and you'd be a goner. The guard would fire his rifle close to the bear to frighten them off. Sure enough, some fool would shoot one for a trophy. There was no place to skin a bear as our quarters were small, so he froze the darn thing. He had to have left the bear behind as I highly doubt he could have fitted him on a plane or been granted permission to do so."

Larry went on to tell Olivia about a few famous people he met while training at Camp X. Ian Flemming was with the British Royal Navy and was sent to Camp X in Canada to further his espionage training. He went on to write the James Bond series. "Your mother and I, and I'm sure you have seen all of the movies. Some were quite laughable, but people seemed to enjoy the shenanigans 007 got himself into, surrounded by the ubiquitous gorgeous women."

The Cold War began shortly after WW2. The two emerging global power countries were Russia and the United States, with Canada being a close ally.

The two leaders, Josef Stalin of the USSR and Harry S Truman had very different ideas of how post-war Europe should be divided. Stalin wanted USSR governments posted throughout Eastern Europe and to destroy Germany's industrial capabilities. Truman wanted stability and democracy.

In 1945, George Orwell published an essay titled "You and the Atom Bomb," which addressed the terrifying implications of atomic warfare and the global political situation in the aftermath of World War II. In this essay, Orwell warned about the illusion of peace in a world where nations possessed nuclear arsenals, stating that it was a "peace that is no peace." It was also in this publication that the term "Cold War" was first coined.

Soon after, an "arms race" began. A race of potential extermination of large parts of the world. The Russians had nuclear capabilities before

WW2 but amped up their effort after the war. It was the same with the United States. It was a continual game of one-upmanship.

In October 1962, the U.S. and the Soviet Union found themselves in a tense, 13-day standoff over Soviet missiles armed with nuclear warheads that had been deployed to Cuba just 90 miles away from American shores. President John F. Kennedy addressed the American public on television on October 22, 1962, revealing the presence of these missiles and informing them of his decision to establish a naval blockade around Cuba, while making it very clear that the U.S. military was prepared to use force if necessary to eliminate this threat to national security. In the midst of this crisis, many feared that the world was on the edge of the abyss of a nuclear war. Fortunately, the situation was defused after the U.S. accepted Soviet leader Nikita Khrushchev's offer, which involved the removal of the Soviet missiles in exchange for a pledge by the Americans to refrain from invading Cuba. Notably, Kennedy also agreed secretly to remove U.S. missiles that were stationed in Turkey. Olivia remembered that day. She was young but recalled the tense situation watching the news with her parents. She vividly remembers adults telling their children "not to eat the snow" because there may be Russian "fallout" in the snow, which Olivia could never understand. Then there were the drills when they lived on the Air Force bases. Out of the blue, it always seemed to Olivia that the emergency horn would blare, practically giving people a heart attack. Everyone on the base had to take cover, with students jumping under our heavy wooden desks. The only thing we, as children, knew was that the Russians might attack.

The Barlows lived on the outskirts of Vancouver until Ben graduated from high school three years after Olivia. Then Millie and Larry sold their place without telling Olivia or Ben, bought a one-bedroom townhouse in a fancy area of town, and joined the local golf course at exorbitant member fees. Millie always wanted to show people with money that she was as good as them. She would practically drool around these people, pathetic. But as usual, Millie had a lot of friends, so "what did she know?" thought Olivia. Millie's presentation and demeanor were never angry or stressed toward acquaintances. After Millie's dementia got worse, Olivia was finally able to see what so many others saw after Millie's anger left her body. Ben didn't get a chance to see her during her two years of dementia. He died when he was fifty-seven from a major stroke. His liver had been so damaged by his years of heavy drinking that the neurologist surgeon could not stop the bleeding. His whole body had failed.

Olivia read to the end of Aunt Belle's last letter. There wasn't really anything else at the end of this box of letters except that Olivia needed to contact the lawyer who had sent the documents, as there were more to come. That seemed strange to Olivia. What else was there to say? Aunt Belle had passed away forty or fifty years ago. Her husband, Glen before her. Olivia admitted she did understand Millie better from all of Aunt Belle's letters, but it was too late for Ben to have learned about her past. Would that knowledge have helped his path in life? Or would he have found another reason to drink? He chose his destiny, or did he? Olivia could say, "I've chosen my destiny," but she didn't always know what that might be. Olivia would start down a path and constantly get knocked aside, licked her wounds, and try again. "Destiny has many roads that curl back upon each other. How can a person truly know their destiny when life conspires to constantly change it? Even if we don't accept that change or changes, sometimes there isn't a choice. We can stay stagnant and blind to destiny ringing inside us and let life direct us whilly-nilly without purpose or…or we can stay mired in situations we'd love to change but fear the unknown. Destiny will happen whether you realize it or not. Want it or not."

Olivia contacted the lawyer who had sent the initial letters, not knowing what to expect. Olivia spent all her time reading and thinking about Millie's history and how it had affected not only her life but also Ben's and Olivia's. It was good to know the history, no matter how horrible it may have been. To Olivia, knowledge of just about anything only helps in our understanding of others. It wasn't like there weren't any doctors or psychiatrists who may have helped Millie, but she was in total denial about who she appeared to be to Ben, Olivia, and Dad. How could Olivia ever have said to Millie, "Mom, you are totally screwed up and have so much anxiety and anger you always end up hurting us. Why? Why? I guess we were horrible children who deserved your wrath." At least, that was their mindset. Ben and Olivia were horrible children. She didn't know whether that feeling of inadequacy ever left her.

However, when Olivia went into nursing, she and her fellow students were instructed about every aspect of nursing care, including psychiatry. At the time, Olivia thought Millie was an undiagnosed bipolar patient with her extreme highs and lows. It very well could have been, but in later years, after Olivia's own diagnosis of major depression and complex PTSD and while attending a couple of psychiatrists, they diagnosed Millie in absentia as having "borderline personality." Millie certainly fits that diagnosis, a diagnosis incredibly difficult to treat because the patient never sees themselves as anything but perfect, at least in Millie's case. Outbursts of extreme anger are part of the diagnosis. Unfortunately, all of Millie's stress and anger at her world was taken out on Ben and Olivia. Larry occasionally got in the way, but he was never able to stop her physical abuse of Ben and Olivia. The thing is, it wasn't just physical abuse. Ben and Olivia grew up feeling they were unwanted and total failures. Ben and Olivia both had addictions. Olivia's was men, well actually the thrill of romance. All of her life, Olivia tried to get some kind of love, but as they say, it was "all in the wrong places." Olivia felt abandoned, alone, and unworthy. She knew Ben felt the same. Such a tragedy of life.

Chapter 18

Olivia

Olivia finally got to the point in her late forties to know what kind of life she wanted and needed. Olivia met Tim long after her kids had grown up and had forged their own lives. Olivia could only imagine how abandoned they felt by their Dad, who disappeared from their lives for years and then died way too young, never having reconciled with his kids.

Being a single parent of three, with the youngest just two years old when Olivia's husband left, was a huge challenge. Millie's parenting was by force and fear. Olivia did not want to replicate that with her own children, but nobody is perfect, and learning to be a good parent is a lot of trial and error. Olivia and her kids made it through eighteen years of being a single parent. She loved her children more than she could ever express. Olivia always wanted to make their lives better and more stable, but she had a terrible record of choosing men. All of them were addicts of some sort or flirts, another kind of addiction that never ever made her feel loved and wanted. Finally, she met Tim. Of course, they had their issues. Who the heck doesn't? Men are from Mars and all of that. Any relationship takes a lot of effort and understanding towards a person who grew up with their own struggles. Tim and Olivia were almost opposite in character. "But he grounds me, and hopefully, I bring a bit of laughter and spontaneity to our life together. I piss him off, and he pisses me off at times, but we meet in the middle and have a great life together" figured Olivia.

Olivia decided to go through the reams of photo albums she had been left by Millie. They were definitely educational and historical. Until Olivia read Aunt Belle's letters, she only had a little bit of information about her grandparents and Millie's youth. Olivia only knew that she loved her Grandma and Grandpa. They would take Ben and her camping in the summer. They would meet up with one of their uncle's family and their cousins, whom Olivia loved to be with, and they would spend several weeks in the summer camping at one of the many lakes in the Okanagan. Grandpa taught Olivia how to fish, and of course, she got a hook stuck in her thumb somehow, but Grandpa got it out without too much drama.

Olivia gets very antsy when she doesn't get outdoors where she and Tim live in the country, where it has rained every day for a month or more at times. Olivia got used to walking their dogs rain or shine. She needed her daily dose of green and fresh air, even if she and the dogs soaked when they returned.

"There's so much smoke in the air today from the nearby fires I can hardly breathe outside. Our climate is definitely changing, whether you want to deny it or not. It sure seems clear to me, even in the smoke, that the weather has become much more unreliable to predict, and there have been environmental disasters everywhere. Driving home the other day was like entering an apocalypse. The smoke was so thick I couldn't see the highway overpasses until I was at them. I came close to missing my exit," Olivia told Tim.

Life for Olivia seemed to have taken a break. Ever since Millie died, Olivia had been totally consumed by memories and Aunt Belle's letters. She felt like running away. But where would she go? Her brain felt like mush. Olivia couldn't even take the dogs for a walk today. The smoke was too thick. She had asthma, and breathing the dense smoke irritates her lungs, and then she sounded like a heavy-duty long-term smoker. "Not me. I hate the stuff, regular smoke or otherwise." Olivia had had to treasure her lungs over the years. Asthma attacks can be a very scary ordeal. She ended up in the obstetrical emergency unit when pregnant with her first child. Olivia's asthma got out of control quickly one day. She couldn't even remember what triggered it, but she was suddenly surrounded by hospital staff and doctors. Olivia was wheezing so hard she could not catch a proper breath and felt like she would pass out. Olivia wasn't sure if she had experienced anything quite as scary before. Not being able to breathe is very frightening. The doctors set up an intravenous medication that soon eased her breathing, and she was sent home with asthma puffers, medication she had had to take every day since. Thankfully, it never stopped her from the sports that she loved to do.

Olivia contacted the lawyer's office and asked for the next mysterious set of letters. She wondered what these letters would contain. Olivia didn't know how much more she could take. Recent events, Millie's death, the previous two years of turmoil with Millie's dementia, and now these letters. Olivia needed a break. She really needed a break.

So, she booked a ticket to Prince George, BC, where her oldest son and family had moved last spring. It may have seemed a strange move to some in the family, but the cost of living was cheaper there than anywhere southwest of the Okanagan in BC. Olivia's daughter-in-law's family had lived there forever, so it did make sense for them to move there. However, it meant that we wouldn't be able to see them as often. But that is life.

Olivia had a great mini vacation and returned home much more refreshed and thinking a bit clearer-headed.

Olivia's life slowly returned to her usual. She studies Spanish in the morning, has lunch, and then takes the doggies for a walk somewhere within a fifteen to twenty-minute drive. The big guy, Oscar, is an eighty-pound Bernadoodle. Olivia fell in love with him as soon as she saw his picture on Kijiji. He was the cutest, fluffiest teddy bear of a puppy she had ever seen. Olivia and Tim had set up a crate in their bedroom, but the first night, he cried so hard that Tim lay down on the floor beside the crate to keep him company. Now, that's a loving and caring thing to do. Oscar, as they named him, settled down. Olivia knew neither of them got too much sleep that night. It wasn't long before they let him out of the crate to sleep on his doggy rug beside the bed.

Olivia's brother, Ben, died that year. Oscar had outgrown the lap dog phase. He was twenty-two pounds at age three months, so that didn't take long. Olivia was devastated by Ben's death. She was so angry, but she wasn't sure exactly who she was so angry at, definitely at Ben, who could never love himself enough to stop drinking and destroying himself, but also at Millie. Ben could have made other choices in his life. It wasn't totally Millie's fault Ben and Olivia were so screwed up, but the premise they started from was a disaster waiting to unfold. Ben and Olivia hated themselves. They had absolutely no self-esteem, never felt truly loved, and spent a good part of their lives trying to please Millie and everybody else and get their approval. Not that Millie never told them how proud she was, but those were the times Millie felt Ben and Olivia had shone and reflected her brilliance. It was an extremely difficult and confusing time growing up with Millie. She bragged and was proud of Ben and Olivia in public but would tear them down at home. Olivia never knew what to believe. She thought she was the smartest, nicest, and prettiest person in the world, but at the same time, she was the girl who had no boyfriend in high school, was a loser, was bow-legged, and had a big nose. At least, that's what Millie led Olivia to believe. Ben was just stupid and lazy. Another untruth. He got himself through university and ended up in a very well-paying job. But Olivia knew he constantly thought he was an unwanted failure.

Olivia wanted to get Millie out of her head. Was that even possible? She had been the source of a lot of anguish for Olivia for over sixty-five years. "I'm tired, very tired." Olivia has a medical condition, Myalgic Encephalomyelitis (ME), similar to Lyme Disease or Long Covid, plus fibromyalgia, which is like arthritis of the muscles. Very painful.

Olivia constantly has to watch how much exercise and physical or mental stress she goes through, as too much, which is never much at all, will drastically increase her symptoms. Olivia's energy level drops significantly. She gets "brain fog," which causes her distress when she can't recall words or gets them confused, like saying cat instead of that or losing her concentration. Vocabulary used to be her strong suit. Olivia was glad she had been able to travel, even if she was usually in a wheelchair. Nowadays, she can walk her dogs for twenty minutes a day. "Not bad," she thinks. But she relapses a few times a year.

Olivia used to be able to swim forty-two lengths at the pool twice a week and skied, hiked, and cycled, but that abruptly stopped over twenty years ago. Just like that, she "crashed" and never got her former self back, even after years of all kinds of therapy, western and Eastern. Life is like that. It can change in an instant.

"Time to get her shite together this morning." She read her emails and studied Spanish for an hour or so. Olivia was constantly thinking about the next set of letters that would arrive in the mail soon. She had no clue who they may be from. Aunt Belle is long gone. She can't ask her.

Olivia took the dogs for an extra-long drive and a nice walk on the dyke near the Fraser River. Being outdoors really does soothe the soul, heart, and mind.

She and the dogs got home late in the afternoon. Olivia fed the poochies and waited for Tim to get home.

They had a nice dinner that Tim cooked, and Olivia cleaned up. By the time it's four in the afternoon, Olivia generally loses her energy and gets dizzy and weak if she stands too long. Thankfully, Tim is a great cook and doesn't mind getting dinner together, nor does he mind if Olivia doesn't get the dishes cleaned until morning. Olivia does rinse them the night before, at least. Such is life. When Millie stayed with them on the holidays, Olivia had to do the dishes that evening, or Millie would be "bent out of shape," or she'd get up in the middle of the night to do them, embarrassing Olivia even further. It really seemed to upset

Millie that Olivia wasn't a good housewife because she had expectations of Olivia, and cleaning up after dinner was an absolute must. "But why?" Olivia asked. "What if someone dropped by," said Millie. "Well, Millie, that never happens, and if it did well, too bad, it's my house." Her eyes glowed red, and her mouth became a thin line. Olivia should know better than to contradict Millie, even in her own home.

Two years ago, before COVID "saved" Olivia, she was very sorry to say that she had to bring Millie to their house to stay two or three times a year. The last time she stayed with them was Christmas before COVID struck in March in Canada. Millie literally chased Olivia down the hall in her own house when she refused to tell Millie why her brother's wife and kids didn't want to have anything to do with her after Ben died. They blamed Millie for Olivia's brother's death, which isn't totally correct or fair. Olivia was brought up by the same woman, and she could have been an alcoholic or other, but she worked on improving herself and tried to understand Millie for years. Olivia still didn't understand her, but the letters from Aunt Belle had definitely helped. "Why, oh why didn't Millie ever talk to me about her past"? Thought Olivia. But maybe she tucked those years of abuse at the back of her mind, never to reappear again, at least without the help of a psychiatrist.

Chapter 19

Rose

To Olivia's surprise, the next set of letters arrived the next morning by FedEx. She was sure it would take a few more weeks.

Olivia made her usual large cup of tea in the morning. She had already fed the dogs and sat down with the timer on her desk so she would remember to take a break now and then.

The first letter was again from Aunt Belle. Olivia wasn't expecting that. She wondered what else Aunt Belle needed to tell her. Olivia thought her Aunt's letters were finished.

The letter began…

My dear Olivia, this is my last letter before I pass the baton, so to speak, to another person who will fill you in on your grandmother's daughter, Rose.

As I mentioned in a previous letter, your grandmother's daughter was adopted by a nice couple who were settling in Manitoba. Glen knew the couple, Abigail and George Morgan, well enough that your Grandma and I felt secure that Rose would be brought up with love and care. We weren't wrong.

Abigail, Rose's new mother, and I exchanged letters for years. After she died, Abigail's sister, Silvia, took over. I kept them all. I would at first tell Carys about how Rose's life was going in her new home, but Carys needed to put her energies into her new family, especially after Millie was born, and didn't want to hear more. She was very happy to hear that Rose had a good family, but it brought back painful memories of her dearest love, Henry.

Rose grew up in a small town near Winnipeg, Manitoba. Rose was the apple of Abigail and George's eyes. Such a loving, happy little girl with dark curly hair, sparkling blue eyes, and rosy cheeks. They were never able to get pregnant, so Rose was their sole delight.

Rose went to school on the school bus and met a lot of friends. Her favourite subjects were English, history, and some math, if it didn't get too complicated. "Sounds like me," Olivia thought.

As stories and history go, life never stays the same. Abigail died of cancer when Rose was just seven years old. Rose and George were devastated. Abigail had been their north star, their guiding light. Rose and her Dad felt they had been tossed in the wind to blow them this way and that. Rose was eight and wasn't old enough to be expected to look after the house and have dinner ready when George got home from the pharmacy he worked and owned in town. After a few months of mourning the loss of Abigail, George proposed to a local spinster he knew from church. Rose was sure her Dad didn't love this woman, but George needed a wife.

This new woman in their house disrupted George and Rose's rhythm and evenings together. In the past, after listening to an early evening radio show, George would read out loud to Abigail and Rose from all genres of novels. It was easy to lose oneself in George's deep voice that made the words come to life. Books were full of knowledge and transported oneself to other countries and ways of life. Rose's early favourite books were The Jungle Book and the almost brand-new Winnie the Pooh.

Mildred was a hard woman. She never gave an inch. Mildred treated Rose as her personal maid. Rose never minded doing chores for her Dad, but Mildred never asked her kindly or even thanked Rose for her help.

Then came the babies. Rose loved her half brothers and sisters but, again, was expected to be the nursemaid after school and on weekends. Finally, her Dad, George, put a halt to that. Rose needed a social outlet and not be tied to her half-siblings. George could see that Mildred didn't feel the same way about Rose as her own children. Maybe her heart wasn't big enough. Mildred wasn't cruel to Rose but very strict and expected a lot from her, and George usually kept his mouth shut. He certainly didn't want to upset Mildred; she had a temper, and the words out of her mouth were sharp daggers, and it was hard not to get hit by a few.

Rose had free time from Friday evening to Monday morning. She loved hanging out with her friends from school. In the spring, they would go to their high school's football games to cheer their team but also to look at boys, a favourite pastime. In the wintertime, they would go skating during the day and watch a hockey game at night. There were dances at the high school or the community center on Saturday nights. On Sundays, everybody, and I mean everybody, went rollerblading at the Winnipeg Roller Rink. The place was always packed; it was the best and craziest time to go. There were usually 1200-1500 people there. Nobody fell down because everyone was shoulder to shoulder, pressed together. It really was a hoot.

Some of the boys and girls would somehow find some beer or other alcohol and hold secret parties in abandoned barns or small cottages near the lake. Rose went once or twice with her friends but found the parties boring unless it was in the middle of winter and there was a big bonfire. But it always seemed like the boys tried to outdo each other with how much they could drink. Stupid boys. Rose and her friends heard a story about one party where one of the very drunk guys wandered off on the frozen lake. Whether he got lost in the drifting snow or just decided to lie down, he was found frozen by search parties the next morning. Rose and her friends never went to a similar party again.

Winnipeg suffered during the depression, just as almost everyone across Canada and the United States did. The wheat farms in the prairies had been growing abundantly and the bountiful harvests were exported along with Canada's other natural resources, enriching them all until the stock crash in 1929. Many were forced to sell their farms. Canada was one of the hardest hit, having depended on the wealth of their exports.

The farms dried up, especially during the drought which had begun in 1929. People called it the "Dirty 30s." The crippling drought brought infestations of grasshoppers and a weed called the Russian Thistle. As soon as the farmer planted his seeds, the wind would whip up and blow them away. Many gave up and moved to the cities, but unemployment was so high there usually were no jobs to be found. The marriage rate went down, and people couldn't afford to raise families. Not that there weren't a lot of babies born "out of wedlock." The orphanages at the time were large.

WW2 brought darkness and ugliness to the world again, a war more or less expected for a few years. Still, Canada's defense of the armed forces had been severely depleted over the past twenty years. Defense spending had gone down, especially during the depression. Nobody believed another world war could occur again. The concept of a war to end all wars was highly idealistic. War has been since the dawn of time.

Canadians were not in a hurry to go to war, but after Britain declared war on Germany, Canadians also entered. Canada was the oldest country in the Dominion of the British Empire, after all.

Rose and her boyfriend, Richard Prince or Ricky, which he preferred, as well as their friends, were in their mid-teens when war broke out. He was a tall, dark-haired, and dark-eyed boy. Rose used to lose herself in those dreamy eyes. She had a crush on him since she was twelve years old. Ricky was a year older, but that seemed to make a big difference until Rose matured and entered high school.

Rose grew into a beautiful girl, somewhat resembling Elizabeth Taylor, with romantic sparkling eyes that drew Ricky in like a deer in headlights. He was dumbstruck by her beauty. How had he not seen Rose before? She lived just down the street. Ricky felt tongue-tied and awkward around Rose; she was so smart, and he had competition from a few other guys. He gladly would have fought them off, one by one, or all of them at once. He would not be pushed aside by another. Ricky had no idea that Rose already loved him and had been biding her time until she was older and became more of an appeal to the opposite sex.

Ricky was always waiting by the school door for Rose to appear, hopefully without her band of girlfriends that always seemed to be nearby. Finally, she came out on her own one day, and Ricky grabbed the chance to walk her home.

Rose was secretly delighted. After that day, they walked home together, with or without her friends. Of course, Ricky preferred when her friends, even as nice as they were, not to be present.

Most of the boys in their high school were not old enough to sign up to fight overseas. They would have to wait another year or more.

The absence of men and older boys from their town eventually was noticeable, even to the kids in high school.

They carried on with life as teenagers do, more concerned about who was dating whom, who had a crush on whom, and who went to the second or third base. Some girls went "all the way" and had to carry their fear of pregnancy until their next period. Now and then, girls would disappear for six months without much of an explanation, except they were going to live with a distant Aunt to help out or some other excuse.

After school and on weekends, Rose and Ricky would take long walks beside the Assiniboine River. The gentle breeze in the spring and fall was light and airy, gently blowing ripples in the river. Ricky would hold her hand, and they would sneak kisses when no one was in sight. In the summer, they would fish on the riverbanks and, in the winter, would skate for miles and miles, or the boys would play a good game of hockey while the onlookers practically froze. They would bring flasks of hot chocolate with the occasional shot of Irish whiskey to take the chill off their bones. They would drag wood from the chopping blocks and build huge fires for added warmth when needed.

The evening news on the radio kept them informed on progress, and many had older brothers who had entered the armed forces, air force, army, or navy.

Ricky was Metis but attended regular high school; at that time, it was compulsory for "Status Indians" to attend Residential schools scattered across Canada, but thankfully, Ricky, being Metis, wasn't forced to go there and instead attended regular high school in town. His mother and father were also Metis, and his Dad owned one of the more popular restaurants in town. He was a good businessman, and people were happy to ignore the fact he was Metis to have a great dinner and entertainment afterward. He sure took a financial hit during the depression. He had been saving money to open another dinner/nightclub, but that was put on hold until after the war. He later became a rich man when post-war Canada was in a boom.

Ricky was determined to go into the ever-growing Air Force as soon as he graduated. Patriotism hit the young men who were far too young to understand what they were getting into. Yes, they knew families who lost family members, mostly men who either were killed in the First World War or had rendered men disabled. There weren't many televisions during that time. Information didn't travel nearly as fast as nowadays. Still nobody, especially those who lived through WWI and its high toll of tragedies.

Aunt Belle goes on to summarise how Canada became involved in the war.

Canada, of its own accord, joined the war in September 1939. Canada being part of Great Britain's commonwealth countries, realized that Nazi Germany was a threat to Western civilization's very existence.

Right from the start, Canadians were right in the middle of the fighting on the ground, in ships, and in the skies. That's where Canada made its biggest contribution to the war. As soon as hostilities broke out, the British Commonwealth Air Training Plan was set up in Canada so that Britain, Australia, New Zealand, and Canada could have air forces.

By 1944, the Royal Canadian Air Force numbered in the 200,000s.

The Royal Canadian Navy began from scratch in 1939 but grew to 700 ships and 95,000 men. This force was in the thick of the fight right from the start; it helped rescue soldiers from Dunkirk, and it took on more and more of the Allied convoy work across the northern Atlantic, with half of that by 1943 and most of it by the end of 1944.

The Canadian army had around half a million soldiers in 1944, most of whom volunteered for overseas service. Some of them were part of the force that suffered badly at Dieppe in the summer of 1942. Some fought alongside Americans and the British in Sicily and Italy. But most Canadians went to war in June 1944 with the landing on the beaches of Normandy. From there, they continued fighting through France and into Germany, putting in the biggest military effort of their history.

Theodore Roosevelt didn't declare war on Japan, Germany, and Italy until after two years of fighting by the Brits and others. Plus, repeated pleas from Winston Churchill and his courageous wife Clementine, and finally, the destruction of the Naval base at Pearl Harbor forced Roosevelt's hand.

Then, Canada followed suit, declaring war on Japan and its territories, having already been fighting the Germans. Canadian units were in Hong Kong when the Japanese attacked it on Pearl Harbor Day, and the Canadian declaration of war against Japan was made the evening before Roosevelt's declaration. The whole west coast was now in peril.

On December 7th, 1941, besides the attack at Pearl Harbor, Hawaii, Japan launched simultaneous attacks on multiple Allied targets in the Pacific region. These attacks were part of a larger military strategy known as the Southern Expansion Doctrine, which aimed to take control of Southeast Asia and the Western Pacific Ocean.

Here are some of the other places that Japan attacked on that day:

The Philippines: Japan launched a surprise attack on Clark Air Base and other installations in the Philippines. Much of the US Army Air Corps' Far East Air Force was destroyed on the ground, leaving the defenders unable to mount a significant resistance.

Guam: The Japanese Imperial Navy bombed and devastated the US-controlled island within a couple of hours.

Wake Island: A small US garrison on Wake Island was attacked by a Japanese naval force. Despite being outnumbered and outgunned, the US defenders bravely held out for two weeks before surrendering.

Malaya: Japanese forces landing in northern Malaya through Thailand advanced southward, taking Kuala Lumpur and other key cities.

Hong Kong: In a surprise attack, the Japanese Imperial Army invaded Hong Kong, which was then a British colony. British, Canadian, and Indian defenders held out for 17 days before finally surrendering.

Overall, Japan's coordinated attacks on December 7th effectively crippled the American military's production capabilities in the Pacific and ensured that Japan would have a free hand to make rapid territorial gains in the months that followed. The attacks also showed that Japan was a force to be reckoned with and sparked a new level of fear and anxiety among Allied powers fighting in the Pacific.

In later years, well after the war, one of Nellie's brothers told us about his capture while fighting in Asia. Her family had no idea where he was, whether he was dead or alive. It took six long months to discover he had been captured along with twelve others while fighting in Burma. This is what he said:

"I was a young soldier serving in the British Army during World War II when I was taken prisoner by Japanese forces in Singapore. I was terrified and didn't know what to expect. The Japanese soldiers were angry, and I could tell they didn't look at us with much kindness. Our captors showed us little mercy as they forced us to march to our prison camp. I could feel my feet blistering and my muscles burning. The hot and humid weather only made it worse.

The camp we arrived in was a barren place where we were packed tightly into small huts and were assigned to sleep on the ground. There were at least one hundred more captured soldiers from several allied countries. We were given just enough food to keep us alive but not enough to keep us healthy. Usually, it is just a small ball of rice and questionable muddy-looking water.

Many of the prisoners around me contracted debilitating diseases like dysentery, cholera, and malaria. Many died of malnutrition, dehydration, severe beatings, and the intense heat we were made to stand in for hours either to punish us for an often unknown misdemeanor or while building their bridges, which were often blown up again by our boys.

We were forced to work on building the Burma railroad. A monumental task. We had no proper tools or equipment to work with. Mostly our hands, it was backbreaking labour.

Many of us were so sick from malnutrition, dysentery, or cholera that we were in a long line of skeletons with diarrhea constantly running down our legs. If not diarrhea, then we had horrific ulcers on our legs or back started by bug bites or leeches. Every day, men died on that long road to hell. We tried to prop fellow soldiers up so the Japanese wouldn't beat them, which usually led to their deaths.

We had one break for lunch, one break only after sweltering in the hot burning sun. We were allotted one small tin mug of dirty water and another rice ball. It was amazing any of us lived through such horror.

One Japanese soldier seemed to have more of a handle on what Buddhism should be, or Christianity for that matter. He would sneak an extra ball or two of rice and sometimes a bit of chicken thrown in the dump after the Japanese officer's dinner. That may be the single reason some of us in our bunkhouse managed to live. I never forgot the kindness of that one enemy soldier.

The Japanese officers running our camp were put under tremendous pressure to get the railway built, starting in Thailand just outside of Bangkok to Mawlamyine, the first capital of British Burma. It was to be a deadly task building the line over 415 kilometres.

Construction was extremely difficult, with the route crossing through thick, mosquito-infested jungle and uneven terrain while monsoons kept the workers shivering in the downpours and steaming when the sun came back out.

Rivers and canyons had to be bridged, and sections of mountains had to be cut away to create a rail bed that was straight and level. The Japanese in charge of the camps took amphetamines, endorsed by their army, to enhance their fighting ability. However, it tended to make a lot of those in charge a tad unstable, especially if they ran out, which could happen often due to the shoddy amount of supplies they were able to get, if at all.

Any man faltering would be beaten. One man we were not allowed to help was beaten after he fainted and was sent back to the camp hospital on the ten-kilometre dirt and gravel road.

He crawled the whole way. Nobody could figure out how he had managed to do it.

Aunt Belle goes on to describe in more detail the Japanese "code" and the treatment of Prisoners of War (POW's)

There was a high mortality rate. Japanese treatment of POWs was influenced by the Bushido code, which upheld the idea of honor in death rather than surrender. Conditions in Japanese POW camps varied, but generally, prisoners faced overcrowding, unsanitary conditions, and malnutrition. POWs were often subjected to forced labour, performing grueling tasks such as building infrastructure, loading and unloading ships, and working in mines or factories. Many endured physical and psychological abuse, including beatings, torture, and interrogation. Medical care was usually inadequate, and serious illnesses or injuries often went untreated. Diseases such as dysentery, malaria, beriberi, and tuberculosis were common among the prisoners due to poor hygiene and nutrition. Red Cross parcels that were intended for the POWs were often withheld or confiscated, exacerbating the already dire situation. Additionally, Allied POWs faced the risk of being transported on so-called "hell ships" for forced labour or internment in Japan or other countries under Japanese control. These ships were often overcrowded, lacked basic sanitation, and were targets for enemy attacks, leading to high casualties. One of the most infamous Japanese POW camps was Changi Prison in Singapore, where thousands of Allied soldiers were held. Despite the harsh conditions, some prisoners organized educational activities, sports, and cultural events to maintain morale and preserve a sense of community and humanity.

While some captives were lucky enough to encounter relatively more humane treatment, most endured horrendous conditions and suffered from physical and psychological trauma. The liberation of these camps by Allied forces brought relief, but the scars left by their captivity lasted a lifetime for many survivors.

Chapter 20

Europe

The war was a strange mix of European loyalties. There were mini-wars inside the large war.

During the dark years of World War II, the French were fiercely divided about their loyalties. Some embraced the Vichy government and were pro-German. Others formed resistance groups. There were spies all around. Some could be your neighbor who wouldn't think twice about reporting suspected saboteurs, Jews, or whoever may utter a word against the Vichy government or the Germans.

In the early days of the war, many French citizens believed that their government could negotiate a peaceful settlement with Germany. However, in May 1940, the Germans swept through France, and the French government was forced to make a decision: surrender or flee to England.

The newly-appointed leader of France, Marshal Phillipe Petain, chose to surrender. Petain signed the armistice agreement with Nazi Germany, and the country was split in two. The northern half of France was occupied by German forces, while the southern half was controlled by the Vichy government, which was a puppet regime set up by the

Germans. There was no longer anywhere to run away from the German occupation of France.

Under Petain's leadership, the Vichy government made several concessions to the German occupation forces. They collaborated with the Germans in rounding up Jews and sending them to death camps, and they allowed German troops to move freely throughout France.

This left a dark mark on France's history. The Vichy regime implemented policies that targeted various groups within French society, including Jews, political dissidents, minorities, individuals deemed "undesirable" by the regime, and homosexuals.

One of the most infamous atrocities committed by the Vichy government was its complicity in the deportation and extermination of Jews during the Holocaust. Under the Vichy government, French officials actively participated in identifying, rounding up, and deporting Jews residing in France to concentration and extermination camps. The regime cooperated with the Nazis, assisting in the arrest and deportation of tens of thousands of Jewish individuals, including men, women, and children.

In collaboration with the Nazi occupiers, the Vichy government also enacted laws targeting undesirable groups. These included political dissidents, trade unionists, resistance fighters, and those who did not conform to the regime's vision of a "pure" French/German Population. Thousands were arrested, interned in camps, and subjected to torture, execution, or forced labour. The internment camp at Drancy, near Paris, served as the transit point for many French Jews who were later deported to extermination camps.

The Vichy regime further targeted individuals considered "undesirable" based on their race and ethnic background. The regime began discriminatory policies against the Roma population (also referred to as Gypsies), branding them as criminals, undesirables, and a threat to society. Roma communities were systematically persecuted, interned, deported, and subjected to medical experiments carried out by Vichy officials.

As well as these atrocities, the Vichy government participated in acts of collaboration with the Nazis, sending French citizens to work in Germany, assisting in the German war effort, and suppressing resistance activities. The regime enacted repressive laws, including censorship, propaganda, and limitations on civil liberties, to maintain control and allow the German occupation to continue.

A few brave men and women formed resistance groups to fight against the Nazis and their collaborators. These brave groups of men and women carried out sabotage missions, gathered intelligence, and helped Allied forces behind enemy lines.

A tall, redheaded woman with an artificial leg was hired and trained with England's new espionage division, an act that surely not only shocked many but especially men who felt a woman's place was in the kitchen and had no place or the brains to be involved in warfare.

Boy, did she prove them wrong?

Virginia Hall was a young woman who had lost a leg in a hunting accident. She joined the British ambulance crew and was in Vichy when France fell to the Germans. She managed to escape back to England, where she convinced the powers that she would make a convincing spy. Who would suspect a one-legged woman (she wore an artificial leg) could or would be a spy? Virginia was very intelligent and sent a lot of valuable information back to England by wire. She was constantly on the move because many times, she and her fellow saboteurs had to pull out of locations when the Germans using radar to detect illegal signaling radios would get close, sometimes just down the street.

A Gestapo senior officer, Klaus Barbie, of the violent German secret police, was furious that this woman, nicknamed the "limping lady," evaded them every time they got close to capturing her. Virginia was, after all, an amputee. How could they not spot her or have somebody report her location? Virginia walked down the streets of Paris and other towns without a second glance.

At one point, she had to escape on foot over the Pyrenees to Spain. She endured more pain than most people could imagine on that trek. In later years, she had to do the trek all over again, taking a few of her fellow saboteurs to safety.

It took a lot of convincing the higher-ups in the British army's new espionage unit to let her do her work as she felt called to do. She spoke several languages, had travelled extensively throughout France, and knew the terrain well.

Being a woman, many thought she should be at home, married with a couple of kids, instead of galivanting around Europe doing a "man's job." Some men involved in the spy agency would deny her reports and go with what a man in the field had reported. Much to their dismay, Virginia proved to be the one submitting the correct information every time.

There were many other female collaborators, some carrying out small feats like slashing tires on the German officer's cars or luring them down alleys or apartments with the promise of sex, only to have her partner stab the German soldier in the back with his pants literally around his knees.

Or like a woman named Marie who lived in a small village near Lyon.

Marie knew from the beginning of the war she had to do something. She watched as her male friends and family members were arrested or conscripted to work in German factories. Marie refused to sit idly by, knowing that the path to her freedom from the Vichy and German regimes and all the horrors they were committing demanded courage and sacrifice from all who were able. She joined the Resistance, taking great risks to her life and those of her loved ones.

Marie began by helping Resistance fighters escape the German occupation by providing food, clothing, and shelter. She would shelter the fighters in her small cottage, burying their weapons and ammunition in her garden until the couriers, as the men and women were called, took them to safety in England or Spain. Marie also helped to forge identity documents and transported messages, risking death at the hands of the Gestapo.

In time, Marie became another female key figure in the Resistance and developed incredible connections and networks across the French countryside. Marie also began recruiting other women to join the Resistance, teaching them how to shoot, hide, and communicate secretly. Women were essential to the Resistance, and Marie knew that their bravery would help them bring a swift end to the occupation.

As the war progressed, Marie's work and secrets became increasingly dangerous. The Gestapo started to suspect her, and frequent raids of her house planted seeds of paranoia. It was only a matter of time before they found her underground hideaway.

After helping many English, French, or allied soldiers escape, she knew her days as a female resistance fighter were coming to an end. Marie had moved about different areas and houses, but a woman Marie thought she could trust and who had helped her shelter several allied soldiers was actually a Vichy government spy. The next morning, just after sunrise, Marie had just woken up and was enjoying her tea when she looked out of the window, and her heart sank. She could see three large black cars flying the Nazi flag. Marie dropped her tea and ran towards the cellar door where she was hiding four soldiers awaiting pickup by the couriers. There was nowhere to go. She had failed. They would all be sent to a concentration camp and quite possibly killed.

Marie was brought to Ravensbrück, which was the largest exclusively women's camp in Nazi Germany. Over 120,000 women from various parts of Europe were forcibly imprisoned in this place. Among them were resistance fighters and political adversaries who opposed the Nazi regime. Additionally, there were those who were considered undesirable by Nazi society, including Jews, lesbians, sex workers, and homeless women. But Marie was considered a traitor.

She endured weeks of torture, but she refused to give up her contacts and accomplices who she knew had to carry on this smaller war within a war.

Tragically, the death toll in Ravensbrück exceeded 30,000 women. Some of them met their end in the gas chambers or hangings, while others died due to starvation, diseases, or excessive labour.

Numerous female guards subjected the prisoners to cruel treatment, with beatings and torture carried out daily. The saddest part of this particular prison was that it was run by females, including the guards who carried out unspeakable methods of torture. Some female guards claimed they had no choice in the matter of their duties or they would be prisoners, too. But we found out later that wasn't true as once many women found out exactly what the job entailed against other women, they left. No one knows what happened to these women. Perhaps they had to escape and hide from the SS or Gestapo.

Marie, beaten until almost dead, was sent to the gas chamber as a Traitor. The Germans felt they had given her ample opportunity to confess and give up the names of her collaborators, but she never did.

In 1944, after several embarrassing campaign failures, the Allied forces landed in Normandy and began to push back against the German army. The French resistance continued to play a vital role in helping the Allies gain a foothold in France. They sabotaged railway lines, attacked German convoys, and provided valuable intelligence.

Reading these letters with all the history included was like reading a book. The letters were hard to put down. Olivia was so curious to learn more about her Grandma's daughter, Rose. Aunt Belle never gave Millie these letters, and Olivia could understand why. She didn't think Millie ever knew about the existence of her half-sister. It would have been up to her mother, Carys, to talk about her painful younger life and losses, but she never did. After a break and a walk, Olivia continued reading these remarkable letters. Such a lot to absorb.

Life was sad and terrifying again throughout the world in the 1940's. Rose and her friends were quick to volunteer to do whatever they could to help the war effort, pack parcels for the men overseas, knit warm socks, write letters of encouragement, and whatever else that might help the soldiers.

Rose and all of her friends knew the seriousness and sadness of the war, and they did all they could to help out their families with so many fathers and brothers absent, with too many never coming back.

One by one, families were given news of their children having been killed or severely wounded. Many families were inwardly terrified to hear the death messengers' distinct and horrible knock on the door. Parents cried in their sleep, trying not to wake their younger children with the news they had lost their older brother, cousin, or father. The news was full every night of the atrocities of war. Even though Rose was to be out of the sitting room when the news was on in the evenings to protect her, she assumed that she would sit on the stairs and listen. At least Rose's father, George, was too old to join the Armed Forces and was needed in their hometown as he was the only pharmacist in the area. Her two half-brothers were younger than her. They, at least, would not have to worry about receiving a death notice. Rose's first mother, Abigail and George, had family nearby, and some of their sons were overseas. It was a constant feeling of dread in their bellies.

Finally, Rosevelt had no choice but to enter the war. Pearl Harbor in Hawaii had been attacked by the Japanese. Prime Minister Churchill of Britain had been sounding his cry that Germany was winning in Europe, having overtaken France and other surrounding countries. But Churchill had also been trying to sound the alarm over the invasions of the Japanese, which had successfully overtaken parts of China, Singapore, Mongolia, Vietnam, and Cambodia and were seeking to take over Burma, now known as Myanmar, and looking at India next. The United States had put an oil embargo on Japan, so in turn, Japan decided to (forcibly) take the resources they needed to grow their country from the "weaker" powered countries. They had an inflated sense of what they could achieve. However, they did a lot of destruction all over South Asia. Bombing in India, Burma, and elsewhere has been an ongoing experience since 1937.

Many towns and cities in China, India, and Burna had built bomb shelters even before the start of WW2 in Europe.

A very strange event happened in Winnipeg on February 19, 1942. Rose was sixteen, and Ricky just turned seventeen. It was named "If Day," a mock invasion by the "Nazis" in Winnipeg. If you hadn't been following the news in the papers and had stumbled upon the scene downtown Winnipeg extending to a three-mile radius, you would be legitimately terrified. Everything looked as if the real Nazis had invaded. Churches, schools, and government buildings hung the Nazi swastika, and overhead planes with German insignia whizzed by.

The radio blasted messages from Hitler, and "Nazi" troops stormed the local library, threw books outdoors, and set them on fire. We found out later the books were old and were going to be destroyed anyway. But what a nightmare of a day.

The government had carried out this too-realistic war scene to encourage citizens to buy war bonds. It certainly put the fear of God and war into their already stressed-out heads. Fear was a good motive, apparently.

The Federal Government in Canada invoked the War Measures Act on February 24th, 1942, which granted the government the ability to suspend basic human rights and round up at least 12,000 people of Japanese descent, born in Canada or not, and send them to Internment camps in British Columbia and across Canada. Some families ended up south of Winnipeg, and the men were forced into labour on sugar beet farms, often taken away from their families for an extended period of time.

On one of Rose's excursions into Winnipeg with her family to buy new clothes and shoes, they saw many Japanese families waiting to board at the train station. Rose asked what was going on, but she didn't get much of an answer. Rose had never seen so many people all at once who didn't look like her or even Ricky.

Rose, Ricky, and their classmates finally graduated. Just after graduation, Ricky entered the Air Force and would be flying overseas soon enough. The Metis of Canada was not acknowledged as a separate contributing force, but Ricky didn't care. He was very patriotic and strong in his belief in supporting Canada during this horrific time. Little by little, reports were reaching Canada of atrocities being carried out against the Jewish nation and others forced into labour or gassed in the chambers. It would take years to discover how many Jews were exterminated. A horrible blight on humanity. Never, ever to be forgotten.

Again, Olivia set down the letters. When she was younger and working as a new nurse, Olivia worked night shifts every four weeks for seven, that's right, seven straight nights. She rarely slept during the day, and she didn't think she'd ever made it working seven nights in a row. There was an older nurse who only worked nights. Olivia had been told by a few nurses working on the same unit that this nurse had been in one of the extermination camps. This nurse always wore long sleeves, summer or winter. One night, when Olivia was working with this nurse, there were just the two of them for the whole ward, so they were often incredibly busy. One night, though, they were catching up on their charts, recording each patient's night so far. The other nurse's sleeve rode up a bit but just enough to show that horrible tattoo that marked her as a Jewess. She was the only survivor in her family, according to Olivia's head nurse. Olivia didn't ask why she was the only one of her family who survived. What nightmares had this woman gone through, she hated to think.

Olivia needed a break again. All this information, a lot of it, was new to her, plus the fact the letters involved the heartache of families related to Olivia was just too much. Her head was spinning. How was she to get through the rest of these letters? What really did they mean to her except for the fact Rose was her mother's half-sister whom Millie never even knew about, plus Olivia was adopted and not truly related to these women? "Were these letters given to me to show the differences between Millie and Rose? Was one of their lives better than the other? Was I supposed to be the historian"? Olivia really didn't understand, but she did love history, and reading about family life from the early 1900s to the point she was at in these letters was definitely educational and entertaining. Also, considering the fact that Millie never really spoke about her years growing up, maybe these letters were to help Olivia understand Millie better. "I'm kind of "getting it," thought Olivia. Millie felt she had to be perfect, so talking about anything that wasn't perfect in her life just didn't happen. Olivia's dad also never talked about his early life. "Was there so much inherited pain that it was easier to block certain events out, never to speak of them again? Wipe the slate clean and hope their children never had to endure the atrocities of war and hunger."

Olivia called Tim and told him she needed to take a long drive somewhere, anywhere, to get a break. Her head was about to explode. Olivia was trying not to think about the reasons for these letters. The more she thought about it, though, the more Olivia realized Aunt Belle just wanted to pass down some history of herself, Carys, Millie, and Rose. She knew Olivia loved history and writing. Maybe one day, Olivia could gather all this information and write a book of sorts for her kids to know their history. Maybe they teach history better in schools these days, but there is a lot in these letters Olivia had never heard about in school or otherwise.

She was beginning to understand that even though decades had separated the generations, people were people with desires, dreams, and nightmares. Olivia had not really thought about her elders as having love affairs with men or women or in between. She remembered her hormones raging and the desire for sex when she was younger. Why did she ever think it wouldn't be the same for her ancestors? Biology was biology. Hormones rage, and women get pregnant. Men love women. Men love men. Women love women, and around and around. Due to laws and the attitude of the general public, many things have changed, if slowly and definitely not perfectly.

Millie had tried to be so perfect she probably did not have sex before marriage. To her, that was the very worst thing anyone could do. Well, guess what? Olivia certainly had sex like most of the other kids in high school, especially college. She became a teenager in the sixties, free love and burn your bra era. Millie always had Olivia dressed in the latest fashion and wore items that her friends didn't wear until a couple of years later, like nylons and a garter belt. Olivia also wore elephant pants, bell bottoms, white go-go boots, hippie-style shirts, miniskirts, and a bandana-worn hippie-style. Her hair was very long, down to her waist, and was wavy and golden-coloured.

Millie never told Olivia about sex, so she had to learn from the sex education films they saw in grade school, which were no help whatsoever. It wasn't until Olivia entered nursing school that she learned the details about ovaries, fallopian tubes, tiny eggs, and wiggling sperm bound to connect at some point in a woman's cycle. At least in theory.

Tim got home a bit earlier from work. He agreed they needed to get away, and he booked a cabin beside a small creek. It had an outdoor area for fires and good hiking trails nearby. Tim and Olivia took the dogs with them. They loved running in and out of the water at the clear, shallow water. At the end of the first day, they were all worn out. It was incredibly peaceful. Fancy hotels, crowded beaches, and all-inclusive were not their usual mode of relaxation. Although now and then, it was good to land somewhere tropical and do nothing but sit on the beach with a cerveza. "Listening to the trees blowing in the wind, the water splashing over stones, the eagles soaring overhead puts me in a state of awe and humility. Nature grounds me" said Olivia. Tim most definitely agreed.

Tim and Olivia had done quite a bit of travelling, and they liked finding their own accommodation away from the large hotel complexes. They were going to Cuba in a few months. Olivia and Tim had been there before and stayed in different "Casa Particulares," similar to Bed and Breakfasts in North America. They liked to meet people outside of the huge all-inclusive hotels. Olivia and Tim took Thai language lessons before both trips to Thailand, and Olivia had been learning Spanish online for three years. She figured it kept her brain cells working.

Tim headed back to work the following Monday. It really did both of them good to get away and "change our minds," as Olivia's former French brother-in-law used to say. It made perfect sense to her because that's exactly what is needed: a change of mind, of thinking and worrying.

Olivia wanted to read the rest of the letters but was reluctant at the same time. There was already a lot of information to process, but Olivia was a curious cat and wanted to know more about Rose and her family.

Chapter 21

Rose and Ricky

Rose was not happy that her best friend and boyfriend, Ricky, would be going overseas to war after training in Winnipeg. She was constantly worried and had to be patient like everyone else in Canada for a letter or some news about the war and how Canadian troops were doing in each area of conflict.

After several months of training, Ricky and his fellow airmen were ready to fly overseas. They did not know where they were headed at first but landed in England to await further orders.

The song "You won't know where you're going until you get there" was very appropriate.

He would be part of an airborne troop with the Air Force, working with the British Air Force, dropping bombs, food, supplies, and whatever else was needed. They called themselves the "Burma Bombers". Some missions were solo, but most had a crew responsible for dropping supplies by parachute into target areas for the other allied troops to collect. Or they could be sent on bombing missions, hoping to take out key airfields or roads the Japanese had overtaken.

It was an honor and privilege to be a part of the Burma Bombers. However, in later years, war statistics showed out of every 100 bomber airmen, 45 were killed, 6 seriously wounded, 8 became prisoners of war, and 41 escaped unscathed physically. Emotionally, it was another story.

Ricky was good at writing letters when he could.

June 20, 1943

Dear Rose

I'm sitting in the tent with a few other mates, trying to get some letters written back home before lights out. We're on a strict schedule, having to shut down all lights by sundown so we aren't spotted from above, if you know what I mean.

After our training in Winnipeg, several of my mates from the Air Force Academy were flown overseas to continue training as radio operators in England. I've been shadowing a guy who has been over here for a year, and I have to learn fast, as we're expected to go on drop flights soon. Next week, we're being transferred to Burma. Can you imagine that? A country that's mostly jungle.

It's not as bad as you might think. We're pretty safe in our big heavy planes, and all we're doing is dropping supplies. Oh, there goes the dinner gong. Time to go. I'll finish this letter later.

I'm now somewhere in Burma. I'm afraid us radio operators are sworn to secrecy. Not that we peons know what is really going on. We're just told what to do.

It's hot and sticky here. The humidity is as thick as rain. We're constantly drenched in sweat. There are bugs here as big as our fists, and we have to watch out for snakes that lurk in the dark. Taking a walk to the latrines during the night is risking your life.

There are some Burmese men and women who are on the allies' side and come to camp to do the laundry and help prepare meals. They seem very humble and are always bowing to us. I think it's their religion or something.

I wrote you a poem. I know you love poetry, and I'm going to try my best. It's a bit cheesy, but the truth is

Each night, I dream of you, of your smile, your grace,

I long for your embrace, the warmth of your face.

The days are long and hard, and the heat is fierce and strong,

But your love keeps me going, and my heart beats true and long,

I think of you in every moment, in every breath I take,

And I pray to God that soon, this war will end, for all our sake.

The sounds of war surround me, the cries of wounded men,

And in these moments, my thoughts turn to you again and again. I imagine you beside me, holding my hand tight,

And I find the strength to keep fighting, to keep up the fight.

So please, my love, keep me in your heart and in your prayers,

And I promise to come back to you, safe and sound, no matter where,

For you are the light that guides me, the reason I fight this war,

And I'll come home to you, my love, forever and more.

Well, the lights will be out soon. I love you, and I don't want you to worry. I will come home in one piece, I promise you. I'm also enclosing a poem written by a pilot, a true poet, who captures how I feel.

Oh! I have slipped the surly bonds of Earth

And danced the skies on laughter-silvered wings;

Sunward, I've climbed and joined the tumbling mirth

of sun-split clouds and done a hundred things

You have not dreamed of-wheeled and soared and swung

High in the sunlit silence. Hov'ring there,

I've chased the shouting wind along and flung

My eager craft through footless halls of air...

Up, up the long, delirious, burning blue

I've topped the wind-swept heights with easy grace

Where never lark nor ever eagle flew-

And, while with a silent lifting mind, I've trod

The high untrespassed sanctity of space,

Put out my hand and touched the face of God

by John G. Magee on September 3, 1941

Lovingly

Pte Richard Prince

Rose loved getting Ricky's letters. She thought about him all the time. It was so hard to keep her thoughts of all the things that Ricky could be facing, including snakes. Yeeeeeeuk. She always knew Ricky was smart and brave, and she would just have to believe in him. Trust his words that he would come back to her, preferably in one piece.

Rose had finished school and just celebrated her eighteenth birthday with her girlfriends, as most of the boys were overseas. They went to a movie that had recently come out in Canada. Casablanca. What a great film it was. Ingrid Bergman was so sultry. Those eyes. What a dreamboat Humphrey Bogart was, a powerful actor.

Rose's Aunt Silvia, one of her mother's younger sisters, came to visit. She had been in England with a troupe of Canadian entertainers, singers, dancers, and comedians. Silvia's job was coordinating the costumes, ordering, fitting, and repairing on the fly. She was in Canada for just a couple of weeks gathering material and other supplies for use in the sometimes big productions put on for the boys and women overseas. Silvia loved the excitement these shows brought to the soldiers in the army, navy, and Airforce. It gave everyone a break from the death and destruction of the war. Silvia didn't talk about the almost nightly air raids when they were billeted in people's homes in England. Silvia wanted Rose to join her. The troupe had a high enough turnaround of support personnel that more women were always needed. Her former assistant went and got married, and her husband, a soldier from Canada, wanted her safe and at home away from the nightmare of war. Can't say I blame him.

So Aunt Silvia convinced Mildred and Dad to let Rose travel with her overseas. I really don't think they had a clue what life in a war zone was like. But Rose being Rose, when she was offered an opportunity to stretch her wings, she was the first in line. She got bored easily.

Two weeks later, Rose and Silvia boarded a plane to jolly old England to entertain the troops. Rose was so excited she could barely sit still. It was her first time on a plane of any sort. This was one of the Air Force's transport planes, so before take-off, Silvia introduced her to her friends. Once they were in the air, the plane engines were too loud to carry on a conversation.

They were an eclectic bunch, full of excitement for the upcoming new show. They were joining an American entertainment group, and they were all dreaming of meeting Bob Hope or, Bing Crosby or anyone from Hollywood. Maybe they would be "discovered" and get a role in a Hollywood movie. Wasn't that everyone's dream?

Silvia looked like a younger version of Rose's adoptive mother, Abigail. Rose still missed her Mom badly, and sometimes, when she glanced up and saw Silvia, she would startle, and her heart would skip a beat.

Rose, Silvia, and four other women were billeted in a large house in central London. Part of the roof was missing, and one bedroom was exposed to the air after being bombed a few weeks ago. Rose was wide-eyed, wondering what she had gotten herself into. This was not a holiday. This was not romantic. This was the reality of war. What if the house got bombed again? Suddenly, she was losing her nerve about being her Aunt's assistant, but it wasn't like she could walk away. She was so far from home. Rose would stick close to her Aunt Silvia and try not to cry.

Rose shared a modest room with her Aunt. There were two twin beds, a commode, and a wash basin. Pretty wallpaper adorned the walls. There was a small armoire and chest of drawers.

They had a quiet night and slept soundly.

The next morning, they found out they would be joining the Army Show with Wayne and Shuster, a comedy team from Canada.

Rose was beside herself with excitement. She would be meeting stars. After the show finished in England, some of them would be joining the United Service Organization or the USO with the likes of Bob Hope, Judy Garland, Mickey Rooney, and Marlene Dietrich. Silvia was hopeful they would be chosen to go. She had been part of the entertainment to encourage the morale of many soldiers since 1941, so she had the experience and knowledge of what it takes to run a large show. Like Rose, she thrived on excitement and challenge. She had been involved in so many shows here and back home she had been pretty sure she would be chosen. Rose, of course, would accompany her. One thing Silvia didn't mention to Rose's Dad, Glen, was that they may be protected by soldiers and guards while on a base entertaining, but some of those bases were close to the front. Nothing had happened to them so far. You just had to get used to the sound of planes, gunfire, and the occasional bomb going off in a field.

Silvia did explain the possible dangers to Rose, but as she figured, Rose was ready for excitement and to do her part in this ugly war and wouldn't be sent back home. Rose had known Abigail's sister for years. Silvia was only twelve years older than her, and they always laughed together at family events. Rose trusted her Aunt would take good care of her.

A week later, when the Canadian show was on hiatus, they boarded two planes, with a few other Canadian men and women of the entertainment support staff, the equipment, and costumes bound for Italy.

There were risks flying anywhere, and as the plane flew into Palermo, Italy, they were attacked by German fighter planes.

"Rose, I'm so sorry. I am sorry I got you into this. I promised you and your Dad, I would protect you. I never thought this would happen."

Both planes were weaving, dropping, and turning, trying to avoid the guns firing death and destruction at them.

One plane took some bullets, but both planes landed without tragedy. Rose and Silvia were shaken, but a round of rum was provided to everyone on the planes in the mess hall. It was the first taste of real alcohol Rose had up until then. She was given one small glass of sherry on family events and holidays since she was sixteen, to the horror of her stepmom, but her father believed it was better for young people to learn to drink properly at home before setting out to parties and whatnot.

The rum warmed their bellies and calmed their nerves. This was one experience Rose nor Silvia would be writing home about.

Five thousand miles away, as the crow flies, Ricky was immersed in his duties as a radio operator and sometimes gunner over many parts of Burma. Every second day, he was on duty, hoping to get his flight hours up so he could take a break and maybe get back home to see Rose. He hadn't received a letter from her for a couple of weeks now. He missed her so much when he was in downtime. Maybe she found someone else. He couldn't blame her if she did. He had been in this hellhole for months. He felt dirty and sweaty. As soon as he finished showering, he was hot and sweaty again. The Air Force food was boring, with hash and corn, but when he tried the food prepared by the locals, which smelled heavenly, it was too spicy for his stomach, and he ended up missing his flight the next day as he had sat in the toilet most of the night. The food was delicious, but maybe next time, he would ask for less spice. It turned out to be dysentery, not the food that felled Ricky for weeks. It was a common ailment, along with cholera and malaria, that affected men for years.

The days flew by. They were always busy, which was great because sitting around, you got melancholy and tearful for home. He had been getting letters from some of his cousins entrenched who knew where, listening, transcribing, and breaking codes. Ricky was incredibly proud of his cousins, but he never knew where they were stationed. He had a central address where he sent his letters back to them. The mail ran well at times, and Ricky would receive four or five at a time, then nothing for weeks. He and some of his mates would share their goodies and any news from back home. Some parcels contained warm sweaters or wool socks. It seemed the folks back home weren't aware of how bloody hot it was here.

During his off hours, Ricky would write letters and poetry every second day to keep his mind off the stench, mosquitoes, and pervasive mud during the rains.

In the dense jungle far below,

A war was raging against an unseen foe,

A plane appeared in the sky

Bringing comfort to those nearby

The pilot, skilled and brave,

Guides the plane its cargo to save,

Dropping the supplies with precision and care,

Knowing they could mean life or death down there.

Food, medicine, and ammunition too,

All delivered from the sky so blue.

The plane roars on, its mission clear,

To bring support to those held near,

Behind enemy lines, they lay,

With hopes and prayers for a brighter day.

The parachutes blossom just like flowers,

Descending gently, defying the powers,

Of nature and war and all the strife,

That threatens to take away their life.

The fighters on the ground cheer and yell,

As the supplies fall, their spirits swell,

In the jungle, the war rages on,

But with supplies dropped, they can carry on,

With thanks to the Burma Bombers,

We'll forever hold their bravery with honor,

We'll raise a glass. We shed a tear,

For those Burma Bombers who flew without fear.

Finally, he received a long-awaited letter from Rose. He ran behind the showers and sat on a stump.

Dear Ricky

I miss you so much I could cry.

I haven't received any of your letters because I'm overseas too! I became her assistant in England with Aunt Silvia a month ago. She's the main wardrobe coordinator. We left England a week ago and landed in Palermo, Italy, to join the USO with Bob Hope! I'm beside myself with excitement. (Rose purposely left out the part of getting shot at by the Germans).

We work hard, and there's no time for rest, but I love being a part of the show. The costumes we put together are beautiful. They spare no expense to entertain our troops. It seems some Canadian soldiers are a part of several attacks orchestrated by the American troops. I don't care. I'm just so blessed to be a part of the war effort to bring some joy to our troops.

I'm feeling well, except I must be losing weight as my clothes seem a bit loose, but I have no complaints. It's definitely worse for the troops who give so much, sometimes their lives, to keep us safe and free.

Listen to me prattle on. Forgive me, but there's so much to catch up on.

Obviously, if you've sent me letters in the past month, I didn't get them, but Dad informs me that you are somewhere in Asia, India or Burma. He didn't know exactly. I hope you are doing well and haven't had any complications or setbacks. I constantly worry about you and remember fondly our time together on dates, dancing and laughing. I miss our long walks, holding hands and kissing behind the bleachers at school. I loved watching you and your pals playing football on Friday nights. You were always a hero to me.

Please write to me as soon as you can at the address below.

I send you a million hugs and kisses. Be safe, and keep me in your heart. I wrote a poem for you like we used to do at home.

My dearest love, so far away,

My heart aches for you each and every day,

I pray to God to keep you safe and sound,

And that soon, you'll be back on solid ground.

The war rages on, and I fear for your life,

But I know that you're strong, you'll survive the fight,

I send you all my love, all my hope and care,

And I promise to wait for you, no matter how long or where.

Each night, I look up at the stars above,

And I think of you, my brave soldier, my love,

I imagine you beside me, holding me tight,

So, hold on tight, my love, keep up the fight,

And know that I'm with you through every day and every night,

For you are the light that shines in my heart,

And I'll be waiting for you, even if we're worlds apart.

Forever your sweetheart,

Rose

Boy, oh boy, did that perk Ricky up. He was losing sleep not hearing from sweet Rose, the only girl who loved his goofy self. Well, she could be goofy, too. She really was a free spirit in spite of her grumpy stepmother. Rose always saw the best in people. It didn't matter who you were or your status in life. She accepted people at face value, although at times, it would turn against her. But she at least was secure enough to brush the negative people off and carry on. Ricky wished he could be more accepting of people like Rose, but being Metis, he had been on the receiving end of abuse from ignorant people far too many times. He had a hatred growing in his belly, constantly trying to prove his worth even to some of his fellow brothers in arms. Are they really brothers? Would they leave him behind if he got injured? It was a lonely and frightening thought.

The mission for Ricky and the other soldiers in his squadron was to drop supplies to the Allied troops located in Eastern India, Northern China, and Burma, flying over the "Hump." Flying over the foothills of the Himalayas was the most dangerous route for planes, but it had to be done. Ricky's job was manning the radio.

The Japanese had taken the famous Burma Road, the only route for transporting all goods from the port of Rangoon. The Northern route was also occupied by Japanese troops. There were pockets of Japanese-occupied areas throughout India, Burma and China. Chiang Kai-shek was the supreme leader of the Chinese and did not want the loathsome Japanese to take over their land.

The Japanese were more adept at fighting in this harsh land. They were totally dedicated to the Emperor of Japan, their divine leader. To die in battle was an honor. To kill or brutalize enemy captives was acceptable. Stories from captured Allied soldiers tell of prisoners being eviscerated, crucified, or beheaded. After success in capturing a village or town, it was normal to slaughter the villagers after raping the woman.

The Japanese soldiers and fighter pilots gave no thought to giving up their lives for the Emperor.

Burmese people, caught in the crossfire, suffered greatly. Villages were destroyed, families displaced, and lives shattered. It was heartbreaking to witness the toll that war took on innocent civilians. As they were later called, the Burma Bombers did their best to protect them and provide aid and support amidst the chaos.

Due to the many tribes in Burma, there were divisions in loyalty, which made soldiers' lives more difficult, not knowing which villagers to trust. Generally, the Musselmen or Muslims were pro-British, and the Maughs, the Hindus, were for Japan. It was a complicated array of support systems.

Burmese farmers, mostly women, still plowed their fields. People had to eat in spite of the danger of getting blown into a million pieces by the Japanese attacking or inadvertently stepping on an unexploded shell.

Day after day, Ricky was either on his time off or boarding the plane. The pilots liked to fly at night when the moon was covered by clouds. The problem with night flights is they were flown almost by memory. The land was not flat but very hilly. A pilot better know what he is up against.

They suffered in deplorable conditions. For years, the fight in Asia had been inadequately supplied with men, armory, planes, and tanks. When the USSR agreed to enter the war, Stalin made it clear he wanted Germany defeated first, so a lot of men and equipment had been diverted to Europe.

Even their tools to fix the planes were inadequate; they used flashlights and coins to remove loose screws and, with make-shift tools like these, accomplished the impossible and kept the planes flying.

There was a huge attrition of men anyway due to the many perils of fighting in the jungles. Along with malaria, cholera, and dysentery came the threat of poisonous snakes or insect bites. They had Mepacrine to combat malaria and had their immunization shots against cholera, typhus, bubonic plague, and yellow fever, but like any vaccine, they were not 100% effective for various reasons.

Rose was now getting frequent letters from Ricky, now that he knew where to send them.

c/o the Canadian Entertainment support group

My Dearest Rose

I feel so much closer to you now that I know you are on "this" side of the Atlantic. I'm so happy that you are doing your part in this war. I'm so proud of you and always will be. You are my apple pie a la mode, my cherry pie, and my honeybunch all rolled into one.

Although our day-to-day work here is similar and can be boring, we take turns flying every second or third day, dropping supplies to our ground troops on hilltops near the jungles where they would be fetched in the middle of the night.

Our squadron of bombers are delivering devastating blows to enemy positions and disrupting their supply lines. But our missions are not without risks, as we usually face anti-aircraft defenses and skilled Japanese pilots attempting to shoot us down.

As a radio technician, I am responsible for keeping our aircraft's communication equipment in top condition. I work to ensure that the radios are calibrated, the frequencies clear, and the tubes get replaced regularly.

During those harrowing flights, my role extends beyond radio maintenance. I'm part of a crew working alongside the pilot, navigator, and gunners. We rely on each other's skills and expertise.

I listen carefully to the messages that crackle through the speakers in the plane, which relay vital information about enemy positions, weather conditions, and mission updates. It keeps me focused completely, and I don't have time to worry about what Japanese fighters are in the skies nearby.

There are moments of triumph hitting the "bull's eye," so to speak, dropping supplies and getting the target right. We always let out a big cheer while the pilot quickly turned us around back to our home base.

On one mission, our squadron successfully destroyed a critical bridge, cutting off Japanese supply lines. The effort between the aircrews and ground forces is a testament to the power of communication and collaboration. It was a victory that filled us with a sense of purpose and pride. I knew then my job was something to be proud of.

Yours forever,

Ricky

When the monsoons hit, they carried on making their drops at times through severe winds and pounding rain. This had been a recent change of tactics. All manner of fighting, bombing, and air supply was now a 24/7 job, upping the danger tenfold.

They flew Dakotas and the newer American Air Liberators, big transport/cargo planes. The flights would take them to drop sights marked out by the allies on the ground. It was heavy work pushing the boxes of food or medical supplies attached to parachutes. It was through this campaign they kept the Japanese soldiers at bay. By the end of the war, the Japanese in this part of Asia were in very poor health, not having had the same support, and were expected to continue the fight until death, even without food or supplies.

Ricky was on a regular rotation, flying over hills and valleys to deliver rice and medicine to their designated spot or to drop bombs on Japanese targets.

It was always a dangerous flight. One of the pilots that rainy day was determined to take off because he only had to fly two more missions before he could hang up his wings in Burma and head home by Christmas. Ricky was along for that flight.

They had just dropped their last supplies on a hilltop when they spotted Zeros, Japanese fighter planes coming straight at them. The planes they were flying were heavy and slow.

The Canadian pilot, Johnny Miller, had a few years of experience flying in less-than-optimal missions and had avoided being shot down until that night.

Zeros, we're headed straight at them. Kamikaze pilots bent on total death and destruction.

Ricky's plane took several hits, but they kept going, trying to reach base. Ricky frantically sent out Maydays for help on his radio, not knowing if it was received before the wing was shot off. Ricky could see the fiery eyes of the Japanese pilot shortly before that pilot crashed into the wing of their heavy, large plane built to withstand these pesky mosquito bites.

The wing on their plane was badly damaged. Their pilot furiously attempted to find a suitable landing spot. They were still over the jungle, not at all an ideal spot to land. He maneuvered around the high trees, trying to see through the low-lying clouds. He prayed he remembered the placement of hills in this area. That would be their grave if he hit the side of a hill.

Johnny, the pilot, literally shut his eyes and prayed furiously to whoever would listen. He tried to lean the plane to the left. He was sure there was a field farmed by the locals a few miles from their base camp. If only they could glide over the next hilltop.

Ricky kept pumping out Maydays and SOS, hoping someone would hear and respond before they went down.

The plane was shaking violently, the seams ready to blow. Ricky kept shouting into the non-functioning radio. Mayday! Mayday.

Everything went dark. The plane lost its engine. They hadn't flown too high; they were closer to the ground than the Japanese fighter planes.

The last few moments were like a dream or a nightmare. The plane became silent, gliding towards the darkness of the hillside shadows. Nobody breathed. The silence seemed to last hours, but that quiet ended suddenly when the plane skidded on dirt and the nose tipped into the ground brutally.

The plane flipped upside down and came to rest. Two crewmen and the pilot died. There were three left.

"Evacuate! Evacuate! Shouted one of the men. "The plane might blow."

They slid out the side of the plane where the wing had been completely sheared off. They fell on their bellies as had been taught in case of a plane down and shimmied to the nearby copse of palm trees.

The Japanese kamikaze plane with its dead pilot lay embedded in the side of their plane.

The three survivors had injuries from deep wounds to broken arms. Somehow, Ricky escaped serious wounds. His arm was sore, the muscles shot, and parts of his skin torn away, but he crawled back into the plane after they determined it wouldn't blow up to retrieve the medical kit and check the ones left onboard, hoping it hadn't been sucked out when the wing had been sheared off.

The kit was there. Ricky made his way back to the two other survivors and the pilot and patched them up as best as he could, then cleaned and patched his own wounds. They would have to hunker down in the makeshift tent they made from parachutes. They had no time to jump and deploy their chutes.

Ricky would have to set out on his own to try and make his way to a road so he could assess exactly where they were. He had grabbed some maps from the plane, but without seeing the moon or stars through the clouds, he couldn't place their location relative to their base camp. At least he knew they had crashed into a small field. He was hoping a road wouldn't be far.

Survival in the Burmese jungle relied on adaptability and ingenuity. Ricky always had to be vigilant about disease-carrying mosquitoes, leeches near rice paddies and in the wet jungle, and venomous snakes, which terrified Ricky more than other threats.

He walked across the small field beside the hill. It was empty of farmers or Japanese soldiers. It was an eerie calm. Several times, he fell into holes that didn't look like holes on the red dirt road. He was full of dust and had twisted his ankle. He certainly looked like an apparition, a rust-colored monster risen from the dead.

The silence didn't seem appropriate after the recent noise of the Dakota and the zeros buzzing them. He hadn't heard such silence since hunting in the woods back home.

After an hour of hobbling across the fields, he saw another track, a little larger than the one he was on. It had to lead somewhere, hopefully, a main road.

He limped down the dirt road for another hour. Did these farmers really have to walk this far to tend their crops? Such as they were, having craters blown into the soil by indiscriminate bombs in many areas. Ricky walked by some unexploded bombs tilted in the earth. He hardly noticed. He kept walking as if in a trance.

The sun was starting to rise. The steam from the recent rains was lifting over the jungle like a shroud. Ricky wondered if he was about to be exposed to hidden Japanese troops on this road to who knew where.

He hadn't realized he had lost a boot, probably in the bottom of a muddy hole. It didn't matter. He hurt all over, but his survival instinct took over. He had to live to see Rose again.

The sun did rise along with the mist. He was definitely exposed, and a group of farmers were walking up the dirt road towards him.

Ricky was praying to whoever might listen, the heavens, the stars, and all of his ancestors, including his code-talking uncles, that these farmers were friendly and not on the side of the Japanese. Burma was a divided nation with the top brass changing sides at whim.

Ricky fell to his knees and passed out on the ground, watching the farmers run towards him, yelling in their language.

When Ricky came to, he was on a straw bed of sorts in a hut. He had been cleaned and his wounds bandaged. Some very stinky poultice had been put on his lacerations. He was trying to tear them off when an older woman entered and started shouting at him. He had no idea what she was saying, but obviously, she was upset at him for trying to remove his bandages. He instantly stopped and stared at this round-faced peasant woman.

She had kind eyes and was no longer shouting at him. She had brought him some hot tea, which he drank down as fast as the heat allowed him. She adjusted his bedding and pointed to his poultice-covered wounds. She indicated the stink with hand gestures but smoothed her hand over his legs, arms, and head, soothing his pain. Soon, he was asleep again.

He must have slept for two days. Waking only for a change of bandages and to sip tea or spicy soup. It was the best-tasting soup ever.

One morning, maybe a week later, he had lost track of time when he heard English voices outside. His company had found him. He was so grateful he could cry, and he did, a ton of tears of relief.

Word had gotten out from the locals to the base commander that Ricky had been found. A rescue unit would be sent out, and because there was no place to land close by, two airmen and a medic parachuted into a field near the small village.

Ricky gave the location of the downed plane as best he could, where the two seriously wounded men were hopefully still waiting to be rescued.

Unfortunately, they had died due to lack of food and water, and one poor bugger had bled out. Ricky would never get over this crash. He constantly questioned his decision to set out on his own to find help. He should have stayed and helped his flight mates. It didn't matter that Ricky would have died, too. He always carried that guilt around like a noose.

With the assistance of two villagers, the men set out on a hike through the jungle. Ricky wasn't strong enough to walk the whole way. He kept stumbling, so the men, including the small, statured but incredibly strong villagers, took turns carrying him on their backs. Over the days of walking, Ricky got stronger. The guides were good and knew their way through the jungle following man-made or animal-made paths.

They hunkered down at night under makeshift lean-to's and listened to the night sounds of the jungle, including the howls and screams of a kill. Finally, after several arduous days, they came to a road that led to the air base. All the men had lost weight, and a couple contracted malaria from the evening mosquitoes they couldn't avoid. Even the campfire smoke from cooking what had been hunted by the guides didn't keep the buzzing cloud of mosquitoes out of their hair and eyes. Any exposed skin had numerous bites.

Ricky was bruised and battered but didn't have to be sent to the field hospital. His lacerations had healed better than the camp's doctor could believe. It must have been those horrible, stinky poultices. Go figure.

While he was healing, he spent a lot of time catching up on his letters home and to Rose. They must be out of their minds with worry. They may have thought him dead. He had no idea he had been missing in action and presumed dead for close to a month.

While he sat on the stump behind the showers, he heard a couple of guys talking about him and the crash and his rescue. One guy, Ricky, couldn't quite place a face to the voice, said loud and clear, "It figures the redskin made it out. He probably scalped the other two and gnawed on their bones."

The other guys in the shower laughed. It hurt Ricky to the core, causing more pain than his injuries ever had.

Rose realized she had to keep working to keep her mind off her worry over not hearing from Ricky for so long. There wasn't a problem about the lack of things to keep all of them busy. Costumes to fit, repairs to sew. There were nightly shows, but until Bob Hope and his backup entertainers arrived, the shows were smaller and with less-known entertainers. This was practice for the really big shows.

Finally, Bob Hope arrived. There was a lot of excitement among all the stagehands and support staff like Silvia and Rose.

Mr. Hope always put everyone at ease. He never seemed to be anything but happy, putting smiles on all men and women watching the shows. He would always take time to visit the hospitals where he would say his favourite line, which always got a hoot, was "Don't bother to get up, " as if any of the soldiers laying on cots could even try.

Rose, Silvia, and the other women were asked to visit the men in the makeshift hospitals on the days there wasn't a show. They may be extremely busy on show days, running off their feet and crashing on their bunks to fall into a deep, dreamless sleep, but the visits to the hospital exhausted them in a different way. The emotional toll was beyond belief. For the less injured, sitting by their side and sharing a pot of tea was easy. For the severely injured, it was a different story.

When casualties arrived, they were "triaged" into priority of medical needs. For those who were deemed too far gone to be saved by any surgery or medicine, the overwhelmed doctors had to literally leave them, call in the priest or minister, and carry on to the ones that could be saved.

Even hardcore soldiers who had fought for years cried out for their mothers, a cry so deep and heartbreaking that you prayed for their peace, even if that meant death. The cries nearly broke the best doctors and nurses. The sorrow was felt to their core. Years later, in the warmth of their homes back in Canada, they still felt the chill of those cries in their chests and bones. Rose and Silvia would never forget.

Finally, after the long days, weeks, and years of the war, there was news of Germany's surrender. Hitler had been pushed out of France, and the Germans surrendered, with Russia pushing from their side.

Ricky's troupe celebrated with an extra ration of rum, which seemed a tad watered down, if you must know, but things were looking up except for the war with the Japanese, which carried on. This horrific war wasn't over in Asia. Japan was still determined to win the territories it desired.

Another of the Burma squad's supply planes went down somewhere unknown. They did several reconnaissance flights over a large area, but neither the plane nor any survivors could be found.

The remaining men on the base mourned their loss. The huge loss of men and planes was taking a toll on all of them. They had no spirit left after this loss. Half of the men on the plane, including the pilot, should not have been flying in the worst storm of the monsoon season. But they all wanted to get their flight hours in and get home.

Just a week later, the US. Dropped a bomb on Hiroshima, killing over 80,000 Japanese men, women, and children immediately. More would die of radiation poisoning in the following months and years. Two days later, the US dropped a second bomb on Nagasaki, killing around 40,000. The Japanese/allied war was over.

It took time, but eventually, all the Canadian soldiers, Army, Navy, and Air Force made their way back home. Those who lived. Over 43,000 men died and 55,000 were wounded. The loss of life in every nation was beyond numbers.

Chapter 22

Rose and Silvia

R ose wasn't informed about Ricky getting shot down for several weeks due to the difficulty of getting letters to the right place.

Poor Rose could barely sleep or eat from worry. Was he dead or alive? Did he get captured by the Japanese? His poor family must be terrified.

Ricky's plane had been shot down, and he and five other men were missing and presumed dead. Rose would not believe it. Ricky was her soul mate. She would know, somehow. Her heart still felt her missing half, but not as if a life had snuffed out. He just had to be alive.

Rose and her Aunt stayed with their entertainment group and continued working with the shows in Italy, Berlin, and England. The war had finished, but it would take a while to get all the soldiers home, so their entertainment carried on. It certainly was a lot more relaxing without bombs going off all around them. A person, maybe even soldiers in battle, had to push the thought of dying out of their heads in order to carry on. Getting through one day was a blessing, and every night, their prayers were thankful.

Both Rose and Silvia knew the bravery they had to maintain, especially during shows at the front during an active war. They couldn't imagine the soldiers in battle. How did they keep going?

The Bob Hope show, and others similar helped maintain morale amongst the Allied troops.

It was a huge reward for Rose and Silvia, watching the soldiers' eyes light up and the laughter emanating from the crowd during performances. At least it gave these brave men a break from the dark, cold, bloody mud and shadows of dead men hunting the battlefields. I wonder if their phantoms are still crying out for relief from the pain and horrors of mankind.

One of Rose's favourite songs was from Vera Lynn in 1942. It made her cry and have hope at the same time.

There'll be bluebirds over

The white cliffs of Dover

Tomorrow, just wait and see

There'll be love and laughter.

And peace ever after

Tomorrow, when the world is free

The shepherd will tend his sheep

The valley will bloom again.

And Jimmy will go to sleep

In his own little room again

There'll be bluebirds over

The white cliffs of Dover

Tomorrow, just wait and see

The shepherd will tend his sheep.

The valley will bloom again

And Jimmy will go to sleep

In his own little room again

There'll be bluebirds over

The white cliffs of Dover

Tomorrow, just you wait and see

Rose and Silvia carried on as always, although Silvia noticed that Rose was worried no matter what she said. Rose was losing weight again. It's a good thing they were seamstresses, as clothes had to be altered often.

Silvia loved having Rose with her and knew that Rose had matured a lot this past year and a half. War did that to a person. They were lucky to be in entertainment, although travelling from place to place could be very risky. Recently, before the war had ended, one of the transport planes carrying entertainers and equipment was shot down while flying over England.

Silvia and Rose spent more than one evening talking about Ricky and what they could do to hear any news from his troop. Rose talked about her love for Ricky. They fit together like peas in a pod. Sure, she had met other boys and dated, but once she and Ricky danced together at one of the high school sock hops, that was it. He kissed Rose after he walked her home, and she could have sworn fireworks had gone off.

They had been side by side through the rest of high school up until Ricky left to serve.

Silvia told Rose that she had been in love once.

Silvia was in her twenties and had been focused on her career as a fashion designer. High school had not been a positive experience. She wasn't bad looking. She was only 5' tall and 110 lbs. She had beautiful green eyes that would draw people to her but never to love. She would get bored with the "juvenile" high school boys who were too shy during school days to talk to her, but on weekends before dances, they were as drunks as skunks eating fermented food. Pathetic boys trying to act like big men. It wasn't unusual for fights to break out when the dance was over. Male lion cubs did not get their catch and growled at the lions who had caught their prey. At least, that's how Silvia thought about the dating game.

When Silvia graduated and entered a fashion college in New York, her life certainly changed. She went to parties with her friends and had a great time with the men and women involved in fashion. It was mind-boggling. She could see many of the men were more like women, but not all. Some men looked like "normal men," but they spent time with men, and some of the men looked like women. It really was confusing.

Silvia had been attracted to men, and so she spent time dating and having sex with a few. She didn't care if she met her true love right away. There were definitely more frogs than princes in her mind. Until.

Silvia was at another gathering of designers and hung owners when she spotted a woman, a girl really, and something about her caused Silvia to pause. Her heart was beating faster, and she couldn't take her eyes off this gorgeous young woman. No, she wasn't beautiful, but there was something about her spirit, her laugh, and her joie de vivre that ignited Silvia's passion. She didn't understand why she was attracted to this girl. She was supposed to meet her true love, a man, to marry and have several kids with. Why was her lower belly vibrating with this warm sexual feeling, a need to be closer to her, to wrap her in her arms and be there forever?

Silvia left the party totally confused and ashamed. What was happening to her? She had to meet this girl and figure out her crazy feelings and imaginations of the two of them together. She had never felt this sexually aroused by the men she had tried to forge a future with.

The next time there was a party with most of the same group, Silvia followed along. It had been a few weeks since the last party, and she was hoping beyond hope that the young woman would be there.

Silvia spent a couple of hours wandering around the gathering at the fancy two-level apartment with its gorgeous view of the harbor. What a life some people enjoy. Rich beyond imagination. Some of these rich people just loved to hang around the art world, people in fashion or theatre or starving artists so dark and droll in their artistic presentation.

After a few hours of wandering, Silvia was heading to the coat room, ready to leave this dull party. She got her coat and was about to go when the elevator doors opened, and out came the young woman and a man.

Silvia went to the side of the elevator doors so the two could come out. The young woman saw Silvia, and a huge smile appeared on her face. She waved at her friend to carry on, grasped Silvia on the arm, and said, "Follow me." Silvia was so shocked she followed the young woman to a sitting area obviously set aside for her.

The two women sat on a sofa side by side. Silvia was so nervous she couldn't even look at the young woman whose name she still didn't know. Her name was Giselle, and she was the most recent top model in New York.

Giselle ordered champagne, and soon Silvia was relaxed enough to look her in the eye. They talked about mundane things and what brought them to the fashion world. Giselle had been "discovered" in Montreal at its fashion houses that were growing rapidly after the depression. It wasn't long before New York came calling with incredible offers of employment with generous benefits with the stipulation she be seen in the arts and fashion district almost every evening. It was exhausting. The day began early at the fashion house with fittings from early morning until mid-afternoon. They would break for a few hours to rest. Then, off to the elegant restaurants for more exposure. The problem was the models never got enough sleep, and they had to keep their weight down to the impossible low that fashion show directors deemed the best to show off their newest trends in fashion.

Silvia couldn't believe what was expected from this young woman. She vowed she would stand by her and protect her from the constant demands on her being.

Silvia met Giselle every evening at some nightclub or another after Giselle had finished her constant publicity tours around different events and fashion shows. Too many people seemed to want her time of which she had very little, even for herself.

Silvia occupied her time in the evenings. It wasn't long before Giselle asked her to move into the hotel room she was staying in to help her organize her life and keep the sharks at bay.

At this point, Silvia was over the moon in love with this gorgeous creature. She and Giselle talked well into the night about their hopes and dreams. They needed each other in different ways, but they fit.

There wasn't any sex involved, although Silvia was more than ready to kiss every inch of Giselle's body.

Giselle was very lonely and was so grateful for Silvia's presence in her life. Silvia had the right technique to see reality and what others wanted from her.

One evening, they came "home" to their hotel suite. They both had drunk a fair bit after a successful show. Giselle couldn't have looked more delightful in each gown she wore. Her eyes sparkled, and everyone in the audience could feel her joy. Especially Silvia, who knew that every look from Giselle at her was filled with love and wanting.

They left the ubiquitous after-fashion show party early, ignoring the pleas from Giselle's agent that someone famous was about to arrive and she needed to stay. Giselle's reply was that some things in life were far more important than waiting around for some pompous new actor to appear who was more likely to be gay.

Something was sparkling between the two women on the drive home, but they stayed apart from each other. The sexual tension was thick and vibrating.

They had had a lot to drink, but not so much that they didn't know what was about to happen between the two.

Giselle took the lead, undressing Silvia as soon as they shut and locked the door. Giselle laid Silvia on her bed and fetched the bottle of champagne brought to her room every evening on ice.

Giselle Popped the cork, and the champagne fizzed all over Silvia's naked body. Giselle began to lick it up from top to bottom, causing Silvia to moan with desire. Giselle managed to remove her sexy dress and lay down beside Silvia. They spent the rest of the night exploring each other's bodies and finding each other's path to ecstasy over and over until they were too exhausted to continue. They fell asleep in each other's arms until morning. They woke up to a loud banging on the door.

Giselle's manager had arrived and was yelling at her to get up and dressed as she was late for a luncheon being held at some fancy restaurant where agents from Hollywood would be attending.

Silvia and Giselle jumped out of bed, hoping not to get caught in their passion from the past evening and apparently all night.

Silvia agreed to hide in the bathroom until Giselle left with her manager.

Giselle didn't come back that day or night. Silvia went everywhere she could think Giselle might be. She asked at all the parties and fashion houses and heard some bits of gossip but nothing concrete.

Silvia was heartbroken but couldn't believe Giselle would vanish without a word of where she might be.

Silvia returned to her previous job in one of the fashion houses. Everyone knew she had been Giselle's personal dresser, and she was rehired in an instant.

Soon enough, the gossip had turned to concrete news about Giselle. Apparently, the meeting she nearly missed the last day Silvia was with Giselle was with a Hollywood agent looking for new talent and wanted Giselle to go to Hollywood the next day and try out for parts in several movies Warner Brothers had planned. Giselle, being the beautiful, captivating woman she is, got gobbled up by Hollywood. She tried many times to contact Silvia by phone or mail, but unknowingly to her, the agent intercepted all calls and took Giselle's mail from Silvia.

Silvia finally understood what had happened and just knew Giselle's manager had wanted to keep them apart. It just wouldn't do. If any word got out about Sivia and Giselle's affair, well, his career would certainly be ruined.

It wasn't until several years later that Giselle and Silvia ran into each other at a party in New York. Giselle acted nervous and standoffish until she beckoned Silvia to follow her to a room at the other end of the huge apartment where the party was being held by some rich woman who "wanna be hip" in the fashion world.

Giselle started crying and hung onto Silvia, pleading for forgiveness. Giselle's manager had figured out the growing romantic situation between her and Silvia and had put her on a direct flight to Los Angeles, where they immediately went to her new Hollywood agent dealing with the scout who had "discovered" Giselle.

If Giselle wanted to be a movie star, then she had to appear sexy and into men. To Giselle, getting a big part in a Hollywood movie was everything she dreamed of and had worked towards since she was twelve. Giselle was "matched" with a male rising star, and they married two years after Giselle left for Hollywood. The couple had two children.

There hadn't even been an offer to bring Silvia out to Hollywood to be Giselle's assistant. Too risky, she supposed. Nevertheless, Silvia's heart was broken beyond repair. She never felt the urge to love again, man or woman. Silvia had died inside.

Rose listened to her Aunt's story and then got up from her chair to give Silvia a heartfelt hug. Such a tragic story, but now she understood her Aunt more than ever and was so grateful she trusted Rose enough to bear her story. It was an honor to have been the only one in the whole family with whom Silvia had shared this very personal story.

Remarkably, Silvia found love again in a most unusual place, the makeshift hospital where Rose and Silvia volunteered.

Emily was a courageous nurse stationed at the hospital, tending to wounded soldiers who returned from the frontlines. Her warm smile and compassionate nature provided solace to so many who had lost so much in the war. Her heart, however, yearned for something more.

Silvia was drawn to Emily's unwavering dedication and found a sense of peace in her calming presence.

Silvia had tumbled and opened the skin on her knee and needed to go to the makeshift hospital for antibiotics and to have her wound wrapped. Emily was on shift and doing "intake" for minor injuries.

As Emily tended to Silvia's wounds, their eyes met, and a connection sparked, one that defied societal norms and expectations of that time.

Their love blossomed discreetly. They stole fleeting moments together, stealing glances and exchanging secret smiles. In a world consumed by war and hatred, they found solace in each other's arms, a sanctuary from the chaos that surrounded them.

Their love, however, was not without its challenges. The fear of discovery loomed over their heads like a dark cloud. Society's prejudice and the harsh consequences of being caught in a same-sex relationship threatened to tear them apart. Yet, their love burned brightly, refusing to be extinguished. Both Emily and Silvia were good-looking women and had had many requests for "dates" and even some proposals from the many young soldiers.

Together, Emily and Silvia found strength in their shared commitment to love. They navigated the treacherous landscape of war, offering each other continuing support and encouragement. In the darkest of times, their love served as a beacon of hope, reminding them of the beauty that still existed in the world.

Chapter 23
The End of WW2

Horrible stories were starting to come to them about the Nazi concentration camps in Germany and Poland, and perhaps more places. From the terrifying images and stories came disbelief. This cannot be true. What kind of monster would do this? To children, too. But the stories and images kept coming. Many Canadians felt shame, not because of what they had done, putting Japanese and others in Internment camps, but because at least they were fed and taken care of. At least, that's what they convinced themselves, but this was beyond any monster's imagination. Some stories about such camps had leaked, but nobody really wanted to believe it.

The following poem gave Rose the inspiration to begin her own writing. It was written in the Warsaw Ghetto during the Holocaust. The poem tells the story of a small child who supports his starving family by illegally smuggling food supplies from outside the ghetto. The end of the poem shows the author's fear, not of his own death but of leaving his mother without a source of food. Poetry can change hearts.

Through walls, through holes, through sentry points,

Through wires, through rubble, through fences:

Hungry, daring, stubborn

I flee, dart like a cat.

At noon, at night, in dawning hours,

In blizzards, in the heat,

A hundred times I risk my life,

I risk my childish neck.

Under my arm, a burlap sack,

On my back was a tattered rag;

Running on my swift young legs

With fear ever in my heart.

Yet everything must be suffered;

And all must be endured,

So that tomorrow, you can all

Eat your fill of bread.

Through walls, through holes, through brickwork,

At night, at dawn, at day,

Hungry, daring, cunning,

Quiet as a shadow, I move.

And if the hand of a sudden fate

Seizes me at some point in this game,

It's only the common snare of life.

Mama, don't wait for me.

I won't return to you,

Your far-off voice won't reach.

The dust of the street will bury

The lost youngster's fate.

And only one grim thought,

A grimace on your lips:

Who, my dear Mama, who

Will bring you bread tomorrow?

Henryka Łazowertówna

Translated by Patricia Heberer,

from Children during the Holocaust

Again, Olivia put down the letters. She had been reading about Canada's history or knowledge of the Holocaust. It seems Canada and other countries worldwide had their own means of shunning the Jews and keeping them "in their place." In Eastern Canada, some businesses put signs above their doors reading "NO JEWS OR DOGS ALLOWED!" In the Western provinces, the signs read "CHRISTIANS ONLY!."

Antisemitism was rampant during those years and, unfortunately, is rearing its ugly head nowadays. Olivia understood that there was a long history of resentment towards the Jews because Jesus was crucified, and the world's religions seemed bitterly divided. There are many religions, and each one seems to think they have the correct way of believing. Germany, under Hitler, set out to exterminate all Jews and other "undesirables". To Olivia, the world's power struggles have always been and will always be. However, one of these days, one of these men in power will blow us all up. Then what! Ridiculous. They think they are so smart. They don't just want to rule their own countries. They want the world. Olivia pictured all of them with tiny little penises, trying to overcompensate with their brutal ways.

Finally, just before the war with Japan was declared over, Rose received a letter from Ricky. He was alive, just like Rose always knew. Their hearts were intertwined, and they would know. They just would if something had happened to either one. Soon they would be home. Home to get married and have a dozen kids, well maybe two or three.

Post-war in Manitoba, there were a lot of changes. Men had jobs, and women did, too, but they were never paid the same as men in the same position. Ricky continued on with the Air Force, at RCAF Shilo, near Brandon, Manitoba, learning to become a pilot. It's what he loved, the freedom he felt in the sky. He was intent on proving he was better than the words that came out of his fellow soldiers in Burma. He would be the best pilot anyone in the British Commonwealth.

Rose took a job nearby but close to the airbase where Ricky was stationed. They were happy and settled in their small bungalow on the base. They made enough money to go dining and dancing or to see the latest Hollywood movies, which often starred her Aunt's former love, Giselle. Rose wondered how she would handle life if Ricky ever left her. She loved him so much, and he loved her the same. She was positive. They had dreams together. Life was great.

Rose and Ricky had been married and living together for a couple of years but still weren't pregnant. They hadn't been worried at first, having been so busy getting married, going to Vancouver for their honeymoon, and then settling in their house on the base. Ricky worked shifts from 0700-1500 (7 am to 3 pm), 1500-2300 (3 pm to - 11 pm), or the infamous graveyard shift from 2300-0700 (11 pm to 7 am).

So, Rose and Ricky blamed it on the shift work and lack of proper sleep. They weren't in a huge hurry to get pregnant as life was fun right then, and they didn't want to lose the love they shared in every room of the house. The walls were thin, and they tried to keep themselves to a certain decibel so the neighbors wouldn't overhear and figure they were a couple of sex fiends. But why would God make sex so pleasurable if they weren't meant to express their joy completely? Kids could wait another year.

Ricky was surely having nightmares about the war and the plane crash. He never slept more than three to four hours. Rose didn't know how he kept going. On evening shifts, Ricky often came home much later than the shift ended. He told Rose he went with some of the boys on the same shift to the mess hall to have a beer or two and wind down before heading home. Rose could understand that, but Ricky always refused to have her pick him up after he had a couple of beers. Ricky started to disappear on his days off and would come home smelling of beer and stale cigarettes.

One Saturday, doing the weekly laundry, Rose noticed a different odor coming from one of Ricky's shirts. It smelled like perfume. It couldn't be thought Rose. Ricky and she loved each other intensely. How could he even have the energy to have an affair? Rose vowed to keep her ears and eyes open. She'd have to confront Ricky if any more evidence came her way.

Several weeks went by, and everything seemed to get back to normal. Rose and Ricky went out to dinner and danced at the officer's mess hall. Ricky had proved to be quite intelligent and excelled at each level. He even seemed to get his drinking under control. He had been warned by his superiors if he showed up for any shift smelling of booze, he would be tossed out of the aviator program. His love of flying was what got him straightened out.

Like many addicts before him, it wasn't long before he would sneak shots of vodka from his skinny flask. Nobody seemed to suspect he was constantly at an inebriated level, but Ricky was getting very good at acting when needed.

Rose suspected Ricky was drinking again, but he didn't smell like day-old beer and stale cigarettes anymore. Rose never thought Ricky had sunk so far down to hide his drinking from her. Ricky and Rose had always talked about everything good or not so good in their life, sharing deep fears but also dreams of their future. What would their children look like, how many would they have, and where would they travel to teach them about the rest of the world?

Recently, though, Ricky had been closed to these conversations, actually getting up and leaving the room if Rose started to share her day, then would ask about Ricky's day. He always used to respond, but not for the past couple of weeks.

Christmas was a challenge. They were staying with one of Ricky's uncles, who had been one of the Code Talkers, and Ricky was eager to hear some stories. Although Rose was also intrigued by Uncle's stories, she eventually felt neglected by Ricky. Rose spent almost the whole Christmas holiday in the kitchen cooking with the women. She didn't mind helping out, but the holiday seemed to segregate the men from the women.

Uncle Liam's stories from the war were fascinating, sometimes humorous, sometimes awe-inspiring. He disappeared to his room for a while.

Uncle Liam returned to the room and sat near the Christmas tree, adjusted the feathers on his headdress, tried to look as serious as possible despite the absurdity of the situation, and gave his talk in an exaggerated "Indian" accent.

"Rose and Ricky, eh! You see, I'm a Cree code talker. Now, ya might think that bein' a code talker is one heck of a serious business, eh, and ya wouldn't be wrong 'bout that. But that doesn't mean that we didn't have our fair share of laughs, eh, along the way, ya know."

It all started when the military approached our Cree community, asking for volunteers to use our language as a secret code during the war. At first, I thought they were pulling my leg. Me, a code talker? I was more known for my jokes and stories of old times than my tactical skills. But they insisted, so I thought, why not?

I remember when I got the call-up. Being just a young fella, still am. Full of dreams and spirit. I had to leave my family and my rez and go fight for our country. They told us it was for the greater good, to protect our way of life. We were ready and excited.

At first, they didn't understand us, the military folks. They didn't get why our languages were so important. But we showed 'em. We showed 'em how we could talk right in front of 'em, and they wouldn't have a clue what we were sayin'. Our rez accent, our words, became like a shield, keepin' our messages safe from the enemy.

Our elders taught us their ancient languages, passed down from generation to generation. The military boys couldn't grasp the complexity of it all, but we could. It became second nature to us, like breathin' or walkin'. They even invented some words and gave us nicknames. Me, I was Mooseberry. Don't I look like a big ol' berry fit for a moose?

Then came the day we went off to war. We were scared, no doubt 'bout that. But we had each other. Brothers from different nations, united by our languages and our purpose. In them trenches, we spoke in our tongues, creatin' codes only we could decipher. And we sent those messages, tucked away in our rez accents, to save lives.

It wasn't easy, though. We saw things, and experienced things that still haunt me to this day. Friends lost; families back home torn apart. War is a brutal thing, ya see. Ricky knows all about it. But we held strong and carried on with our duty. We knew our rez languages could make a difference and protect our fellow soldiers.

Trainin' to be a code talker wasn't no cakewalk, let me tell ya. We had to learn all about radio communication and memorize all these secret phrases and codes. It was like learnin' a whole new language on top of our Cree tongue. But my fellow code talkers and I didn't let that get us down at all. We turned it into a game.

Picture a bunch of Cree warriors, runnin' around the trainin' camp, shoutin' secret phrases at the top of our lungs. We had a hoot comin' up with ridiculous code names for ourselves, like "Swift Squirrel" and "Moody Moose." Who knew savin' the world could be so darn fun?

Out in the field, things got even funnier. We're out there in enemy territory, tryin' to send critical messages while avoidin' capture. But it ain't easy when you got a fellow code talker who can't stop cracking jokes over the radio. We had to keep our laughs in check, worryin' the enemy might hear us and think we'd gone batty, which wasn't far from the truth.

One time, we were stuck in a muddy ditch, hidin' from enemy fire. Our radios were our lifeline, but they chose that moment to go haywire. So there we were, caked in mud, tryin' to fix the radio while one of our guys starts doin' impressions over the airwaves. I couldn't help but chuckle, even with danger all around us.

Sometimes, we had to come up with code words on the spot. I remember one mission where we were caught off guard, and the only word that came to mind was "BigJoeBlow." So there we were, sendin' messages about troop movements and artillery positions usin' a code word that had the whole team tryin' not to giggle.

Lookin' back, I can't help but grin. The Cree code talkers were a bunch of misfit jokers turned wartime heroes. We might not have fit the mold, but we made our mark with a twinkle in our eyes and laughter in our hearts. So if ya ever hear the word "gooseberry" over the radio, know that there's a Cree code talker out there spreadin' a little joy in the midst of it all.

Bein' a code talker was serious business, don't get me wrong. We took our job seriously. But sometimes, you gotta find humor in the midst of it all. Laughter became our secret weapon, keepin' our spirits up even in the worst situations.

But there's no denyin' the gravity of our part in the war. It wasn't anything to joke about. When we were sent to the front lines, I found myself in the thick of chaos and danger. Gunfire and explosions were all around me, but I stayed focused on my duty. Hidin' behind trees, I sent messages that determined the fate of so many young soldiers. Yes, a serious job indeed.

I'm proud of my part in the war, but I still feel the weight of it all. I saw the destruction and loss it brought on so many. But I stood firm, knowin' our efforts wasn't in vain.

Months turned into years, and that war kept goin'. But we kept on, too, our code stayin' unbreakable while the enemy got more and more flustered. They couldn't crack our messages, and we kept on winnin'. The Cree code talkers became a force to be reckoned with.

When that war was over, I went back to my community. We were honored and hailed as heroes who helped win the war. But the government and the Armed Forces didn't give us the recognition we earned. We were back to bein' "lazy, dirty" Injuns

---

Olivia put the letters down once again.

A couple of Ricky's uncles were part of the Code Talkers, whom, to this day, at least in Canada, have not been given acknowledgment and thanks at least until 1963. First Nations men and women code talkers were not spoken about. They were under strict orders not to reveal anything about their work in Canada or overseas. Many, but not all, were from the Cree Nation.

It was a huge accomplishment. The Code talkers were very successful because they used their own words and not written messages, so there wasn't a paper trail.

Olivia set the letters down again. Time for a break. Olivia had found out a few years ago that Larry, her Dad, was a descendent of a prominent Cree, Chief Peguis, who had descendants named Prince, like Ricky's last name.

It's interesting that Olivia's Dad was also involved in communications and spying during the Cold War, sort of a Code Talker himself. He was a bit too young for full service in WW2, but part of his training was onboard the huge Hercules aircraft patrolling the skies and learning communication skills. He was not ever able to talk about his work as it also was "top secret." When Olivia saw a photo of Chief Peguis, it was clear that her Dad could have been his brother or son. They looked so much alike. Larry was part of the air force patrolling the west coast of British Columbia for enemy aircraft or submarines.

Olivia had only heard about the Code Talkers from the States. Incredible stories and a few Hollywood movies brought her knowledge she had not learned in school. That's sad.

Olivia knew many First Nations men had entered the war, certainly for various reasons, but their hope was they would prove their dedication to Canada, be acknowledged as true members of Canadian society, and receive the same benefits. That did not prove to be true.

Olivia took the dogs for their walk. They went to the river, and the dogs had a nice dip in the cold water. Except they absolutely smelled stinky when the dogs got back in the car. So Olivia had to hose them down before she would let them back in the house. Dogs! But she loves them.

Chapter 24

Darkness Sets In

After Rose and Ricky return home from their Christmas trip, life turns back to silence. A chill hung in the air, and it wasn't from the snow outside. Ricky still refused to talk and disappeared for hours at a time after work or on weekends.

Finally, Rose had had enough of his silent treatment and confronted Ricky one evening after dinner. They just finished washing the dishes, and we're about to turn the TV on for the evening shows they used to love to watch together.

Ricky broke down in tears. He wept like the whole world was sitting on his shoulders, trying to wear him down. He told Rose what had happened in Burma, what his so-called brothers-in-arms had said when Ricky overheard their horrible remarks about him. He wept and wept, and Rose held him all night. She was absolutely devastated that men could be so cruel. Rose kept telling Ricky that he was a hero for surviving not just the plane crash but healing and returning to camp. Ricky never did receive a medal for his part in trying to get help for the men left behind. He had done everything he could to get help to the severely injured men, but by the time he was found, it was too late for the other men. Did the powers that be not understand how hard he had tried? Ricky was devastated having to leave the men behind, but what choice did he have being the only member of the flight crew that could walk even with the bleeding wounds on his legs and torso from the shrapnel, flying metal parts of the plane piercing him? He had removed as much metal as he could stand from his body in order to walk to find help. The airplane radio had been blown to pieces, so he couldn't relay their location. Ricky felt stuck between a rock and a hard place. He knew if he didn't at least try to find help, they would be all dead soon anyway. He repeated over and over to Rose that he had no choice. He wasn't abandoning the men. He was trying to save them.

Rose held him and soothed his brow. She told him over and over that he was a hero. Every mission he went on, there was over a fifty percent chance of not making it back to base. He should not ever feel guilty about living. Rose needed Ricky. She told him over and over throughout the night that he was loved not just by her but by all of her and Ricky's family. Even his code-talking uncles, also not officially recognized for their incredible help in the war effort, tried to tell Ricky not to think about the losses but what they had achieved. They were all an important part of finishing the war that threatened not just Canada but Kanata, their homeland, since before they were pushed onto the reservation land, usually not fit for farming and traditional hunting. Canada chose to turn a blind eye to First Nations and Metis involvement in the war. Maybe the government didn't want to applaud their achievements and have to deal with the Indians as human beings. Human beings the government kept pushing onto reservations and confiscating the rich fertile land they had inhabited for centuries before the white man came. The white people in charge told the proud First Nations people that they were uneducated, dirty pagans.

Nothing seemed to help Ricky come out of his darkness. He continued working on the Air Force Base and became an excellent pilot.

A couple more years went by, but there were no babies. Rose wanted Ricky to go through some tests from their family doctor as she had done. Ricky refused and would get upset anytime Rose suggested it. Rose was sure Ricky had started drinking again, but she wasn't sure, so she never said anything to Ricky about it. Rose was sure she must be wrong and turned a blind eye to Ricky's erratic behavior.

One evening, Ricky was later than normal from his evening shift. She started getting an ugly feeling in her stomach. Something was off. Rose got up from bed, put her coat and boots on, and stepped outside in the middle of the night in the middle of winter to see if the car was back. Maybe Ricky fell asleep when he got home but didn't get out of the car. No, he wasn't there. Rose heard sirens and tried to block the dreadful feeling in her tummy. No, that's not Ricky. It isn't him in the accident on the highway. Ricky always drove the back roads home.

Rose went back into the house. She lifted the telephone receiver and called the base operator. The woman who Rose knew told her yes, there was a terrible accident on the highway, but Ricky had left an hour ago, and it couldn't possibly be him.

Rose waited and waited. Scared to death because Ricky still wasn't home. Where was he? Had he gone to some woman's place? Was he so drunk that he didn't know or care where he was? Was any woman, especially a stranger, easier to have sex with than the one he loved with his heart and soul.? Rose was losing her mind. Too many horrible thoughts she couldn't control.

The phone rang. No! Shouted Rose. Oh my God, I can't answer the phone. I don't want to know who or what was waiting on the other end. The ringing stopped. It was probably a salesman of some sort calling at this ridiculous hour. Didn't they have any manners calling at this hour of the night?

After a few minutes, the phone began ringing again. Insistent and intrusive. Finally, Rose summoned up the courage to answer.

There had been a serious accident between a semi and a car. Both drivers were taken to the local hospital emergency room. The officers believed the driver of the car was Ricky, but she needed to come to the hospital to confirm.

The man calling hung up after telling Rose a car would be at her house in ten minutes to take her to the hospital. There wasn't a mention of Ricky's medical status, and Rose was so overwhelmed with emotions she forgot to ask.

Two soldiers came to pick Rose up exactly ten minutes later. She wasn't at all surprised because, if anything, she learned that being involved in the Air Force meant everything was run precisely on time. Rose had time to get back into her day clothes. It was winter and a lot below zero than anyone liked. The cold literally froze their breath, and it was difficult to breathe with a frozen airway. Rose wrapped her scarf over her nose and mouth, which helped filter the frozen air.

They reached the hospital within fifteen minutes, located in the town nearest the Air Force Base. Rose jumped out of the car almost before the driver had it in the park.

She raced into the lobby frantically, looking for someone to tell her where Ricky was. The driver and the sergeant who had driven Rose to the hospital caught up and took Rose to a small room. She was asked to wait there for a minute before she could see Ricky. She nearly screamed at them to take her to Ricky now, but she realized she would probably get further if she kept a sound mind.

The sergeant returned with a couple of coffees. Rose didn't want to waste time chatting and drinking coffee. This was getting ridiculous. Just when she was ready to jump up and demand to see Ricky, the sergeant began to speak.

There had been a horrible accident involving Ricky and a semi-truck. Both were driving fast, too fast for the road conditions and the time of night. There was black ice everywhere, even though the highway was constantly plowed. People forgot that deadly, almost unseen black ice lay below the plowed road.

The semi lost control after hitting a black ice patch, and the tail end of the truck swung out into the oncoming lane.

Afterward, when the truck driver recounted the incident to the officers and doctors attending him, he described Ricky's piercing gaze, a defiant stare met with a disconcerting tranquillity and acceptance. It was as if Ricky had anticipated this very moment as if he had been waiting for it to happen. This encounter haunted the truck driver's dreams for the remainder of his days, as he witnessed the person he had taken the life of, utterly unbothered by the consequences, showing no inclination to grab the steering wheel and steer away from the impending crash towards the vast emptiness on either side of the road. Ricky had the chance to survive, yet deliberately chose not to.

Rose was twenty-seven years old and childless. She was shattered. Her hopes and dreams were gone in a flash. She didn't want to believe Ricky chose to die, but she knew that Ricky still had nightmares from the war, horrific dreams where he'd wake up screaming. His physical wounds healed but left an ache in his muscles where the shrapnel tore through his skin and muscles. A constant reminder, which, aside from lack of sleep, would exhaust him. The war years had killed Ricky well before he returned home.

Silvia, who was living in Edmonton, came to stay with Rose and helped her pack all her belongings and move to the nearby town of Brandon, where Rose worked. Rose and Ricky had been living on base, and although adequate time was given to move out, she still had to vacate.

With Silvia's help, they found a cute bungalow to rent. Rose preferred a small house to an apartment as a garden was important to lose herself in the summer months. Just like her mother, Abigail, Rose loved having her own garden of dark red roses with their heavenly fragrance. Ricky bought Rose her first rose bush after they were married and moved on base. She would dig this one up and replant it in her new cottage, which she called her new home.

Nearly a month after she lost Ricky in the accident, Rose returned to her job. Everyone was so kind and encouraged her to take more time off or work part-time. Rose needed to immerse herself in her job. She worked at the small city hall but was kept busy doing research and lots of typing and filing. After work, she would usually go out for dinner with some other single people from work.

Rose didn't feel single. She was still attached to Ricky; at least, her heart was. She would go for long walks on Sundays after church. Rose felt she had lost her faith but had gone to church since she was young with George and Abigail when they attended the nearby Anglican church. Rose always had felt such peace at church and had a strong faith in God, but she was having a difficult time reconciling men who would kill others in the name of God and Country while in her quiet little church with the quiet little minister preaching about loving thy fellow man. Weren't the Germans Christians? Weren't the Italians? How can we all be wrong and right at the same time? Life was confusing. She vowed if she ever had children, she would protect them from the literal hell of any war. Perhaps, she mused, hell does not reside in some infernal realm "below" but manifests itself right here on earth. Jesus sacrificed himself to redeem humanity from their sins, but suffering still persisted, unabated by His sacrifice. Rose, who was always reading about other lands, people, and customs she had heard, said from a Buddhist point of view, "Life is suffering." That statement was true, at least in Rose's mind.

Rose certainly wasn't the only war widow, and several of them formed a group that met every Wednesday evening to share, commiserate, and learn how to live alone again. Some had been married longer than her and Ricky, some only a year or two. Most had children who were presently whooping it up in the next room where they had hired a "babysitter" who earned every penny.

Day by day, week by week, time rolled on, and Rose found her way in life again. She started taking writing lessons. Rose loved to write poetry. She hadn't realized she even liked to read poetry until she took a literature class held in the evenings by a crazy old Einstein-looking professor who loved to share his vast knowledge of seemingly all things written.

Rose loved to read and was fascinated by the professor's teaching and had attended several night classes held at the town high school. The old professor was retired, had never married, and didn't know what to do with himself after he had finished teaching at the University in Winnipeg. He moved to a small town and lived in a cottage overlooking a lake. Professor Theodore Solomon (or Teddy to his close friends) was an avid fisherman and thought he would spend his retirement years fishing almost every day, summer or winter. He was "hooked."

Professor Solomon grew weary of the ceaseless fishing, the aggravating experience of rarely catching fish, so when his friend, the present high school principal, approached him with an opportunity to teach adults in the evenings, he eagerly snapped up the offer.

A few years went by, with Rose becoming content with her life. Her poetry had been published in the local paper, and she even won a contest, first place in the poetry division. Rose made friends with the old professor and had him over for dinner every Sunday evening. He encouraged her writing and helped find other poets similar to Rose's for her to read to better understand the rhythm and flow of her words. All his assistance was so helpful. Serving him dinner once, sometimes twice a week, was a small payment as far as Rose was concerned.

The following Sunday, Professor Solomon came to visit Rose and was practically jumping out of his suspenders and pooping his bow tie. Rose, Rose, you must go, you must go! She had no clue what he was going on about. He did tend to overflow with excitement when reading passages from the great authors of the past. Maybe he found an original publication from one of his favourites.

Rose, I have signed you up for one of the greatest poetry workshops held across Canada. This year, they are holding it at Lake Manitoba. There were only two spots left, and you needed a sponsor, so I have signed you up for a fascinating weekend.

Rose was dumbstruck. She hadn't really gone anywhere on most of her vacations; she just travelled home to visit her Dad, who was not so young anymore. Rose's step-mother Mildred had died of cancer two years ago. Rose attended the funeral to support her Dad and half-siblings. She knew about losing loved ones. However, she could never say that she had loved Mildred. She wasn't connected by blood like she and her Dad were. Abigail and George always meant to tell Rose that she had been adopted, but her birth mother, Carys, had asked that she never be told. Carys wanted Rose to believe her new parents were her parents to love completely and to never feel she had been abandoned by her. Rose never ever knew about Carys, and after George, her Dad, died, there wasn't anyone left to know.

Professor Solomon, or Teddy as Rose called him now, calmed down enough to speak a little slower. Rose, I'm sorry, you, of course, don't have to go to the conference but it is a great opportunity for you. The expenses are covered as you qualified as a war widow for the scholarship. Looking at Rose's face turned pale, the poor professor thought Rose might faint. Yes, she was about to, but out of incredible joy. She grabbed the professor and hugged him so hard he thought he would pass out.

So she set out for the resort near Gimli on Lake Manitoba the following August. The workshop was for four and a half days, but participants were invited to stay the weekend at a reduced rate. Rose jumped on that opportunity. After all, she hadn't had a real vacation since the war, if you could call the war anything close to a holiday.

The workshops proved to be intense, yet Rose relished every moment spent there. Prominent Canadian poets of the time, including Anne Wilkinson, Selma Gay Bartlett, Elizabeth Smart, and P.K. Page, delivered exciting and informative lectures and graciously took many questions afterward. Rose formed lasting friendships with several aspiring poets despite their scattered locations across Canada and the United States. Rose's mind was reeling after nearly a full week of immersive learning and networking. The fact that most of the group managed to stay at the resort from Friday afternoon until Monday afternoon brought joy to Rose's heart. A gathering was organized that evening at the pub conveniently situated across the street from the resort.

A group of those female poets-to-be was full of joy after attending the course. They had a large roast meal with dumplings, potatoes, baby carrots, and a constant supply of corn on the cob, sweet as can be with a lot of butter and salt. They drank lots of cold beer in icy glasses. Rose was having so much fun. She started to feel free and happy again. Rose felt incredibly grateful to her friend Teddy, who had set up this poetry workshop and mini holiday.

Chapter 25
Rose Meets a Man

There were several servicemen at the bar, too. They had just finished their own conference on aspects of the Cold War. They were radio operators like Ricky, who had started out in the Air Force. They were about to be sent to the far north to a station in Churchill, Manitoba, to listen to any communication picked up from the Russians. This would be their last weekend of freedom before heading north. They would be stationed there throughout the fall, winter, and part of spring until the weather conditions were more stable for flying and landing.

The two groups of people, the poets and the radiomen, danced, played pool, and generally had a blast. Rose hadn't had so much fun since Ricky, and she went to the dances on the base. They both loved music, and dancing just opened up your inner joy at living.

Rose danced quite a bit with a really nice-looking guy. He had dark hair and deep brown eyes. His name was Donald, but he went by Don. He was originally from Alberta but had been transferred to Manitoba to train as a radio operator. Rose told him all about Ricky and his love of planes. Don was amazing. Took his time and actually listened to Rose. Don had never been married before but was engaged to a woman in Edmonton. It would be a long separation from Sarah, leaving her behind for probably nine or ten months. Sarah didn't want to get married before Don was transferred out. She wanted a big wedding as she was from a large family of six brothers and three sisters. All her siblings were already married. Sarah was the youngest and a bit, well, a lot spoiled. What Sarah wanted; Sarah usually got.

Rose and Don talked well into the late evening. When the bar closed, Don walked her across the street and gave her a kiss at her door. Rose was a bit surprised but definitely wanted more. More of anything. She missed having sex and waking up beside her lover in the morning. Rose could have kicked herself for not inviting Don inside, but he did seem like a gentleman and was engaged. She would just have to be happy with his presence and conversation. He said he was impressed with anyone who could write novels or poetry. Don asked Rose to show him some of her work tomorrow, so she went through her portfolio to find her best.

Rose saw Don at the breakfast buffet, but he was sitting with his pals, so Rose did the same with her friends. After they finished eating, Don and his friends approached and asked them to join them at their BBQ and dance that evening at the same bar. The pub was BBQing a huge pig. It would roast on a rotary set up above a slow-burning fire. Rose and her friends quickly accepted. It sounded wonderful.

Don and his friends were going fishing soon. Although fishing was better in the early morning, they didn't care. A few were hung over from the night before. Nothing that a case of beer wouldn't cure.

While they went fishing, Rose and her four remaining friends were tired and a bit hungover and decided to lay on the beach or in the hammocks tied in the nearby trees in the shade.

Rose was already very tanned from the amount of time she spent in her garden. It took hours of tender loving care, especially during the long hot summer. Professor Solomon was more than happy to water Rose's lovely garden while she was away. He also loved the colorful and fragrant assortment of the annual and perennial flowers and bushes all around her house. He sure figured Rose had a true green thumb to be able to know what to plant where, what natural fertilizers and compost to use as well as which natural species attract monarch butterflies and honey bees.

Rose and a couple other girls/women brought their towels and bathing caps down the lake. It was a beautiful day, and they all loved to swim out to the dock on a waterslide. Again, Rose couldn't believe her good fortune. Her life was looking up. She was becoming a poet and meeting new friends. It was unfortunate that Don was engaged, but she still had a lot of fun with him, dancing and talking the night away. Rose was sure she wouldn't like his fiancé. Sarah did sound selfish and demanding, but that was Don's problem, not hers. At least Don hadn't said nasty things about her, other than she was the youngest of many and spoiled. Rose didn't understand Don's situation; really, she hardly knew him. He did have deep thoughts and a mind thirsty for knowledge. He would stay in the Air Force to eventually get trained as a pilot, and then after five years or so, he would leave the forces and hopefully become a pilot for a major airline. At least, that was the plan Sarah came up with. Strange, strange situation, but it was his life. There may be more to the story than she knew. Maybe they would have a chance to talk again this evening.

Rose and her friends had lunch at the well-stocked buffet at the resort, then went for a round of mini golf close by. Two of the male attendees at the poetry workshop joined them, and they had a riot of a time. Rose and one of the guys were absolutely not good at this mini sport and kept hitting the ball way off target, landing in the sand or small water traps. Rose figured she would take golf lessons next summer if she ever came back to this resort.

They went to the small lounge at the resort for a beer or two. Soon, Don and his friends appeared and joined Rose's group to share fish stories. They really had caught several trout, which they cleaned, put on ice, and brought to the chef at the bar where the BBQ would be held. Everyone was in a celebratory mood. Many of them worked full-time in various occupations. One of the male poets, Stan, was a medical doctor in training, having been almost pushed into the profession by his father, a surgeon at Winnipeg's largest hospitals. His mother was a professor at Winnipeg University teaching English literature. Rose thought his mother probably knew her friend, Professor Solomon, very well, but she didn't mention that to him. Rose remembers Professor Solomon telling her about a female professor he could hardly stand. She was in the same department as him, but she was a bully. Pushing her way to almost the top of the university. Rose figured if this woman was Stans's mother, then maybe she was a nasty pushy person, but on the other hand, there weren't many women, at least in Canada, who held top positions in any profession. No wonder this woman was not the nicest person. She'd had years and years of pushing for her right to teach and move up in her profession, constantly banging her head against the "glass ceiling" and men who felt she had no right to take their jobs.

Stan said he actually liked learning to be a doctor, and even his parents were quite happy with him becoming a family doctor specializing in Obstetrics. Poor Stan would probably never get a good night's sleep. Stan loved the arts. He invited all to visit him in Winnipeg and would take them to the museum or a play. The group all cheered at that, well, mostly the literature/poets who would love any chance to see an opera or play. That was a thrilling prospect.

All of them headed to their rooms for a nap after the hot sun and a few beers. Rose had a nice, cool shower and washed the lake water out of her hair. Rose was wearing her hair shorter nowadays. She had kept it long and tied up during the war years and several years after. Rose was tired of the same look she had had for too many years. Her enjoyment of life had been returning, and she wanted a change, even if it was a small thing. Her golden-brown hair often looked messy when she tied it up. By the end of the day, she would have curly tendrils sticking up all over her head. Off to the beauty parlor, she went and got it "chopped off." Her hair was short but became very curly in a pleasing way. Rose liked the change.

Rose lay down on the bed naked with the room fan blowing gently across her back. She heard a soft knock at the door but ignored it, thinking it was for the next room. There it was again, another knock. "Rose, come out and play with me." It was Don. Was he crazy or drunk? Rose grabbed her robe and opened the door partway. Yup, drunk as a skunk. Oh boy, how was she going to handle this? Rose said very gently, "Don, go to your room. It's just down the hall, four rooms." "Rose, I am a gentleman and would never push myself upon a fair lady. I merely stopped by to let you know I'm looking forward to our (hiccup) oops, excuse me, evening together. Don't you worry your little head off. I'll be sober as a judge when I come courting."

Oh gee, thought Rose, he really has had a few in the hot sun and probably hasn't eaten much. Rose re-directed Don's direction toward his room with a gentle push. Oh well, they had a few hours before the BBQ, so hopefully, he'll be right as rain then. If not, well, it was nice knowing him.

Two hours later, there was another knock on the door, and Rose opened it to a freshly showered, freshly shaved, and sober Don. "Yay," thought Rose. "I do enjoy his company."

The roast pig and freshly caught fish were so tender, and both melted in their mouths. Again, there was sweet corn on the cob and strawberry shortcake with real whipped cream for dessert.

Rose danced the rest of the evening, mostly with Don but with her other friends, too. They twisted to Chubby Checker and danced cheek to cheek to crooners like Dean Martin and Frank Sinatra. Rose was having an absolute ball. It wasn't just Don who gave her a roving eye that evening. She felt free and admired again after so long in the "desert." As soon as she finished dancing with one guy, Don would snag her and dance with her so many songs. There were more men than women, so Rose and the other women in her group felt obliged to dance with a few and not just the one they came with to the bar.

Soon enough, it was midnight, and the bar had to close. Across the street, they trekked to the resort. It was apparent some in the group had paired up and were retreating to one of their rooms to carry on partying.

Don and Rose were still in good spirits from all the fun of the past two days. This time, after Don kissed Rose, she invited him in. The evening had built up a sexual tension between the two. As soon as they closed the room door, they began passionately kissing, causing moans from both. They began undressing each other on the way to the bedroom. Don had a gorgeous body, strong and tanned from the summer. His hair was darker than hers but with definite golden blond streaks, again like hers but more distinct from the sun.

They lay down on the bed and caressed each other, kissing each other and exploring every inch of each other's bodies. Thankfully, Don had brought a sheath or condom with him because she sure didn't think of packing her old diaphragm from her early married days. It was probably full of holes or dried out from non-use, if that was possible.

She and Ricky got rid of diaphragms and condoms after a couple of years of enjoying each other and trying for a household of kids. Well, that didn't happen. Rose had, after all, been a married woman. Sex wasn't new to her, and neither did the experience seem new to Don. Much later, Rose did wonder at Don's expertise at sex. He was gentle at the start, kissing and licking Rose all over, especially on her sweet spot, causing her to moan even louder. Don flipped on his back, pulling Rose on top of him. Oh my God, she was coming and strongly. Rose ground herself against Don's still-hard cock. She came again, and then Don flipped her over one more time and came inside her. Rose felt she had never had such wild and satisfying sex. She had no idea what she had been missing with Ricky all those years, especially the many years of no sex because he was too drunk or exhausted from life. Wow.

They stayed together the whole night. Don had only one condom with him, but he promised to "pull out" before he came. Rose figured that should work. She really didn't care at that point. There was no way she was going to push him out of the bed when she had been transferred to a feeling of pure bliss.

They made love several times throughout the night and early morning. They also took a few breaks for rest, but they talked about life mostly.

Don had been engaged to Sarah since high school. They had been caught sleeping together, and there was a demand from Sarah's family for them to marry right away, even though Sarah didn't get pregnant. She was from a strict Catholic family. Don had already applied to the Air Force and had been accepted. Sarah refused to marry him until he returned from the northern post. Sarah wasn't at all keen on Don entering the Air Force and possibly being transferred to any small base across the country. Even in the Northwest Territories or Nova Scotia. The end of the world for Sarah, literally. At least Don had stood up to her about his career, at least to this point. He also wanted to be a career pilot but had wanted to grow and move up in the Air Force. Housing was always supplied, although not nearly as large as Sarah's family home, a huge cattle farm just out of Calgary, Alberta. Don readily admitted he had lost his high school crush on Sarah. He was in a real mess and was thankful for the time away from her to figure out how to get out of the engagement. He told Rose that she had re-awakened his passion for life. He loved that she was a poet and a gardener.

They were exhausted from their sexual escapades but knew they had to leave each other today. Rose and Don exchanged addresses. Somehow, they pulled apart long enough for Don to leave to pack his gear. Ten minutes later, he was back in Rose's room for another huge kiss goodbye. "I think I'm in love with you, Rose. I will cherish you forever, my beautiful rose, or at least until I see you again." Then Don was gone. Rose sat for several minutes, gathering her thoughts. She really didn't know Don that well, but he did seem like a true and honest man. They had both spoken with so much passion about their possible future together. He was another soul mate for Rose. She really never thought she would meet a man with so much in common with her. He also loved kids and wanted a houseful. Don was six years younger than Rose, but that didn't seem to be an issue. Some men grow up emotionally quite slowly or never at all. Some men or women quit growing after their first drink of alcohol. They stayed stuck in a party mode and ended up losing everything, children and all.

Ricky quit growing up after the crash in Burma and subsequent verbal abuse by his so-called brothers-in-arms. The war and booze destroyed Ricky long before he returned home.

So Rose packed up with a song in her heart. She was full of that warm, sunshiny feeling of being in love. Rose was still dumbfounded. At her ripe old age of thirty, she was able to see a bright future again between her love of poetry and having the biggest crush on Don, which was reciprocated. Rose was absolutely positive Don would find a way out of his engagement with Sarah.

Chapter 26

Professor Solomon

Rose got back to her usual routine. The Professor, returning to Rose's house for the usual Sunday dinner, could see the new light in Rose's eyes. He knew when a woman was in love. After all, he had read all of the love stories, including the tragedies from the earliest writers and poets. Just read the Bible. Psalms are full of the most romantic stories of love, let alone the classics. He had never met a woman he was deeply in love with. He had met many people all over the world during his education in literature research, but not one woman stole his heart. He attended many parties held by rich people involved in the arts, but not one woman thrilled him. Sure, he had sex with them, wasn't that expected? But not one woman thrilled him. And then he met Ricardo, a stunningly handsome young man. Bronzed from the Mediterranean sun. Professor Theodor Solomon's heart almost stopped. He'd never really been attracted to a man. This was something new. But he wasn't queer, he was pretty sure. He loved being in the presence of women, lots of lovely, sometimes beautiful women. He especially loved spending hours talking with an educated woman. That's where he saw their inner beauty.

He was enjoying a Campari on an outdoor patio with another lecturer for the European literary conference held in Monaco that summer. Teddy looked up, having the feeling somebody was watching him, and his eyes connected with the golden man, boy, really. So much love and depth in those eyes. Teddy nearly cried out but contained himself. He lost track of what his companion was saying and tried to turn back to the conversation, but it was difficult, having been mesmerized by this boy's golden eyes. He was a god. Teddy finally turned his eyes to his companion and responded to what he thought the conversation was about. However, his companion gave him a strange glance and carried on with his spiel about some minor character in one of Shakespeare's plays. A redundant and pompous man he was.

Teddy turned his head in the direction of the young man, but he was gone. "That's probably best," he thought, having remembered a lovely wealthy lady involved in philanthropy in the "arts of literature." Whatever that meant. He wasn't absolutely sure, but he wanted to find out.

So, after a nice siesta, he made his way to the conference cocktail party, followed by another boring dinner, and then off to the casinos for a bit of fun.

Teddy chatted up with the wealthy woman at the cocktail party and found her to be a very dull lady who had no idea what philanthropy or the arts in literature meant. Maybe she was looking for a husband, having been widowed just a year ago. A dangerous combination, thought Teddy, a lonely, dull woman with so much money she thought she could entice a man with money. No, Teddy would rather marry a pauper with a brain. Although most paupers with a brain usually find their way out of poverty. What did he know, having been a wealthy single man for all of his adult years? He really ought to look into the situation of awarding bursaries to young widows or divorcees with children. He inherited a lot of dough from his very wealthy parents. He was an only child. They were both young, just in their fifties, when they caught some nasty flu and simply died one night after the other. There was the question about the missing half bottle of morphine, but the exhausted nurse probably forgot to mark all of the doses down. Teddy figured his mother probably drank the bottle on purpose. Her chest congestion was beginning to clear, and she managed clear broth for dinner; there didn't seem to be a reason why she wouldn't continue to improve. But Teddy knew his mother loved his father and would be lost without his care and guidance. So, Teddy became an orphan at age twenty-five. He is a good age to travel and continue his education all over the world.

Lo and behold, the golden boy, as Teddy now referred to the young man he saw earlier that afternoon, was one of the waiters. Heavens, Teddy couldn't quite look at him. He caused the poor boy to spill a tad of wine, just a couple of drops of white wine, but the head waiter gave him dagger eyes. After that, Teddy kept his eyes to himself.

While dessert was being served, the young man dropped a piece of paper in his lap. All it said was, "Club Tango 2300 hrs. Well, Teddy knew what that meant. He was to meet the young man, boy really, at a certain club at eleven pm, which was still a couple of hours away, so he ventured down to the hotel's casino.

Teddy entered the smoky, hazy club, vibrating with energy. He spotted a seat at a small table and sat down. It was a good spot as he could see the door as well as the dance floor. Teddy glanced around and saw that there seemed to only be men here. A lightbulb went off in his head. "Oh, it's a bar for queers and homosexuals." Teddy was completely unsure if that's what they were called, but he didn't seem disturbed by this fact at all. He looked at some men who looked just like him and others dressed more like women. It was definitely a new experience, which Teddy absolutely loved. He believed you only live once after having listened to his scientist friends, or if he was a Buddhist, he may come back as a baboon, which would serve him right after all of his escapades and "experiences" he sought out in life.

Teddy didn't spot his golden boy until nearly twenty minutes later as the poor young man, boy really came flying in the front door, stopping to look around. He found Teddy sitting quietly, unfazed by his surroundings.

"I'm so very sorry, signor, I was delayed at work," Teddy asked him if he got into trouble spilling the wine, and Ricardo replied that he did, but it was his first infraction in two years, so he was forgiven but put on notice. Teddy suggested he calm the waters with the head waiter, but Ricardo, with his lovely, sweet, melodious voice, replied that he was just fine. Teddy asked what Ricardo wanted to drink and went to get himself one and for Ricardo, too. Ricardo figured, very incorrectly, that Teddy was queer and was used to these types of bars.

After a couple of drinks and a bit of conversation, Teddy found out his young friend was twenty-one, certainly the age of consent for any country. Teddy, by this time, was forty-five, ancient really, but he kept himself fit and up to date with the ways of the world through news and literature. There was a brilliant book, The Well of Loneliness, written by Radclyffe Hall in the 1920s, it was very, very controversial about a woman, a lesbian, and her love of a flighty young woman and a friend, a man who wanted to marry her until he understood what being a lesbian meant. He stuck by her side throughout her heartbreak.

Teddy even asked Ricardo if he wanted to dance, and yes, he certainly did. They danced and drank and laughed and closed the bar down. They jumped in a cab, and both being quite drunk, they almost giggled all the way back to the hotel as the cab driver glanced disgustingly at them in the rearview mirror. Teddy tipped the driver well, and they went to his room.

Teddy didn't get too much further describing his night of falling in love with Ricardo with Rose. Rose was a very open-minded woman, and after years of friendship, he felt free to talk about more personal issues.

Like in Shakespeare's plays or in life, tragedy strikes us all.

Teddy and Ricardo spent a month making love and falling in love. Teddy felt he had fallen down the rabbit hole. This was a whole new life to him, mostly hidden behind closed doors, even their meeting places, out of the scrutiny of the "other people." It was all so bizarre but exhilarating at the same time. Illicit love affair.

It seemed like anything goes in those days, especially in the Mediterranean. But that was far from the truth.

One night, leaving the "bad boys bar," as they called it, they took a cab back to the hotel as they always did. They didn't recognize the driver as having been the one to give them dirty looks.

As usual, Teddy and Ricardo were in a happy celebratory mood. They weren't paying attention at first, but it wasn't long before both realized the cabby had taken them on a different route than usual. They asked the driver why he was taking a different route. No answer. The men sat back, trying not to panic. Something didn't feel right. Both of them had been in situations before where paying attention to their body, feeling the fight or flight adrenaline increasing but trying to remain logical. But the logic became clearer and clearer the further away they got from the hotel district. Teddy tried to open the back doors when they slowed down around a corner, but both doors were sealed shut.

Teddy started shouting about having money and would pay the abductors anything to let them go. He didn't want to think there was something worse to deal with if he couldn't bargain for a release. The cab kept driving and finally stopped behind what looked like an abandoned wooden house. "Shit," thought Teddy and Ricardo at the same time. What was going to happen to them?

They were led out of the car by four men, two on each side of them, into the house, which was abandoned. They were thrown to the floor, and the men started kicking them over and over. They kicked them from head to toe. They never said a word in any language; they just kept kicking with their hard boots until they ran out of steam and were left in a cloud of dust.

Both Teddy and Ricardo were unconscious and didn't move for several hours. Teddy came to first, and the recent past came back with full force. He rolled over onto his back, shouting in pain, then he saw Ricardo. "Ricardo," Teddy shouted. He crawled over to him. Ricardo didn't look good at all. "Oh no, no, nooooo." Ricardo's head had been kicked in. He was dead.

Teddy passed out again and again from the pain, but his head finally cleared enough to get himself upright. What was he going to do? He looked at Ricardo again. He had to get out of there and find help. He had no idea where he was. He stepped outside into the bright sun. His watch was gone, as well as his wallet. He limped up to the dirt road and had to make a decision to turn left or right. He tried to remember which way he felt the taxi turning as he had been trying to keep tabs.

Teddy went with his intuition and turned right, remembering that Ricardo slipped beside him from the right seat in the back. He didn't have any water and was limping and hurting everywhere. He limped along the road, not seeing a car or people for more than half an hour. He didn't know how he would be able to carry on. He sat down on a large rock at the side of the road. Eventually, a cart with horse and driver, a gaggle of geese in a couple of cages, and a pile of hay. Thankfully, the farmer pulled over and spoke French as Teddy had learned after English.

The farmer helped Teddy into the back of the cart, making a soft bed of straw. A half-hour later, Teddy woke up when the farmer stopped, and he heard people talking. The farmer had taken Teddy to the small village medical clinic. There, the doctor tried to patch Teddy up as well as possible. He set his broken leg in plaster, but Teddy would need surgery later when he returned to Canada.

The clinic called the local constabulary, and a policeman came to take the report. Teddy told them everything he knew about the cab driver, even the name that was hanging on a plastic cover on the rearview mirror. Teddy was transported back to the hotel he was staying in Monaco, and the owners allowed him to stay for free for the following week, as Teddy had stayed at their establishment several times over the years. They brought him his meals, and the mayor insisted that nursing care was provided twice a day until Teddy healed.

Teddy returned home. His leg had been too damaged for any operation to have his leg return to full functioning, so Teddy limped and used a cane.

When Teddy stopped talking, Rose sat quietly for several minutes, absorbing the magnitude of what Teddy had just told her. She got up from her chair and gave Teddy a long hug with tears in her eyes. Rose asked Teddy if they ever caught the men would do that to him and Ricardo.

Teddy told her that he returned home without any progress made by the local police. He wondered how hard they tried. Ricardo was a known homosexual but had always kept his head down. All the police could surmise was that the cab driver was working illegally, as all of the registered cab drivers were cleared of suspicion. None of the other men who were at the wooden house that night were ever found. It was located in a remote location. A small farm that had been abandoned. It seems nobody knew or saw anything. It was very late at night. Teddy tried for years to get either the government in Ottawa or Monaco to keep searching, but after several years, even Teddy admitted it was a hopeless endeavor.

"Wow," Rose thought. You never knew what the story was behind anybody, even close friends. It had taken Teddy several years before he knew and trusted Rose enough to tell his story. Teddy said he never loved again. Ricardo was his angel, his golden boy, and he wanted to keep his love for him as homage to his brutal death.

The evening conversation had been long, and it was getting late. Rose wanted to share her good news with Teddy about Don, but that could wait until next Sunday.

Which rolled around pretty fast. Rose still kept herself busy after work, attending more night school courses. They had become very popular among the widows and otherwise single Moms.

Professor Theodore Solomon, Teddy showed up at Rose's door the following Sunday at four in the afternoon for "cocktails" and then their Sunday dinner with a wonderful bottle of wine chosen by Teddy when he knew what the fare would be. They always had a great time together, laughing and chatting about what matters in their week or life. It was time to tell Teddy about Don.

Rose had already received two letters from Don, and she replied back as soon as she could. He always professed his love and the hopes of their years together after he finished training in the North. He was sending a letter this week to Sarah as well as her parents to explain why he couldn't fulfill his promise to marry Sarah. He was sure they would understand why any of them would want to force this marriage between Sarah and him when he didn't love her at all. He would have to tell his parents, too.

Rose told Teddy how she had fallen smack in love with Don, which had taken her by surprise. She told Teddy how they met and talked all night and their plans for the future. Teddy, as usual, was always interested in Rose's life and was very happy to hear she had found love after all the years it took her to get over Ricky.

Chapter 27

The Nightmare

Rose and Don changed letters, usually two a week, for a couple of months. Rose kept sending letters, but it would be a week or longer before she heard from Don. His explanation was he was getting tired and having to study for their weekly exams. Rose could understand that and tried to be patient with his infrequent letters. Then, they stopped altogether. Rose was getting more and more concerned. Another month went by with nothing. Rose kept writing letters anyway with hope. He was on some mission where he couldn't get letters written or sent.

Finally, a letter arrived from Don. The news wasn't good. His "fiancé" was pregnant, about four months on. Sarah declared that Don was absolutely the father, and he had to fulfill his commitment to marry her, especially now that she was having his baby. They would marry next summer after the baby was born. It was a done deal, and Don wondered at Sarah's honesty regarding the baby, but with both families adamant, he had to fulfill his commitment. Don professed his undying love for Rose, but they had to part forever.

What a nightmare for Rose. She cried herself to sleep after screaming into her pillow that life was too cruel. She vowed never to love another man.

Teddy came over a couple of times a week worried about Rose. She had lost some weight and wasn't looking like her normal perky, happy self. He would get Rose out of the house on Friday or Saturday evenings to a movie, play, or dinner. Time heals all wounds, he thought and then remembered his enduring love for a young man. Boy, really, he understood that phrase was definitely not true in all cases.

Another month passed, and Rose realized she must have missed her period in the past month or two. Her periods were never regular. Part of what her doctor said was why she probably couldn't get pregnant, although she suspected that it was more because Ricky's sperm count was on the low side. Rose had been feeling squeamish in the mornings, and her breasts were tender. Never having been pregnant before, she wasn't exactly sure how she was supposed to feel. Rose made an appointment with her doctor. Now wouldn't that just take the cake, getting pregnant at thirty, a widow, left by another man whom she put her faith in, someone who would grow old with her, share their secrets and dreams with. "Why, oh why?" Rose knew she was feeling sorry for herself, but life always seemed to take a sharp turn just when you thought things were moving along nicely, happily, with a sense of purpose.

She couldn't even write her usual poems about the joys and love found in life. Nothing seemed happy and cheerful at this point.

Just as Rose had feared, after seeing the doctor and having blood tests, "the rabbit died".

She was about three months pregnant. Rose was beyond belief. "I'm too old. I can't do this alone". Rose wrote a letter to Don telling him about the pregnancy. She did feel badly for his situation, but he needed to know. Rose had decided to follow through with the pregnancy. What other choice did she really have? Abortion was not only illegal; Rose had always believed in God and the bible and didn't want to go against her beliefs. She had plenty of female friends she had met through the "widows and single mother" night school classes she had attended over several years. Plus, she had Teddy, who was like a slightly older single uncle. Teddy had already told Rose he would do everything in his power to help her through the pregnancy and help raise the child should Rose decide to keep the baby. At this point, Rose was sure she would give the baby up for adoption, thinking it would be so much better for the child to be raised in a two-parent family, but Teddy had a good point, and her Aunt Silvia was also ready to help in any way she could.

Rose had a lot to think about. Truly, everyone was happy for her, even though just her very close friends knew the full circumstances of what had transpired with Don. He just wasn't mentioned.

Rose had a good pregnancy after getting over her morning sickness, which seemed to last forever. She didn't gain a lot of weight, although she tried. Rose had lost a fair amount of weight in her early pregnancy and couldn't seem to gain more than eighteen pounds by the end of her seventh month.

Teddy or one of her girlfriends would come over many evenings to bring or make her dinner. Rose felt spoiled, but she knew she was always exhausted lately and still working full-time. She fortunately had maternity benefits from work, but the longer she was able to work before the birth, the longer she would have to rest afterward.

One afternoon after lunch, Rose started getting cramps. She couldn't be in labour. She was a month early. She had just been checked by the doctor last week, and all was well. Maybe these were "Braxton Hicks" contractions which she had been told could happen a month or more before the real labour and contractions happened. Rose tried to put this out of her mind until her workday was finished. She suddenly had a cramp so strong she cried out. The woman she was working with at the time, having had four of her own children, came over to support Rose, who was trying to stand up to the pain. Suddenly, Rose's water broke, and she had another strong contraction. Her workmate, Julia, called for help and an ambulance.

After an eight-hour labour, relatively short labour for a first-time pregnancy, her child was born and immediately whisked away to the Special Care Nursery to be assessed as the baby was small, as expected for an early birth, but would need oxygen and special formula feeding.

Rose was devastated. She hadn't even been told the sex of her baby. She fell asleep on the narrow, hard hospital bed, totally exhausted from the labour and birth and after pains which were almost as bad as the labour. Rose had been given some medicine for the pain and completely zonked out.

The next morning, Teddy came to see how she was fairing, plus a string of friends, male and female, wishing her well. Rose had already declared she would be giving the baby up for adoption, still feeling a two-parent family would be the best and most loving choice for her daughter. Rose was able to see her beautiful daughter once a day until Rose was released from the hospital. She and the nuns at the hospital decided to name her Rose Marie after her mother, but also, being the month of June, there were roses in full bloom. Such an appropriate name, even though her daughter would never ever know not just her name but how much her mother loved her. It was a huge and horrible decision to leave her behind when Rose was discharged from the hospital.

Rose was able to take maternity time off from work. She had had too much heartbreak in her life and needed to get back into her flower garden and walk in nature on the many trails surrounding their town. She went from horrible spells of deep grief then bouncing back to feeling she made the correct decision regarding her daughter. Rose felt like a yo-yo, but with the help of close friends, especially Teddy, she slowly became stronger in her determination to move forward past her misery of life's events. She certainly knew she was not the only one who had suffered in this life. She thought of all the young widows; yes, they had financial assistance, but the life of a single mother was one of the most difficult challenges in life. She admired each and every one of them. They all looked exhausted and frazzled but somehow happy with life. They explained that getting out to night school and meeting other windows and single mothers had changed their lives. They helped each other out with babysitting, picking the kids up from school, and with whatever else was happening in their lives that might need assistance from others in the same boat.

259

Chapter 28

Close to My Heart

Time passed, and Rose kept in touch with two of her aunts, her dad's sister Silvia, and her mother Abigail's sister Glynnis.

Two years later, Rose met another man and got pregnant. This child was a boy Rose kept but not the poor excuse of a man she had ended up with. Four years later, Rose met another man, was soon pregnant with her third, a girl she also kept, and married this man who turned out to be a shit of a husband. Life seemed to have gone drastically sideways, including her hopes and dreams for her future. Rose stayed with this man but also fell out of touch with her Aunt Silvia, who had moved back to New York with a contract to design at one of the top fashion houses. Rose found herself in a marriage with no love, a man who was a drunk and a womanizer, but Rose had sunk into a depression that lasted years. She just didn't care anymore. But she always remembered her Rose.

Olivia put the last of the letters down. Aunt Belle had died, and the letters either stopped or got thrown out. She sat there, almost numb. What about the rest of the story? Where did Rose live with the last husband? Did she have more children? Olivia was full of questions, but how would she get the answers?

What a horrible situation to be given an incomplete story. At least Olivia knew a better story of her grandmother, Carys, and her two daughters, who never knew about each other. Olivia's mother, Millie, was now dead, and quite possibly Rose, too. She would have been about the same age as Millie. A sad story without a complete ending.

Olivia started searching for her birth mother forty years ago. At that point, the registry in Manitoba was "closed." Olivia had been able to receive very little information, no names of her birth mother or father. Olivia was told that her mother loved to write and had many other interests. At school, she excelled in English literature and art history, which she continued learning at workshops and night school for years. There wasn't much written about Olivia's birth father. He had been in the Armed Forces, as had many men back then. That was it.

Then Olivia's files were lost, but nobody had realized until she decided she needed to find out what was going on, so the file was reopened. Apparently, Olivia's birth mother had died, and her birth father didn't want to have anything to do about releasing his information except that he was happily married with four children and nobody knew of his "indiscretion." Well, that just made Olivia almost hate the father who had literally tossed her aside. "Oh well," I thought. "I guess I was never meant to know who my birth parents were."

Epilogue

Not long afterward, the Manitoba Registry was opened. Olivia didn't think it would help her to find any of her relatives if her birth Mom had died. Any living relative would have to have contacted the Winnipeg Registry, then maybe, just maybe, the stars would align, and Olivia might meet an Aunt or uncle. Olivia didn't even know if her birth mother had stayed in Winnipeg, married, or had other children. Or whether she ever told her family about her. Obviously, Olivia's birth father, now a "Christian," as he told the registry, didn't want to have anything to do with his child.

The Registry had been open for a while, and Olivia was ready to give up hope. She felt like she was grieving about what might have been all over again. Then, out of the blue months later, Olivia received a letter from the Manitoba Registry.

Dear Ms. Olivia Harrison McDonald

We have some news for you. You have been on our registry for several years, and we're contacting the Registrar's list of adopted children in order of application.

You have a sister, Annamarie Wilson, who also registered over ten years ago, but due to Manitoba's governing laws regarding the Registry, we had to wait until the laws changed to an open registry so family members could find parents or siblings. Your sister has asked us to contact you for a face-to-face meeting at your convenience.

Olivia waited and waited, and she finally received another letter from the registry telling her the following information:

Dear Ms. Olivia Harrison McDonald

Your half-sister, Annamarie Wilson, will call this Sunday morning, March 21st, to set up a face-to-face meeting. Ms. Wilson is very happy we have connected with you and is very excited to meet you face to face.

Your shared birth mother passed away in 1999. Our condolences. In our opinion, the Registry has taken too long to open its files.

I've enclosed a letter from your birth mother, Rose Prince, written shortly after you were born.

Dear Baby Rose,

I write this letter with tears in my eyes but love in my heart. You have been a part of my life for the past nearly eight months. I'm sorry I couldn't keep you longer, but you wanted to meet the world a bit early. You were such a beautiful tiny baby with rosebud lips and dark curly hair. I have loved you more than anything in the world. However, I've made the very difficult decision to give you up for adoption.

Please understand the decision was not made lightly. I spent many sleepless nights tossing and turning, trying to decide what the best decision for you would be. I've come to the conclusion that I'm not in a position to raise you properly and give you the life you deserve. I want you to be a part of a loving family that can give you everything I cannot.

My decision was not and will never be a reflection of my love for you. I will always love you and carry a piece of you in my heart.

I hope your adoptive family will give you all the love and support you need to grow up happy and healthy. I hope they teach you everything I cannot and show you our wonderful world of wonder. I hope they love you as much as I do.

I hope someday, if the adoption laws change, we will meet, and that will complete us. I feel I'm missing a part of me, a hole that cannot be filled until I have you in my life someday.

I'm sorry if this letter brings you sadness, but please know my decision was made from love. I believe giving you up for adoption is the most loving thing I can do for you right now.

Please take care, my sweet baby, Rose. I will always love you.

With all my heart,

Your mother,

Rose Prince

Also enclosed in the envelope was a poem written by my birth mother.

Welcome, sweet baby Rose,

To a world of wonder and light,

May your life be filled with love,

And all that is good and bright.

Your arrival is a miracle,

A bundle of joy and grace,

A precious gift from above,

A blessing to embrace.

May your eyes sparkle with wonder,

As you explore this earth, we share,

May your heart be filled with love,

And kindness beyond compare.

May your laughter ring like music,

And your smiles light up the sky,

May your dreams be big and bold,

And your spirit will fly high.

May you find joy and peace,

In all the moments life brings.

So welcome, little baby Rose,

In this world of highs and lows,

May your journey be blessed and bright,

Filled with love, hope, and delight.

Olivia dropped the poem and letters. "Tim," she yelled. Tim and the dogs came running.

Tears were falling down her eyes. Olivia kept shaking my head, trying to clear her thoughts.

"Please read these letters, Tim, and tell me if I'm right. Am I the daughter of Rose, who was the daughter of Carys? How can that be possible?"

"Oh, but it makes so much sense. There must be somebody who can shed light on this situation."

"Remember you'll be meeting your half-sister soon. I'm sure she can shed light on your mother and what happened the rest of her life. It's very exciting, Olivia."

A few months later, Olivia did meet her half-sister. She found herself and filled the hole in her soul that had been there for decades when Olivia came to the realization that she really didn't love Millie, who had been chosen to adopt her and Ben.

Everything fell into place almost.

Olivia's half-sister told her the story of her mother as she knew it after Olivia was born.

Rose took a turn for the worse for several years. Rose kept meeting men who ended up hurting her in one way or another. Rose finally met a man whom she married, and they had Annamarie eight years after my birth. Rose never fully recovered emotionally from having given up "baby Rose" and her subsequent choices of men. Rose often suffered from depression.

She lost Teddy in the eighties from HIV/AIDS and several other friends from the same. Rose often volunteered at hospitals where mostly men were dying of HIV/AIDS. Rose, as always, had no fear of medicine or death, having seen too much during the war.

Annamarie had not known that Rose, her own mother, had been adopted and was the daughter of Carys. It was a family circle of loss that ended with me.

Olivia, after putting together the trail of letters and information from Aunt Belle and Silvia, believed she was the daughter of Rose, who was the daughter of Carys.

Her story was now complete.

Photos:

Feminine hygiene was a euphemism for birth control. Kills all "organic" matter.

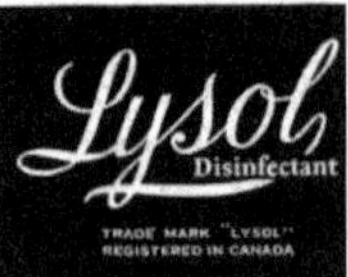

1918 multiple murder   near Grande Prairie

Uncle Percy is among these soldiers somewhere

Bystander copyright.
"MY DREAM FOR YEARS TO COME"

Grandpa playing baseball and looking at an upside down toilet seat

My beautiful grandmother

Grandpa

The little white clapboard house in White Mountain

Uncle Percy: he was a handsome man

CHRYSLER
Plymouth
FARGO
MOTORS LTD
TEXACO
ALLIS-CHAL

Grandpa's gas station and repair and my brother and I outside of one of Grandma and Grandpa's houses with beautiful red roses.